Zane Pre[illegible]

Twisted Vows of Seduction

Dear Reader:

I recognized N'Tyse's writing talent when I selected her short story, "Caramel Latte," for my anthology, *Missionary No More.* Later, her story, "Swirl," appeared in my *Z-Rated: Chocolate Flava 3.* Now N'Tyse returns with a sequel to her fascinating novel, *Twisted Seduction.*

Follow the twists in the life of Greg Adams, who believes he's reunited with his deceased lover, Denise, once Naomi enters his world. After creating her image and identity, she is the epitome of Denise and Greg falls into her trap. Meet Jeff who's entangled with two women, Naomi, his former wife's best friend, and Ménage, a stripper. Discover their ploys in this exciting adventure that will keep you guessing until the dramatic conclusion.

N'Tyse truly spins a tale about what her name represents: **N**ever **T**ell **Y**our **S**ecrets.

As always, thanks for supporting the authors of Strebor Books. We try our best to bring you the future in great literature today. We appreciate the love. You can find me on Facebook @AuthorZane and on Twitter @planetzane.

Blessings,

Zane

Publisher
Strebor Books
www.simonandschuster.com

ALSO BY N'TYSE

Twisted Seduction

ZANE PRESENTS

Twisted Vows of Seduction

N'TYSE

SBI
STREBOR BOOKS
NEW YORK LONDON TORONTO SYDNEY

Strebor Books
P.O. Box 6505
Largo, MD 20792
http://www.streborbooks.com

This book is a work of fiction. Names, characters, places and incidents are products of the author's imagination or are used fictitiously. Any resemblance to actual events or locales or persons, living or dead, is entirely coincidental.

ISBN 978-1-59309-520-8
ISBN 978-1-4516-4864-5 (ebook)
LCCN 2013933671

First Strebor Books trade paperback edition December 2013

Cover design: www.mariondesigns.com
Cover photograph: © Keith Saunders/Marion Designs

10 9 8 7 6 5 4 3 2 1

Manufactured in the United States of America

For information regarding special discounts for bulk purchases, please contact Simon & Schuster Special Sales at 1-866-506-1949 or business@simonandschuster.com

The Simon & Schuster Speakers Bureau can bring authors to your live event. For more information or to book an event, contact the Simon & Schuster Speakers Bureau at 1-866-248-3049 or visit our website at www.simonspeakers.com.

ACKNOWLEDGMENTS

It never fails. When I get to this part, I have to sit back, hope, and pray that I don't leave anyone out. However, I do seem to get better with every book that I write, because those that were there for me since the beginning of time, are still here, supporting, and cheering me on every step of the way. So there will always be a permanent place in my heart for you, even when the ink on the paper fades. For those that don't know, writing can be very lonely. So when I receive a phone call, an email, or even a shout on Facebook telling me how much you enjoyed one of my books, it reassures me that what I'm doing is all worth it. The late nights, the exhaustion, the sacrifices, etc. All worth it! So there's no doubt about it—I do it for my supporters. I am so grateful to have been blessed with such a powerful gift. Only God could have known what I would do with it. So I thank Him for his favor and I know the best is yet to come.

To my dear loving husband, Cory, I don't know where I would be without you. You bring out the best in me. I pray that our love will last forever and that our fire will continue to burn. And to our beautiful creation, Zanaiah, you are everything I imagined you would be. You are my greatest blessing. The beat to my heart and my sun when it rains. I love you with all my heart. I want to thank my mom, Shirley, and her other half, Joe, for passing out my business cards to every single stranger they see. LOL! So when I received that phone call from that woman saying she got my card out of the chicken shack, I knew who was behind it. Gotta love my family. To my sisters Satoria (Lady Mink) and Nina, thanks for having my back and proofing my work whenever I need a second pair of eyes. Tanasha, Shaquadra, Donyell, April, Natasha, and Keyome, thanks for reviewing my work as well and listening to my endless wild ideas. You're the best! Adowri, Angelique, April, Aunt Letha, Aunt Brenda, Trish, Crystal, and Drina, thanks for always looking forward to my next project. Thank you to my Strebor family and extended literary friends, Shakir Rashaan, Allison Hobbs, Cairo, Pat Tucker, Shelia Goss, Suzetta Perkins, Curtis Alcutt, Sincere, Anna Black, Abdul, Marcel Terrell, Sanquinta, Paulette Carter, Sh'Moore, Michelle Cuttino, Jada Pearl, Shontrell Wade, Nefarious, Tyiavory, Niyah Moore, C.J. Hudson, Kai, Anna J, Treasure, Nyah Storm, and all those that are on their grind with me. To my agent, Maxine, thanks for all that you've done and continue to do to take my writing career to the next level. Charmaine and Zane, I could never thank you enough. Zane, I treasure every bit of advice you've ever given me and I am so grateful to be a part of the Strebor family. I look forward to what's to come.

And to all the book sellers, libraries, book clubs, bloggers, reviewers, and avid readers that love and share what I do with the world, I appreciate you from the bottom of my heart. Johnathan Royal, OOSA, The Dock Bookshop, Sista 2 Sista, Black Expressions, Sisters of Essence, Ms. Poetic, Sonja Powell Cooks, Mz. Lady Stiletto, Martin Roy, Readers Paradise, Ella Curry, EDC Creations, Delta Reviewer, AAMBC, TaNisha Webb, and Joey Pinkney, thank you for promoting literacy and assisting in building an author's platform. We couldn't do it without you.

Prologue

"Don't you get it? Neither of those women gave a damn about you. You were nothing more than a paycheck to them, but you were too stupid to realize that. That was *my* money and you had no right!"

"It was ours!"

"No, it was mine!" Vivian lashed out. Greg nearly lost his composure. "But I'll be reimbursed for my troubles once the life insurance pays out, which by the way, I increased after learning of that slut, Denise." She bestowed upon him a twisted condescending smirk.

Greg detested her. The love and compassion he once felt for his wife, seemingly deserted him. He felt nothing. Only saw her for the true evil bitch that she's always been. The raging veins that protruded from his neck looked more like tiny snakes. His breathing became unsteady as his anger intensified.

"You'll never get away with this!"

"Correction. I already have."

Greg lunged for the gun and when he did…a loud bang echoed off every wall in the house. He collapsed onto the bed as blazing hot lead tore right through his skull. The earsplitting clap of the gun had his ears ringing, but it was a far cry from church bells. It sounded more like a stick of dynamite had exploded right in front of his face. His vision became a clouded blur, somewhat like a thick fog, and everything around him seemed to be happening in slow motion.

John Mayer's lyrics sounded as if they were being played backward as he lay there in excruciating pain. Resistance was futile. His wife wanted him to hurt and he was. She'd sought retribution and with every agonizing breath he took, he knew she'd get that and a lump sum of money too. Out of the corner of his right eye, he vaguely saw that their wedding video had been frozen on the part of them sealing their vows. That eternal kiss was the last thing Vivian wanted him to see. The last image she wanted to slow burn in his mind before he succumbed to the fatal gunshot wound.

He couldn't see all the blood spewing from the hole in the left side of his head, but he felt every ounce of it, leaving him weaker by the second. Instead of focusing on the pain, his efforts had been reserved for breathing and trying to remain calm in order to prevent going into hypo-volemic shock.

"Tell Denise I said hello!" she antagonized as she hovered over him. She fumbled around him for a second, then placed his gun in his hand, staging the scene as a self-inflicted gunshot wound to the head. That's what she wanted the police to believe. That's what she would tell family and friends. And that's what she would take to her grave. No one but he and God would really know what had happened here today.

"Please help me," Greg desperately cried out to his wife. He was at her mercy.

He blinked his eyes and Vivian was gone. He couldn't move. He couldn't speak, only writhe in pain. Death had a chokehold on him and he could feel himself slowly losing consciousness. For now, he still had a rhythm to his heart. But that rhythm slowly became fainter with every breath that he took. He was unsure of the minutes or seconds he had left as he began to strangle on his own blood. His body started to grow numb. Then cold.

Just before he closed his eyes, he heard a loud yell. It came from a man.

"Dear God! Umm…hold tight, man. I'm going to get you some help. Hello, operator. My next-door neighbor has been shot." He rattled off the address. "Yes. It looks like he attempted suicide!" Pause. "Yes, he still has a pulse." Pause. "Okay…okay…please hurry! This man is dying!"

1

"A new beginning…a new beginning…" Nadine murmured repeatedly. A soft subtle smile played on her naked thin lips as she settled a warm captivating gaze on her long-time lover and friend, Jeff Jackson. This was that incredible moment that she had been waiting for and the day she had prayed about every single night for four long years. It was all happening now, and while she was flushed with so many different emotions, the only one that truly mattered to her was the joy she felt burning in her heart for the man she had been predestined to marry.

An anxious energy moved intensely through her entire body all while her mind stood calmly at peace as Jeff's proposal sank in. She inhaled every single word like a breath of fresh picked roses in the exact order in which they left his full mahogany, chocolate lips.

"Nadine Collins, will you make me the happiest man in the world and do me the honor of becoming my wife?" Nadine didn't answer him right away. She wanted to savor this moment for as long as she could.

Jeff's speech leading to his proposal had come out so perfect. Almost as though he had rehearsed what he would say to her for months. It was so genuine, touching, and heartfelt that she would have bet money that he'd stolen the lines right out of a romance movie. But stolen or not, at this profound moment and time, they belonged exclusively to her. And nothing mattered more to Nadine than the crystal-clear picture of their future together, finally, as husband and wife.

Suddenly, a loud wail resonated in her ears, causing a mask of confusion to settle on her now tear-stricken face. Her eyelids twitched but her eyes refused to open. Nadine tried her hardest to focus on Jeff's doe-shaped, bright amber-colored eyes as they stared deeply within hers. Seconds later, he proceeded to slide the platinum two-karat diamond ring on her left finger. Her entire face lit up all at once.

The racing of Nadine's heart sounded like a marching band at a Juneteenth celebration. It was as loud as her thoughts. And as uncontrollable nerves climbed up and down her spine, her arms broke out in chill bumps and the fine prickly hairs on the back of her neck stood tall. His bleared eyes danced within hers, and his dick secretly serenaded her pussy, causing it to blush and sprinkle the crotch of her panties. It was surely beyond obvious to everyone witnessing *her* moment that they had been lovers for some time. But Nadine was mesmerized by her husband-to-be, and oblivious to everyone and everything happening around them. She had chosen to forget about all the drama. She was ready to leave the past behind them so that they could concentrate solely on rebuilding their lives together as one big happy family.

"Yes! I will marry you, Jeff. A new beginning," Nadine carried on as she intentionally ignored the constant crying for as long as she could until finally, she popped both of her eyes open in dire panic.

Somewhat dazed, she looked around the colossal, excessively furnished bedroom she shared with her son, Canvas. It was lit partially by the moonlight that peeked through the slight opening of her balcony blinds. She had expected to find her entire staff of Platinum Crest Investments and their clients surrounding her.

Expected the women to be crying tears of joy and happiness for her while Jeff was still positioned on one bended knee, pouring out his heart to her. Besides the day that she'd given birth to their son, this was supposed to be one of the most happiest moments of her entire life. Nadine had waited all of her life for *this* man. Been through hell and back for *this* man. But as she slowly came out of her stupor and her vision grew much clearer, she sighed in aggravation. A brutal reality slapped her senseless and shattered her delusional thinking before she could entertain the idea of marriage to her child's father any further.

She disappointedly looked down at her left ring finger—no engagement ring. Worse, no wedding ring! It didn't take her long after that to realize that she had been dreaming all along. And like all the other dreams, this one felt just as real.

Jeff had not proposed to Nadine the previous day at work as she had dreamt. In fact, she had not seen or heard from Jeff at all this week, which may have been the prime reason behind all her imaginings. She rationalized that her dreams were a sign that he was getting ready to propose. A premonition, or maybe it could have been that right now at this very moment, he was tossing and turning in his own bed, trying to figure out the best way to ask her for her hand in marriage, and she was only having a telepathic moment.

Nadine inhaled sharply before expelling a bout of wishful thinking. After all of those years of being the other woman, the mistress, the silent partner and puppet in an orchestrated three-way affair, she thought by now she would be inured to waking up in her own bed, without him there next to her. She assumed she was acclimatized to the disappointment, the hurt, and all those other hopeless feelings that she occasionally allowed to take center stage. However, the truth was that she would never allow herself to be content with any role other than wife. Hell, she was even ashamed that she'd let him string her along this long.

Nadine eased herself from the bed and walked over to her screaming baby. Their son, Canvas Demond Jackson, was eleven months now and was starting to look more and more like Jeff every day. He had his warm mahogany complexion, thick and defined brows, mesmerizing brown eyes, and soft black hair. Whereas Jeff's natural wavy hair was kept in a Caesar, Canvas had baby-fine, soft tight curls. Even the way Canvas smiled was identical to his father.

Nadine didn't regret her decision to keep her son after strongly considering putting him up for adoption, but she couldn't help but question how things would be between her and Jeff if she had. She hadn't done herself any special favors getting involved with Jeff, and since she was being totally real nowadays, the Mandingo dick wasn't worth any of the heartache and drama she had sustained during the course of their fucking-while-pending-marriage-courtship. She silently cursed the time and energy she had wasted on him. It had been all for nothing, or at least almost nothing.

"Mama's here, baby," Nadine sang to Canvas as she scooped him up from the toddler bed, a cherrywood bed frame complete with yellow, green, and baby blue bedding that clashed with all of her bedroom décor. Her entire room had been transformed into a nursery, which was all the more reason why she felt the exigency to upgrade to something more comfortable for her and Canvas. She loved her contemporary 3,500 square-foot, one-bedroom condominium, which was situated in a secluded back quadrant of an elegant enclave in uptown Dallas. It had been home for over five years, but ever since she'd had her son, it had felt more and more like a shotgun shack.

"Did you have a bad dream?" she whispered softly, rocking him in her arms. She walked Canvas over to her bed and cuddled right next to him. She sang lullabies and stared at him until he drifted right back off to sleep.

Fully awake now, Nadine glanced over at the clock on her fireplace mantle. She wondered where, what, who, Jeff and his dick were inside of at this very moment. It was one o'clock in the morning and she struggled with whether or not she should call him so late in the hour to talk about what was still bothering her and depriving her of much needed rest.

She laid her head, which was covered in a purple silk scarf, back against the pillow and watched the ceiling fan spin. Her baby's soft snores were perfect reminders of why she shouldn't call, care, or worry about his ass. After all, he didn't bother calling to check up on his son or to even ask if she needed anything for him. It took her back to the conversation they'd had last week right after they'd finished making steamy, sweet, passionate…sex. She had suggested Jeff sell the house so that he and Deandra could move in with her and Canvas. It didn't matter so much that she didn't really have the space, in fact she never gave it any thought. Her reasoning was that it was time they raised the children together under one roof, as brother and sister. Jeff rejected the idea. Said it was too soon. Too soon for him, too soon for Deandra. He came up with every excuse in the book, then drove his point home by reminding her that Denise had only been dead a year, as if Nadine had somehow lost all recollection of her best friend. How could she ever forget the day they'd buried her best friend.

Nadine decided not to press the move-in issue any further, but she refused to give up entirely. They still had another bridge to cross. She argued that Canvas needed his father's time and affection as much as Deandra did. She felt that Jeff was showing favoritism between the children and she wasn't afraid to confront him about it. Canvas was his child too and he didn't deserve his father's neglect. If it weren't for all Jeff's empty promises, maybe she wouldn't have felt the void she was feeling now. The contempt. She had been robbed of everything she had imagined for them, and for that reason, she despised Jeff. She sank into a deep sulk as she recalled how he'd reacted when she brought up marriage.

"When will it ever happen? Every time I try to bring it up, you skate around it. I want a husband, not a boy toy, Jeff," Nadine retorted. "Is that too much to ask of you?"

"I keep telling you to give me more time."

"Pssst! I've given you plenty of that already. You either want to marry me or you don't."

"Nadine, I don't need the extra pressure right now!" Jeff matched her tone. "I'm not rushing into this. Time! That's all a brother's asking for."

Nadine shot daggers with her eyes. She marched right into the kitchen and snatched the photo calendar of Canvas off the refrigerator door so hard the magnetic piece fell off in the process. She walked over to where Jeff stood, slapped the calendar on the counter, then located an ink pen and practically shoved it in his right hand. As unannounced tears slid down her face, she looked him dead in the eyes. "Your time is up." There was a moment of pause as her words hung in the air. "When are you going to make me your wife?"

Nadine had asked Jeff that question in the midst of their most recent discussion, stressing that she needed a specific date because she and Canvas had been on the back burner long enough. Jeff hadn't responded to her liking. She'd given him an ultimatum. One thing had been said after another. It hadn't ended well, and now, she hadn't heard one single word from him.

While she loved Jeff with every fiber of her being, she hated how selfish and inconsiderate he could be. How he was able to shut her out of his life, and how he always made her feel guilty for wanting more. Guilty for loving him. She hated feeling needy, and at times desperate for his attention. His love. It wasn't fair and she was tired of trying to rationalize her misplaced feelings. She deserved better than this, she told herself as many times as she needed to.

Nadine reluctantly picked up the cordless receiver. She didn't really know exactly what would come out of her mouth if he answered, but she dialed the number anyway, telling herself that she shouldn't be the one calling. Again.

She promptly placed the receiver to her ear and cleared her parched throat. Despite the introspective pep talk, she hoped to get on one accord with Jeff, if nothing else. There was no reason they couldn't be civil to one another.

Hello, you've reached Jeff Jackson. Unfortunately, I'm away from my phone. Please feel free to leave your name, number, and a detailed message, and I will get right back with you at my earliest convenience. Beep!

Nadine took a deep breath, pressed her lips together, and tried to stomach that perturbed feeling resting in the pit of her gut. She stumbled over what to say, being careful not to piss him off more than he might have still been. Then she could guarantee he'd never call back.

"Jeff, this is me, Nadine. We haven't heard from you, and I… just wanted to make sure you were okay." She rested on that last sentence before continuing. "I'll be up for a little while if you'd like to talk…" She closed her eyes, reopened them, then shifted her position in the bed, "or come by. Just please…don't do this again. Don't shut me out." She juggled the tears in her eyes. "We love you," she said lastly, disconnecting the call.

She placed the phone back on the cradle, and as if on cue, it started to ring. She waited for the caller ID display to register the name before answering. Seeing that it was Jeff's number, she pressed TALK before the second ring, not wanting it to alarm her son and disrupt his sleep.

"I was hoping you would call right back because I was just sitting here thinking about what I said last week, and I want you to know that—" Nadine's apology fell incomplete once the angelic moans of a woman's voice soared through the phone line. "Hello," Nadine uttered barely as she eased out of bed. She stopped in her tracks once she was completely out of Canvas's earshot, and pulled the phone closer to her ear.

"That's right, daddy. Fuck me! Harder!" the woman screamed.

The loud grunts were all too familiar.

"Jeff?" Nadine called out in the weakest of tones. Her breathing was jagged and shallow. The words that came to mind were unexpectedly clogged in her throat.

"Whose pussy is this?" Nadine heard Jeff ask the woman.

"It's yours, daddy!"

Nadine hung up. She couldn't handle any more. She walked hastily, further into the main room. Her feet swept across the cold hardwood floor before arriving at the oversized Persian rug that covered most of the living area. She flopped down on the sofa and tried to catch her breath, but it felt as though the air had been knocked out of her lungs. Felt as if her heart had been ripped right out of her chest. Her body stiffened and her fists balled tightly at her sides.

"Why is he doing this to me?"

Nadine couldn't bear the thought. Her bottom lip began to tremor and she felt a tingling, burning sensation in the back of her throat as she tried her hardest to suppress the inevitable, but it was useless. Within seconds, tears rounded her beautiful brown face, flowing like an endless river. It was that deep. That heartbreaking. Four years out of her life was what Jeff had taken from her. She had put her life on hold waiting for him, and this was the reward for her patience.

Nadine began to mumble something that not even her own ears took seriously enough to translate.

"I can't do this anymore. I can't," she said indistinctly, shaking her head at the truth revealed. More tears collected on her face, blurring her vision, even as she sat in the dark. She asked herself if this was another round of karma coming back to visit. Wondered if this was her punishment for having an affair with a married man—for bearing his child—for still sticking around long after the whistle had been blown. Or was it Denise, her longtime best friend and Jeff's former deceased wife, haunting her for payback?

The answers to those puzzling pieces escaped Nadine as she tried to come full circle with this once and for all. A trail of tears formed a puddle in the corners of her mouth. She drew in her bottom lip and her warm wet tongue got a taste of yesterday, last week, and the past four years. It was the taste of bittersweet memories, love, pain, and everything that fell in between. While Nadine knew it would be difficult to move on from Jeff, she realized it was time. It was apparent that he had no interest in taking their relationship to the next level, and for once in her life, she was tired of pushing the issue. It wasn't getting her anywhere.

The distress from the outcome of it all weighed so heavy on Nadine's heart that she began to experience light chest pains. These exact pains were the onset of blood pressure problems that she had experienced throughout her entire pregnancy which caused her to threaten a miscarriage. It was a result of the subconscious stress she had inherited the second she'd gotten involved with Jeff.

Nadine placed her left hand over her broken heart. To her surprise, it still had rhythm. Another pain soared through the center of her chest, making her gasp all at once. It validated what she had been thinking all along. It was time to let it go! If she didn't, that man was going to send her to an early grave. She didn't bother wiping away the hot tears that cascaded down her face. She eventually decided to go back to bed.

Nadine vowed that this would be the last time that she'd ever allow a man to play Russian roulette with her heart. The last time that she would settle for a man who was not ready to make her his honest lifetime commitment—his wife. Last but not least, Nadine was taking a vow of celibacy. Sex complicated things and lately, Jeff's mind-blowing, ten-piece of dark meat managed to not only be the fix she needed to knock the edge off, but it was the culprit nominated to incite her poor judgment.

She pulled the covers over her body and stared at her son who was sleeping so peacefully, despite the hailstorm his parents were going through. She regretted believing that she was exempt from this type of pain. She wanted to scream and curse, but couldn't. Wanted to throw things out of rage, but wouldn't. She so badly wanted to pick up the phone and give that no-good-bastard a piece of her mind, but didn't. She refused to reduce herself any more than she already had.

Nadine had dehydrated herself emotionally. Her muscles began to ache and her head began to throb. Her eyelids grew heavy. She couldn't refuse her mind and body any longer. Besides, she would need every bit of energy she had left for tomorrow. She was going to do something that she now knew she should have done a long time ago. She was going to take back her life. And the very first step in that direction was to change the locks on her door. Not only did Jeff hold the keys to her heart, he had convenience store-hours access to her pussy. But not anymore!

2

Jeff walked out of the restroom after flushing the Magnum condom he had just worn down the toilet. His semi-hard, ten-inch dick looked like it had been dipped and coated in several layers of rich dark chocolate fudge, then pumped with steroids as it seemingly hung between his knees. He slowly walked toward the bed, his eyes locked completely on her.

"Ready for another round?" Ménage asked seductively as she spread her long, silky shaven legs into an expanding V, as if she were posing for a men's magazine centerfold. She parted the lips of her juicy, tender pussy with two fingers to reward Jeff with a 3D experience, then teasingly twirled the tip of her pearl tongue.

"Come on and finish playing this pussy like a harmonica," Ménage squealed as she dipped one of her saucy fingers inside her orifice. She was wetter than before.

Tonight Ménage wore her hair slicked back in a long straight Jeannie ponytail that stopped just above the split of her ass, with three-toned colored bangs, a silky jet-black and a strawberry-honey blonde. Her poetic tight hazel eyes, flawless butter pecan complexion, and stallion body was the envy of all the strippers at X-Rated, the popular gentleman's club where she currently worked. It was also the spot where she'd met her lover, slash customer, slash suga daddy, Jeff. He was a godsend if she'd ever believed in one.

Ménage hadn't been in the stripping business long, but for the extent of time that she had, she was ready to get the hell out. She didn't want to become trapped in the lifestyle of fast and easy money like many of her homegirls who had succumbed to it. She'd heard one horror story after another about women who were murdered, raped, beaten, kidnapped, or committed suicide, all because of the lifestyle. Then there were the few dancers whose age had caught up to them. They had lost their youth, their body, and all the money right along with it. And the real big-time spenders didn't want a washed-up dancer. That was a no-brainer. They wanted and had to have the baddest bitch in the club. The chick that had body and knew every pole and pussy-popping trick in the stripper's handbook. Ménage was *that* bitch, hands down. She was an anything-goes-behind-closed-doors type of chick and had the best pussy that money could buy. Most of all, she was known for her creative talent and mad sex appeal. She was undoubtedly the highest-paid dancer at X-Rated. And while her name came with local fame and money like clockwork, there was no way in hell that she could make a career out of stripping, nor was she trying to. She wanted to get in, make a little money, and get the hell out. And now that she had over forty grand saved in the bank and a little extra all-purpose cash on hand, she was ready to chase her real dreams.

She'd had her share of experiences in the industry, but she felt it was time to get out while she still had a chance. Stripping wasn't in her life plan; it sort of happened by accident. She had graduated from high school and was on the right track to a promising future until her dope-dealing boyfriend, Slug, got them caught up. He'd owed his supplier money from a score they'd fronted him, and when he'd failed to cash out, rumors started to spread like wildfire that a hit had been put out on him. So when Ménage had gotten word of that, she'd bailed out on Slug, ditched her hometown, Detroit, and fled to Dallas with the clothes on her back and the shoes on her feet. She didn't even tell her family where she was moving. All they had been told was that she had accepted some high-paying job out of state. That was about two years ago and she never looked back, but the trio of bullets tattooed on the face of her pussy would always serve as a reminder of the life and the man that she'd left behind.

While Ménage possessed the body and talent that made her big money, stripping was far from what she had her heart and sights set on. She was an aspiring actress and she figured it would take a miracle to happen before she ever got discovered in Texas. So this next move was going to put her in the *real* spotlight that she deserved. And whether Jeff knew it or not, he was going to help her get there.

Jeff's eyes never wavered from her hairless pussy. Her swollen glistening pair of lips called out his name, causing his nodding dick to swell and salute her all over again. She couldn't believe that he had this type of effect on her, as much as she couldn't believe that he was still rock-hard after busting that mighty big nut. He was seven years older than her, but his dick had the stamina of an eighteen-year-old. He had put a hurting on her pussy, but she wanted more.

"You see what you do to him?" Jeff asked, pointing to his Gila monster of a dick.

She parted her lips, then rolled her long tongue over the upper one. "I could always use some more protein, but then again, it looks like daddy's dick is still hungry," Ménage teased as her enticing eyes traveled his tall, chiseled, and lean physique. Jeff was over six feet tall, dark, handsome, and could beat the brakes off of a wet pussy. She could attest to his bedroom get-down and she was addicted to the pipe. Unlike her other customers, she never had to pretend with Jeff. He was the only man that could make her hotter than a sauna every single time they were together.

"Tell mama you hungry," she purred softly, bringing her wet sticky finger to her lips. She slid out her tongue and proceeded to suck her own sweet pudding right off of her finger. "Ummmm! Tastes like candy." She smiled. She then reinserted her finger, pulled it out, and made her pussy blow bubbles. He enjoyed watching her do nasty tricks. Especially the different ways she made herself cum. She was sure her being a squirter had everything to do with it.

"Damn, baby. You stay wet." Jeff was obviously enjoying the peep show.

"If you want some, come get some," Ménage ordered him.

Jeff took baby steps forward, his eyes drawn to her sweet carnation pink center as his steel-like pipe aimed in her direction like a loaded Smith & Wesson, ready to cause some internal destruction. Noticing his cell phone on the floor, he picked it up and tossed it back on the nightstand. Ménage watched on sheepishly, wishing she could have seen the look on that bitch's face as she got an earful of the two of them going at it. She bet his baby mama was lying up sick right now after listening to another woman getting dicked down by her man. Ménage gave it her all not to burst out into laughter.

Jeff climbed on the bed and crawled toward her. The desire to have him back inside of her mouth had sweat building on her tongue. She spread her legs as wide as they would go and upon that notion, Jeff lowered his entire face back into her yoni. She wrapped her legs loosely around his backside and fisted the sheets as he drove his tongue deeply inside of her.

"Right there, daddy," Ménage squealed as the tip of Jeff's tongue put a gentle spanking on her clit, driving her insane.

"You like that?" Jeff asked, nudging his nose against her arousal as his tongue seesawed between her slippery folds.

Ménage's eyes were practically rolling in the back of her head. "Oh yessss!" she hollered.

Jeff slid his right middle finger inside of her while his tongue paddled through her recurring waves. Ménage placed her hands on the back of his head, propped a leg over his nice tight ass, and fed it to him right.

"I'm about to cum, baby!" Ménage announced. Soon as the words left her lips, Jeff stopped, flipped her over on all fours, and began devouring her from behind. He slapped her on her ass and reacted at how it bounced back against his face. "Ooohhh shit!" Ménage moaned, pulling at her left nipple ring, loving the pain that it brought.

"This what you wanted, huh?"

"Yessss, daddy. Punish this pussy!" Ménage sang. "Don't cheat me outta my fucking nut!" Ménage could tell by how hard his dick felt against her ass that he was on the brink of explosion. He blindly reached on the side of him and grabbed the last rubber out of the Magnum pack. He slipped it on quickly all while he continued his feast, forcing her to reach a climax so big that she squirted all over his face.

He lifted his face from her crotch and took his tongue skinny-dipping along the river banks of her asshole. "I'ma teach you to stop nutting until I say when—" Jeff stopped mid-sentence when they heard a pounding knock on the door. He was hard as tree lumber and about one second away from making his grand entrance inside of her before the abrupt interruption.

Ménage stiffened all at once and then rolled over onto her side as the second round of knocks came.

"You expecting somebody?" Jeff asked, his face pulled into a scrunch.

Ménage checked the time. "No, I'm not expecting anybody this late." She jumped up from the bed and hurried over to the dresser. She threw on a white tank and a pair of lime-green, low-rise terry shorts that made her ass look twice as big, then practically power-walked toward the front door. She looked out the peephole before cracking it open. It was her neighbor and good friend, Tiffany, from directly across the hall.

When Jeff heard the front door open and close, his guard came up. He cursed under his breath as he threw his boxers and jeans on as fast as he could. A million things ran through his mind as he dressed. One of them was whether it was one of Ménage's customers. A hint of jealousy crept over him, but he quickly dismissed it. Although Ménage wasn't what he would ever classify as his woman, she was indeed his lover, his comforter, and his newest addiction. In only a short year, she had replaced all the things that Nadine used to be at one point, and more. In that short time span, Jeff had grown to care for Ménage, but that was about as far as he would allow his feelings to go for her, or for any woman. His pride had been walked on, his feelings pissed on, and his heart shitted on—all by a damn woman. A woman that he once proudly claimed as his wife. He had been betrayed in the worst way and he didn't know if he would ever recover.

A major chain of events had his mind and his heart in a screwed-up place right now, and all a woman could do for him was reward him with some no-strings-attached-conversation and some have-it-your-way-on-the-go pussy. That was *all* he expected and needed from a woman—pussy and conversation—it was all that he would allow a woman to give him generously. He didn't need or want an emotional deposit. That was a personal investment that he knew she would never get a return on, because emotionally, Jeff had checked the hell out. The invisible scars across his chest suggested that he wasn't built to love or trust anybody else. His player's card had been restored and it was time to put that baby to maximum use and catch up on lost time. The days of feeling obligated to one woman and being boggled down with one woman, were history. He was a free man, mentally and physically, and free men did whatever the hell they wanted to, when they wanted to, without the restrictions.

Jeff headed into the living room and found the front door wide open. He could faintly hear Ménage arguing with someone outside as their voices carried into her second-floor apartment. He hurried down the stairs and trudged toward the commotion brewing in the parking lot, unsure as to what was going on.

"I said don't touch my gotdamn car!"

"Sorry, ma'am, you're going to have to call our office in the morning and straighten this out on your own time. As far as I'm concerned, your name is on my list to repossess your vehicle, and that's exactly what I'm here to do."

"I better not see one scratch on my shit!" Ménage screamed over the loud grinding noise that came from the tow truck as it raised her new black Honda Accord onto the flatbed. The fully loaded vehicle was decked out with custom chrome wheels and dark-tinted windows. It was one of the dressiest cars in the parking lot, with a license plate that read *BOSS B.* With her face twisted in a scowl, she yelled, "I'm calling the police. Your list is a bunch of bullshit!" She screamed loud enough for the entire apartment complex to hear her.

"Go right on ahead, ma'am. I'll leave a card for them too."

Ménage grunted and turned to walk off just as Jeff was coming up from behind.

"Hey, hey, hey. What's going on?" Jeff asked. His eyes darted from a hysterical Ménage to the short, heavyset, and balding Hispanic man who was dressed in plain dingy clothing that had visible dirt and oil stains on both his shirt and jeans. He looked over to the tow truck. One side of it read: *GARCIA'S WRECKER SERVICE.*

"I'm towing this *nice* young lady's car, because she hasn't paid her bills," the man retorted sarcastically.

"That's bullshit! I pay all my damn bills and when I call the bank tomorrow to straighten this shit out, I'm going to see to it that your ass is fired!" Ménage fired back. Her silver spike hoop earrings bounced against her shoulders as she fired off.

The man stopped what he was doing only to smile at Ménage and then went right back to work.

"Asshole," Ménage huffed loudly, crossing her arms.

"Wait a minute, my man. There's clearly some misunderstanding here, Mr.—"

"Tony. Tony Garcia," he said with emphasis, smiling again at Ménage who stared at him viciously.

Ménage rolled her eyes upward, shifted her weight from one side to the other, and as she was about to let loose again, Jeff turned to her.

"Go ahead and go back upstairs," Jeff said in a low tone.

"But this motherfucker doesn't—"

"Ménage, let me handle this." It was only then that he noticed that Ménage's shirt was totally see-through. She wasn't wearing a bra, and with the parking lot being fairly lit, he could see her dark swollen nipples and their costume jewelry. He made a gesture with his eyes, but she was so riled up, he doubted she had caught it. He then stepped directly in front of her and faced Tony.

Ménage let out an exaggerated sigh and headed back to the apartment.

"That mamacita of yours has a potty mouth!" Tony retorted, as he continued to reel her car in.

Jeff placed his hand in his pocket and pulled out his wallet. He had three $100 bills, a $50 bill and a few singles. He pulled out the fifty and held it out to Tony. "Please. Just give us a couple of days to resolve this. We will have it all straightened out by then. You have my word." Jeff had been in the car and sales industry way too long to know that business could always be handled under the table.

Tony eyed the money blowing in Jeff's right hand. Without a second thought, he reached over, accepted it, and shoved it into his jeans pocket. "She has until Monday to handle her business. If not, I'm coming back."

Jeff nodded in agreement. "Understood."

Jeff walked off as Tony proceeded to lower Ménage's vehicle from the flat bed. He went back upstairs and when he arrived at the top, he saw Ménage's flamboyant gay neighbor, Mario aka Tiffany, inside of her apartment consoling her. Jeff went inside and both Ménage and Tiffany turned to him.

"All right, Ms. Thang, I'll give you a call tomorrow, honey," Tiffany said, giving Ménage a hug. "And don't lose an ounce of beauty sleep behind this. Everything's going to work out just fine."

Tiffany smiled as he switched past Jeff as if he were modeling on a runway. His long black hair weave had blonde highlights and his MAC makeup was flawless, as usual. Tiffany's lean, well-toned physique was enhanced by breast augmentation and butt implants that filled out his dark denim Baby Phat romper. He rocked a pair of toe-peeking, red-bottom heels that were so high, even Jeff was impressed. Ménage had shared with him once that Tiffany referred to himself as the Mexican Nicki Minaj. He idolized the celebrity rap star so much that his dress and style was even inspired by her. Tiffany also shared Nicki's Zodiac sign, which happened to be Sagittarius. He had the word *tattooed* on the lower part of his back with an arrow that pointed downward.

"See y'all good peeps tomorrow," Tiffany called out before closing the door behind him to return to his apartment.

Jeff looked at Ménage who was standing with tears filling her eyes.

"Did he tow my car?" she asked, practically in a whisper.

Jeff shook his head no.

"Thank God!" she sighed in relief. "What did you say to him?"

"I held him off until Monday."

"Monday," Ménage repeated softly. She placed a hand over her forehead. Jeff could see every muscle in her face start to tense. Her pupils seemed to shrink as she dropped her gaze. Her mouth was slightly agape, yet her breathing quickened.

"Talk to me. You didn't make your car payment, did you?" Jeff asked her anyway, although he had already presumed that she hadn't.

Ménage looked around her living room and then settled her eyes back on Jeff's. She answered him with a delayed shake of the head. She pressed her lips tightly together and her bottom lip trembled. With hooded eyes, "This is so damn embarrassing," she said as two tears skated down her doll-like cheeks.

"Why didn't you come to me?"

"What was I going to say? That I can't pay my car note because

I'm too busy trying to keep a roof over my head." Ménage chuckled at the absurdity of her revelation. She rolled her eyes upward, batting her extended full black lashes. She then took both of her index fingers and dabbed at the corners of her eyes. "I would have figured it all out," she told him, her voice cracking along the way.

Jeff's face was masked with confusion. "But I don't get it. You work and...," he took a look around her living room, "you make damn good money from what I can see."

Ménage guffawed, twisted her lips and then turned them upward. "So is that what you really think?"

"So you're trying to tell me this is all pretend?" Jeff waited to be convinced because his wallet told a different story. By his math, she made enough money to pay all of her bills simply off what he paid her alone. The lavish upkeep of her suburban apartment also cancelled that lie. She had fifty-inch, wall-mounted flat-screens in every room, furniture that looked like it cost a pretty good penny, and her closet alone housed all of her favorite designer labels. Ménage was living good. Better than most. She had exquisite taste, and with that kind of trait, having access to money was a necessity. He would be a damn fool to believe differently.

"Baby, shortly after I met you, I quit X-Rated," she said, staring him in the eyes. "To be perfectly honest with you, I only have enough money in my savings account to get by for a couple more months, and after that's gone, I don't know what I'm going to do. I may have to move back home," she lamented.

Jeff's face lifted with genuine concern. "Why'd you quit your job?"

"I saw how uncomfortable it made you knowing that I was stripping and serving for other men besides you," Ménage said, taking a few steps closer.

Jeff said nothing, only relaxed his shoulders and inhaled her sweet and sultry scent.

"Tell me it didn't bother you," Ménage pressed.

"Yeah, I can admit that it messed with me a little bit for a while, but I knew that was your money gig. And I would never come between your money," Jeff replied as he watched her blush.

"But you told me," she said, placing her finger on his bottom lip, "out of your own mouth, that I was better than X-Rated. That I deserved more. Remember that?" Jeff watched in admiration as she pulled her eighteen-inch stream of Malaysian weave to the right side of her neck. "I know there's something better out there for me." She spoke with the same confidence Jeff was used to hearing from her in the bedroom. "Stripping is played and I'm getting too old for this shit." She chuckled, looping her hands around Jeff's neck. Even in her heels, he still towered her.

"You call twenty-seven old? Hell, I must be ancient then."

"Dinosaur," Ménage said with a loose laugh as her gaze settled on his. "Seriously though. You helped me to realize who I am and what I want out of life. When I look in the mirror now, I don't only see Ménage. I see the *real* me. Ebony Larue Greer," she said proudly, disclosing her government name to him for the first time. "I see an aspiring psychologist who wants to help people."

"Wow, psychologist," Jeff repeated, in shock by her profession choice. He would have never guessed. "And what made you decide that?"

"People like you."

Jeff drew his neck back. "People like me?"

"Yeah. I like listening to people's problems. I guess I feel like I can help them, ya know. Everyone has a story, Jeff." She paused and measured the look in his eyes. "And everyone has a secret." Another pause. She drew her lips to his ears and slid out her warm tongue and snaked it along his left earlobe. "Wouldn't you agree?"

The way Ménage looked at him, the way she spoke to him, the

way she touched him, gave him a rush. And her warm silky skin against his always made his dick wake up from its nap. She then placed her cotton-soft lips against his.

"I want something new," she said, inching out her tongue again and tracing it along his lips. Jeff watched her eyes drift as she rubbed her nose across his mustache, inhaling the traces of her candy corn. He embraced Ménage as her tongue finally entered his mouth. "I deserve to be happy too," Ménage managed in the midst of their tongue affair. She took her left hand and slid down his zipper. She maneuvered her hand inside of the opening, suggesting that she wanted to pick up where they had left off.

Jeff's head fell back as she stroked his erection.

"I want...you, Jeff," Ménage said, before easing to her knees and taking him inside of her impatient mouth.

Once the tip of her tongue glided over the head of his shaft, Jeff moaned with delight. She slid it along the trunk of his dick, showering it before taking it for a scuba dive back down her throat. She deep-throated him so good he came inside of her mouth in less than five minutes. He nearly lost his equilibrium. Once she was done, she opened her mouth, showed him the flavor of the day, and swallowed!

Ménage stood and went to the bathroom to grab some towels and freshen up. Afterward, she sauntered back into the living room and handed a towel to Jeff. As he cleaned himself, he glanced over at her. She wondered what was going through his head. Wondered if there were any changes of heart.

"How much for today?" Jeff asked.

Ménage looked at him dumbfounded. She let his question soak

in before responding. "So, you weren't listening to anything I said a few minutes ago?"

Jeff zipped his pants and handed Ménage the dirty towel. "Which part?"

Ménage couldn't believe her ears. She fixed her incredulous eyes on his and shook her head. With disappointment and hurt laced in her tone, she said, "Keep your money. I don't need it." With that said, she walked off, headed for the room, and left him standing until he got the picture.

"I'll call you," Jeff called out, but she didn't answer. Instead, she sat on the edge of her bed long-faced. Not even a minute later, she heard her front door open and close. She waited a few minutes, counting to ten before she decided to come out of hiding. She instantly spotted the money Jeff had paid her, on the coffee table. It was the fee she charged for her "special" services. She rushed over to the window that overlooked the parking lot. The spot beside her car was now empty. She turned around and walked back over to the cash. She rolled her eyes at the money, crossed her arms, and told herself that this was going to be a lot harder than she expected.

Ménage picked up her cell phone and dialed a number. On the first ring, Tiffany answered.

"Hey boo, did he fall for it?" Tiffany asked enthusiastically.

"Hell no," Ménage replied dryly.

"Bitch, you have got to be doing something wrong! You ain't throwing the pussy on him right or something, chile! 'Cause if that was Ms. Tiffany, baby, his ass would have been done cashed in on *this* cow."

Ménage's silence went ignored as Tiffany went on and on about her untouchable sex game.

"You have got to do better than that, honey! Haven't I taught you anything?" Tiffany went all off the subject until finally coming back around to the matter at hand. "Wheww, chile! Now tell me again how much money he got from his wife's life insurance policy."

"Ex...wife," Ménage corrected Tiffany without missing a beat. "And he got one million dollars from the policy, plus the house. And *all* the accounts that she had in her name, Jeff was the beneficiary," Ménage said, almost robotic. She called it off to Tiffany just as she had overheard it when Jeff repeated the info to whomever he had been discussing business with on the phone that day. She had pretended to be asleep, but was listening to every single word.

"Damn! You hit a jackpot. You gon' be rich, bitch!" Just as Tiffany was about to go all off the meter again, Ménage interrupted her.

"Tiff, I'ma have to call you back, girl. And oh yeah, tell Tony I said thank you. He did great. It was just like we rehearsed."

"Will do, honey. He'll be creeping back through here tonight to get some of Ms. Tiffany's good lovin'."

"Well, please don't put it on him too damn hard. And your ass better show up for work tomorrow because I'm not covering for you this time." Tiffany was one of the top bartenders at X-Rated.

"Bitch, since when have I ever missed a Friday? Never!" Tiffany answered in her transgressive feminine voice.

"Ha, ha. I'm just saying. And keep the noise level down over there. I don't wanna hear all that nasty shit. You know these walls thin as hell."

"Now look, I can't promise you all that." Tiffany laughed.

"You a mess. Well, I'll see you tomorrow night," Ménage said as she walked over to the table where the three crisp $100 bills lay. She scooped them up, locked her front door, and then walked over to the mini-bar in her dining room.

"All right. Chat with you later, babe," Tiffany hollered back.

Ménage disconnected the call and instead of hanging up the

phone, she entered the two-digit code to block her number, and quickly dialed the number she had memorized from a couple of hours earlier when it had come through Jeff's phone.

"Hello?" a woman answered groggily.

"Hi. Is Jeff in?" Ménage inquired in the sexiest phone voice she could muster.

"No, he isn't."

"Are you expecting him anytime soon?"

"No. May I ask who's calling and what matter this is in regards to this time of the night?"

"Is this Nadine?" Ménage asked, already knowing the woman's name.

"Yes. This is Nadine. Now who am I speaking with?"

Silence.

"Hello?" Nadine asked repeatedly. "Are you there?"

Ménage listened as frustration seemed to build in Nadine's voice. Finally, she hung up. A sinister smile crossed her lips from the satisfaction of hearing Nadine inquire about who she was and the purpose of her call. Ménage didn't have a personal beef with Nadine, but she did have a problem with the distraction she was becoming to her and Jeff's relationship. And she wasn't going to let anyone interfere with this opportunity of getting out the strip game and moving on to a real career in Hollywood.

Ménage took the cap off one of the many colorful liquor bottles arranged on her bar. She rolled the money like a weed joint, then dropped each bill inside a Ciroc bottle. She was now in Boss Bitch Beast mode and her game plan was in full effect.

3

Jeff was yanked out of his good sleep by the deafening sound of raging smoke alarms. Something was burning. Something was on fire. At least he thought. Only dressed in his boxer shorts, he rushed to his daughter's room in a sure panic, only to find her not there. His heart pounded through his chest and his breathing got lost in its own way as he raced through a cloud of smoke and into the smoked-out kitchen where the pungent smell was coming from. There stood Deandra, his ten-year-old daughter, standing on her stepstool in her Hello Kitty pajamas and slippers. She had on her mother's favorite cooking apron. She was multitasking; scrambling eggs in one pan, and trying to fry bacon in another. On the counter behind her was a heap of lopsided chocolate chip buttermilk pancakes.

Jeff exhaled in relief as he shook his head and chuckled at the Kodak moment. He wondered how in the world she managed to wake herself up so early on a school day when any other day he was her alarm clock.

Deandra hadn't noticed him standing behind her because it was clear that she was in her own zone. Jeff surveyed the kitchen and the huge mess that she had made. He quietly grabbed one of the towels off the countertop, walked into the hall and began fanning the smoke detector with it. A minute later, the noise stopped.

Jeff discreetly retreated back to his room, got back in the bed, and waited for Deandra to surprise him with breakfast in bed as he suspected she would. He pulled the covers up to his stomach, positioned both hands behind his head, and lay back against the pillow. At times like this, his thoughts settled on Denise, his ex-wife. He could almost feel her spirit there in the room with him, lying next to him as if she had never left.

Denise's sudden death had been hard on everyone, but Jeff felt as if he had been affected by it the most. After all, Denise was the woman he had considerably made his wife and she was the mother of the child he continued to raise as his own, despite Denise's startling deception.

Even with everything she had taken him through, Jeff told himself that he would have traded places with Denise in a heartbeat. Had God given him that choice, he would have laid down his own life for her with no second thought about it. Denise didn't deserve to die and Deandra didn't deserve to be without her mother. Now, Jeff found himself a single man having to raise their daughter all alone.

While it took Jeff a considerable amount of time to muster up enough strength to be in the same space as Denise after she'd slapped him in the face with her confession, he eventually managed to find it in his heart to forgive her. He had learned during that meeting with her that she had been raped, and that her only intentions were to raise Deandra with a man she felt would make a suitable father for her child. Denise had given him a great deal of credit before being so sure that he was even capable.

However, every now and then, Jeff found himself wondering how *any* woman could look her man in the face and lie to him about the paternity of his child. Wondered how she slept at night with that kind of secret buried inside of her. The day he'd read those paternity test results and found out Deandra wasn't his biological daughter, he'd cried like a newborn baby. Felt like his heart had been ripped out. He recalled barely being able to eat or sleep for weeks. Jeff had shut down mentally and the only thing that helped him survive the madness in spite of the paternity results, was the thought of his baby girl. While it was hard for Jeff to accept that Deandra wasn't his biological child, he dealt with it and tried to move forward. His love for his child never wavered because in his eyes, Deandra was *his* baby, and that was never going to change.

As Jeff's thoughts raced to the role Nadine played in all of it and the downright scandalous treachery that would scar him for the rest of his life, his stomach began to churn. It made him resent Nadine all the more. After loving two women and being hurt by both, Jeff felt he would never recover from that kind of pain. He was a man scorned, but he'd be damned if he ever admitted that shit out loud.

Jeff heard the clinking of the dishes as Deandra came walking down the hall. She was headed right his way. He pulled the sheet up to his chest and closed his eyes, pretending to be asleep. He added a snore for good measure.

"Good morning, Daddy!" Deandra said energetically as she placed the folding tray on her father's bed. "I made you your favorite breakfast, Daddy. Wake up!"

Jeff slowly opened his eyes, outstretched his arms, and raised his body up in the bed. He relaxed back up against the headboard.

"I made breakfast for you," Deandra said again proudly with a smile brighter than the glare of sun beaming through the window. "See!" she said, moving the tray closer to him.

"I see," Jeff said, observing all the food piled on his plate. There were a total of six pancakes, five slices of bacon, and scrambled eggs. He even had a tall glass of orange juice to wash it all down. "All this for me, huh? Courtesy of Chef Deandra." Jeff smiled.

Deandra nodded her head, her big cheesy smile still planted on her face.

Jeff acknowledged that his daughter looked more and more like her mother every day. It seemed like it was yesterday when he was bringing Deandra and Denise home from the hospital. He remembered how small she was. Five pounds, six ounces. A little over seventeen inches long with a head full of silky jet-black tresses. Now his baby girl was half-grown and about to eat him out of house and home.

Jeff picked up his fork to dive in as Deandra flopped on the bed beside him.

"Did you forget what today is, Daddy?" Deandra asked, a drop in her voice.

Jeff thought long and hard before it finally hit him. It was the one-year anniversary of Denise's death.

Jeff eased the fork back down on his plate. He looked over at his daughter. There was a tremble in his voice as he started to speak. He cleared his throat. "No, Daddy didn't forget, sweetheart," he fibbed. He stopped and looked around the large room. Everything was still in the same spot for the most part, just as Denise had left it. In fact, the entire house had remained the same. "And you know what, that's why there's no school today. We're going to go visit your mother," he said. They had gone last weekend, the weekend before that, and the weekend before that. Jeff and Deandra visited Denise's grave as often as she wanted to. Mainly on Sundays, after he picked her up from her grandmother Grace's house after staying the weekend over.

"Is Grandma coming this time?"

"Not sure, but I'll ask."

"I would like for Grandma to come with us. She never comes

with us to visit Mommy, and when I ask she always starts crying," Deandra said.

Jeff knew this had been hard on Grace as well. She had lost her only child and while they never really discussed Denise openly, it was obvious that Grace was still healing from it all. A process Jeff had yet to go through.

"Grandma will come around. It's just going to take more time, that's all," Jeff assured her.

Deandra looked at her father and planted a good smack on his cheek.

"What was that for?" Jeff smiled.

Deandra smiled back. "Mommy wants me to give all her kisses to you now."

Jeff swallowed the burn in his throat, trying to mask his feelings as best as he could in front of his daughter. "What do you say I finish my breakfast while you go get cleaned up? I have to make a pit stop to the barbershop and then we will go see your mother right after that."

"Okay, Daddy." Deandra jumped up from the bed and headed off to her room, closing Jeff's door behind her.

Jeff was glad to see how well his daughter was coping with her mother's death. Furthermore, he was even surprised that he hadn't had to seek therapy for her like he had done for himself. Only he had to spend outrageous money for the kind of therapy that he needed. It was the only kind of *help* that would take his mind off of everything he was going through. Even if it was only temporarily.

❖❖❖

Jeff drove five miles per hour along the trail of Laurel Land Cemetery until finally coming to a spot in close proximity of Denise's gravesite. He pulled in slow and parked right next to a sleek black, chrome-accented, Rolls-Royce Phantom. He called off the make and model right off the bat. He sat in admiration, telling himself that he would never spend that kind of money on a damn car, but he couldn't deny how much pussy he would pull from it. The thought brought a tempting smile to his face.

He leaned over to the passenger seat and grabbed the beautiful flower arrangement he had brought to replace the one from last week. Just as he turned to get out of the car, Greg Adams, his wife's former client and the man that rocked his marriage worse than a California earthquake, was walking toward the luxurious vehicle.

Jeff quickly placed his glasses over his eyes, wanting to be certain of the man's identity. Thankfully, Jeff couldn't be seen behind the dark tint of his car, but he could make out Greg Adams as clear as a sunny day. He would single the man out in a lineup without a problem. It was a face he would never forget, even if he tried.

The son of a bitch was dressed in the same fashion that he had been dressed in at the funeral. His tailored black and gray Giorgio Armani suit, cufflinks, and polished black shoes, summarized him in one word—money. Jeff's face frowned all on its own and an awful bitter taste filled his mouth as he sat there profiling the man that he really didn't give a hot flying fuck about.

"Daddy, what are we waiting for?" Deandra asked.

"One minute, baby. I'm trying to see something," Jeff replied, his voice monotone.

Jeff studied the man from head to toe as he got closer. His hair and face was groomed with precision. His fine designer threads exclusively tailored for his tall, medium-built frame. He had a casualness about him, yet an arrogance that was almost as flashy as that fancy automobile he drove. The wind seemingly stood still as he approached the $500,000 car. Jeff secretly eye stalked the man as he unlocked his vehicle and got inside. He turned his head in the opposite direction once Greg started up his engine and began to slowly reverse out of the parking lot.

To pass time, Deandra began reciting the poem she had written for her mother earlier that morning.

"That's real nice, baby."

"Thank you, Daddy."

Jeff waited until Greg was a half-mile down the path before pulling off.

"Where are we going?" Deandra asked, looking around them.

Jeff's eyes darted from the road to the rearview mirror. "Daddy forgot to do something, baby. Just give me one minute. I promise it won't take long."

Jeff followed Greg at a three-car distance. He didn't know where Greg would lead him or even why he was following him in the first place. After all, he hadn't done anything personally to him accept for fuck his wife. In hindsight, Jeff had a valid reason to want to destroy the man's very existence.

4

After handing the valet attendant the keys to his vehicle, Greg casually walked directly across the street. He felt extremely overdressed compared to those around him, but didn't bother with that thought much, being that he was already running behind schedule.

The weather was surprisingly nice, considering how it had rained most of the week. It was 82 degrees. Perfect weather for a game of golf. However, with all the pandemonium going on in his life, his day was far from perfect. Had been that way for quite a while now, and every day for the rest of his life, Greg knew he would have to live with those badgering reminders of how his life once was before he allowed the only woman who supplied him with a greater happiness and sense of fulfillment, to slip away.

He spotted his lunch companion, Naomi Brooks, right away. Her back was turned but he knew it was her. Would recognize her delicious voluptuous curves from a mile away. Furthermore, she was the only brown-skinned body sitting all alone, nursing what appeared to be lemonade, given how she didn't drink alcohol.

Greg took in the scenery, hoping not to see or be spotted by anyone he knew. He rounded the table in front of him and leaned in to announce his presence with a sensual kiss on her left cheek. To spectators, it was an innocent peck, but only he and Naomi knew differently.

"You're an hour late," Naomi pointed out to him before he could even pull out a chair to sit down. She offered him half of a smile and her piercing brown eyes never wavered as she twirled the top of her straw with her fingers.

Greg looked around the patio of the trendy Oak Lawn uptown's Taco Diner for a waiter. When he spotted one, he lifted a finger and bounced his head to get his attention. The young man scurried over to their table.

"Hello, my name is Jeremy. Can I start you off with an appetizer today?" The tall and slinky waiter whipped out the pen tucked behind his right ear. He looked to be around eighteen years old, free-spirited, and carefree. The next thing Greg noticed besides the young man's lively personality was the numerous piercings in his ears. He had at least six in both ears. Too many damn holes for a man. Too many damn holes for anyone, he seconded that thought. The black polish on his nails was the most puzzling to Greg. As if that wasn't enough, he happened to notice the tattoo on the inside of the boy's forearm. It was a dragon spitting out a ring of fire. In the fire were letters that spelled out *HELL*.

Greg cleared his throat. "No appetizer. Just a Mambo Limo," he said finally, situating himself. He removed his jacket and loosened his tie.

"Will that be all for you, sir?"

"For now," he replied coolly.

"Mambo Limo coming right up!"

Greg didn't really feel up to the lunch date and it's a wonder he even showed up. His mind was still wrapped around his deceased lover, Denise. Before coming here, he had gone to the cemetery and left flowers on her grave. He missed her so much and would have given anything to bring her back.

Greg finally settled his eyes on the strikingly beautiful woman seated across from him. Today she wore his favorite color. A casual form-fitting red dress that exposed just enough cleavage to encourage a wave of new thoughts. Her Nubian shimmering brown skin looked like a pot of simmering honey. She was flawless in his eyes. Perfect skin. Perfect teeth. Perfect smile. Her smile was what he loved the most. It was warm, captivating, and on a day like today, uplifting.

Naomi also possessed the key traits that Greg found attractive about a woman. Confidence, intelligence, passion, and wit. She was all that and more. She was the total package. Which was even more of the reason why he was glad to have her in his life. Especially during times like this when he was missing the hell out of *her*.

Losing Denise had done some damage to him internally. Part of him felt he was responsible for her death after discovering that the car accident occurred shortly after their heated phone exchange. She had told him that she was on her way to tell his wife about them. On her way to expose him and his dirty little secret. But she never got the chance to.

Denise's untimely death forced him to realize how selfish he had been. He had taken her for granted and had regrettably hidden his true feelings from her for the sake of what he stood to lose. He was trying to protect his wife, Vivian, along with his millions of dollars in investments, Adams Companies and all their franchises. Most importantly, he was trying to protect his and his wife's reputation. He knew the discovery of his adulterous affair would set fire to everything he'd worked hard to build. And as he found himself in an identical situation, he knew this time would be different. He would be sure to calculate things carefully due to what was at stake.

Naomi raised a brow at him and a peculiar uneven smirk crossed her lips as she lifted her straw and stirred her frozen lemon drink.

Withdrawing the straw from her cherry-colored lips, she sighed. Frustration settled in every crease of her face.

"I called you several times. I didn't think you'd make it," she said finally.

Greg cleared what he thought was dust out of his throat, his expression unchanged. "I had a business engagement prior to coming here," he replied, shifting in his seat a little. He watched her roll her tongue in between her lips. Any other time his dick would have shot up like a space rocket to get close to Naomi, to be next to her warmth, but at that moment it lay completely limp and hardly motivated.

A playful wind whipped over their table causing Naomi's naturally long, bone-straight black tresses to high-five the air. A whiff of her incredible scent found itself trapped in the breeze. Greg inhaled her femininity. It was the closest connection he had made with her since being in her presence. She was wearing the Chanel perfume he had given her. He loved that fragrance. So did Denise.

Greg removed his sunglasses to catch a better view of the scenery. His wandering eyes began to roam her body. The sparkling diamond earrings, diamond pendant necklace, and the dazzling platinum diamond tennis bracelet on her left wrist, had all been gifts for her thirty-fifth birthday, from him. Unbeknownst to Naomi, the bracelet she wore was an exceptionally special piece to him. It was symbolic, being that it was identical to the bracelet he had given Denise for Valentine's Day the year before.

The longer he stared at his strikingly beautiful girlfriend, the more Greg noticed that all the gifts that he had given her in the nine months that they'd been seeing each other, were now being showcased on her incredible body, knowingly, just for him.

Her almond-shaped golden brown eyes rested on his. "Are you feeling all right today? You look exhausted."

In an uneven tone, "I'm fine," he lied.

Naomi studied Greg's face a few seconds longer. "Are you sure?"

Greg looked to his left for no one in particular. Hysterical laughter coming from a group of chatty women at the next table filtered through his latest thoughts. "I'm all right," he said. He watched people who were people watching until an ash blonde Cane Corso caught his attention. He always wanted one of those but never actually got one. Vivian hated dogs. Hated cats. Hated kids. Hated anything that required too much of her time and attention.

"Will you look at me, please?" Naomi asked.

Greg brought his eyes back to hers. She stared at him as if she were carefully identifying every feature on his face.

"You've been crying, haven't you?"

"Where in the heck is my drink?" he questioned, ignoring her all at once.

"Your eyes are as red as my dress, Greg. You've been crying."

He fell silent, looked around for the bubbly waiter who had taken his order. Finally, he was heading back their way.

"I'm very sorry it took so long, sir. Our machine was giving us a little trouble. Is there anything else I can get for you?"

Greg shook his head, clearly aggravated.

"Would you like a refresher, Madam?"

"I'm fine, thank you," Naomi replied kindly.

Greg took a thirsty sip of his drink.

"Well, if you don't care to talk to me about it, I won't force it," she said.

"Naomi, baby, there's nothing to discuss, furthermore, be concerned about. I said I'm fine." He flashed her that signature smile of his, forcing every bit of it.

"Really?" she asked in a questioning tone.

Greg looked at her more seriously. "What? So you don't believe me now. I told you there's nothing to worry your pretty little head about."

"Well, I can't say I'm so sure about that anymore," Naomi muttered.

"Where's all this coming from?" Greg held up a hand. "You know what, never mind. I don't have time for it right now."

Before Greg could say another word, he watched the tears as they formed in her eyes.

"I'm trying to be patient. I swear I am," she started. "But this is becoming..." She picked up a napkin from the table and blotted the corners of her eyes with it. "Unbearable," she said lastly.

Greg cringed. This was the *last* thing he wanted to be dealing with right now. "All I've asked is that you bear with me for a little longer until I get some things handled on my end. It shouldn't be long now," he said, speaking of the divorce he was secretly trying to position himself for financially.

Naomi brought her pain-stricken eyes to his. "What makes you so sure that she's going to let you walk so easily, huh? That could take months. Years. I mean...are you really going to leave your wife for me?"

Greg was silent. "I know where I want to be."

Naomi didn't appear to be convinced.

"All I'm asking is that you be patient."

"Exactly what do you think I've been doing for the past six months, Greg? I love you and you know that, but I can't keep waiting for you to decide when you're ready to leave her when I'm—"

"Damn it, Denise, what do you want from me!" He fought to remain calm. Fought to not cause a scene.

Naomi drew her neck back as if he had caught her off-guard with his temper.

"I'm doing everything that I can," he continued.

Naomi stared on as if in utter disbelief. Her mouth moved in slow motion as she opened it to speak. "Who is she?"

Greg stopped mid-sentence and stared at Naomi oddly.

"What?"

"Who is she?"

"What are you talking about? I told you about my wife, Vivian."

"No. I'm not referring to her. Who is Denise?" Naomi asked, enunciating the woman's name carefully.

Greg tilt his head and waited for that warm sensation to wash over him like it always did when he thought of Denise or heard her name. "I don't know what you're talking about."

"Don't do this. You know exactly what I'm talking about! You just called me another woman's name and it wasn't your wife's." She paused. "So this woman, Denise. Who is she, Greg? And is she the reason you were late? The reason your eyes are all bloodshot."

Greg lathered his tongue in a boiling soup of lies. He didn't know how Denise's name managed to slip out of his mouth, but it was apparent that it had. Out of the six months that he and Naomi had been seeing each other, he had never mentioned his former lover to her, and it was for good reason.

He measured the brazen look in her eyes. She demanded to know who this woman was that he had never spoken about, and before today he had made up in his mind that she would never know. "She's none of your concern so can we change the subject, please," Greg stated matter-of-factly. "We are supposed to be enjoying each other's company right now. I don't need you hounding me about old flames."

"Are you serious?" Naomi batted her long lashes.

"Naomi, please. She's the past."

"Well then, what exactly am *I?* Because last time I checked, you were still married."

Greg didn't want to disappoint her. Didn't want to tell her that Denise was the only reason he found himself doing this again. The only reason he felt *anything* for Naomi at all. When he looked at her, he didn't see her for her. He saw her as Denise. The woman he had fallen so deeply in love with. Greg was never looking for a woman to replace his wife. He was looking for a woman to replace Denise. And when God sent Denise back to him as Naomi, Greg vowed he would never let anyone or anything come between them again.

"This conversation is over," Greg said. He stated his position and that was that. Her eyes wavered from his. He leaned across the table, cupped her chin in his large right hand and stroked it with his thumb. "Don't I take good care of you?" he asked. Her eyes eventually found their way back to him but not a single word left her lips. "Don't I make you happy?" he asked further. Greg leaned in and gave her a reassuring kiss on the lips. "Trust me. This will all be over soon."

Naomi only nodded as if all were forgiven, but the sketchy look on her face said otherwise.

"I have to go. Need to swing by the office and pick up some important paperwork." Greg stood up. "I was hoping later I could come by your place." Greg observed her unchanging expression.

She pressed her lips tightly together. "Sure. What time should I expect you?"

Greg smiled mischievously. "Same time as last night." He reached for his wallet. He didn't have any cash on him. Instead of waiting for the bill, he laid one of his credit cards flat on the table. "Here. Treat yourself to something nice. And sexy," he added.

Naomi didn't even bother looking at the credit card. Her eyes had been trained on him.

Without saying another word, he placed his shades smoothly back over his face, then turned to leave in the same direction from which he had come.

5

Jeff grabbed Deandra by the hand as they walked swiftly toward the crowded outdoor eatery. He was certain his eyes had deceived him, but as he and Deandra stumbled upon the sidewalk in closer proximity of the mysterious woman, he realized he was far from being fooled. Only five feet away, he thought he was staring at a ghost, or perhaps, Denise, in the flesh.

He and Deandra took a seat under one of the umbrella tables. He watched bug-eyed and discreetly as possible the way the woman's lips moved as she spoke on her cell phone. Shortly after her ten-minute conversation, she placed her phone inside of her purse and got up from the table. Jeff studied her carefully from head to heel. From the way her body curved to the rhythm in her stride. It was too close to home to be a coincidence, but he knew that that's all it had to be. Still he couldn't deny that watching this woman made his skin crawl and the back of his neck hairs stand up. She looked exactly like his ex-wife.

"Wait here, sweetie. Daddy will be right back," Jeff called out to Deandra without really looking at her.

"But you promised we would go see Mommy," Deandra said. He could hear how upset she was at the sudden change of schedule. Her voice seemed to trail off as Jeff picked up his pace. He followed the woman closely as she moved hastily across the street and in the direction of the valet attendants. As she fished through her purse for her ticket, Jeff reached out and touched her on the shoulder. She turned around to face him.

A cold feeling immediately swept over him as he stood there in both shock and amazement. He couldn't even translate his thoughts, let alone speak.

"I'm sorry," Jeff apologized, staring into her bright brown eyes.

"May I help you with something?" she asked, exposing the most beautiful smile.

Jeff's eyes were lit with suspense and self-doubt.

"Are you okay?" she asked, looking as perplexed as he was.

"No…I mean, yes," Jeff said finally. He took a second to gather his thoughts. "You resemble…" His thought fell short. "You're going to think this is crazy. But I thought you were my ex-wife." He chuckled loosely, leaving out the fact that she was dead. His stomach seemed to knot up the longer he stood there.

She smiled softly. "It's okay. Mistaken identity. Happens all the time," she replied coolly.

Jeff squeezed out another chuckle to conceal his true thoughts. "Yeah, I guess you're right."

The valet attendant pulled up with her vehicle. A black Chrysler 300. The same make and model of Denise's car. Jeff nearly shit himself. He watched her tip the man.

"Nice meeting you, Jeff."

Jeff came to. "It was nice meet…ing you…too." She smiled at him once more before waving goodbye and driving off. When he turned around, Deandra was standing right there, her eyes following the woman in the black car.

"I thought I told you to wait for me."

As if in a daze, Deandra's brows furrowed and her eyes fell to a soft squint. "That woman looked just like Mommy," she said, making the same observations he had.

Mistaken identity, Jeff thought. He couldn't shake the uneasy feeling that crept over him. He wondered if this woman had been Greg's wife. If she had been in the picture all along.

"Come on, let's go," he told Deandra. He was so deep in thought he couldn't remember where he had parked. Those eyes, that nose, those lips. He went back through every physical feature of that woman's. He couldn't shake the feeling that swept over him and as he passed others on the crowded narrow streets, his thoughts racing from one new discovery to the next, he mumbled something aloud that caused Deandra and the guy walking his Great Dane to eye him in a strange way. "How the hell did she know my name?" he repeated.

6

Nadine stood directly under a stream of warm water, allowing it to slap her in the face over and over again. The shower jets were on full stream so the water shot out from every direction. The water pressure was perfect but as much as she tried to relax and release, the tension in her body wouldn't relent. The heavy feeling floating inside of her chest was emotionally paralyzing. Nadine had always believed deep down that Jeff was seeing someone else. Call it a woman's intuition, a hunch, or a sixth sense. Whatever that special feeling was that she got whenever he left her place was the instinct she should have been listening to. It would have saved her the exhaustion from guessing games, the paranoia of catching a sexually transmitted disease, and it damn sure would have saved her from the pity party she would have to schedule in time to throw herself later. Damn it, had she really taken the time to trust and oblige her own feelings, she wouldn't be in this predicament, again!

Last night confirmed Nadine's wildest suspicions. Not only had she heard Jeff having sex with another woman, she had received harassing phone calls shortly thereafter. The woman had called Nadine a total of nine times asking for Jeff. Had Nadine not finally turned off the ringer, she was sure it would have continued. The bags under her eyes and the pounding headache were testaments of sleep deprivation. She was like a ticking time bomb. Ludicrous thoughts plagued her and the longer she entertained them, the more she wanted to hurt the person behind them.

Nadine poured more conditioner into her hands and worked it into her hair. Even this felt like a major task to her and in her current mind state, she felt like cutting it all off, simply to expedite the process. Jeff had her so perturbed she couldn't focus at home or at work anymore without him ambushing her concentration. Now to add some inconsiderate immature tramp to the mix who actually thought it was acceptable to call her house and play on the damn phone all times of the hour, fumed Nadine even more. Who in the hell did she think she was? Nadine mused. She had considered blocking the number but there wasn't a number to block. The name had registered on her caller display as *PRIVATE* each time. She had lost mounts of sleep over it, but she knew that as soon as daylight came, she would put an end to it all as she should have done a long damn time ago.

Then again, why should she allow some strange woman to rile her up like this? This was all Jeff's doing. Yes, she admitted finally to that feeling in her gut. The prime source responsible for her drama and distress was Jeff Jackson!

After washing her hair, Nadine finally opened her eyes once she felt the water rise past her ankles. She looked down and as she figured, a clump of her hair had clogged the drain. She turned off the water, bent down, and attempted to pull out all the hair that she had combed out during her shampoo. She had lost a few strands from a handful. An increase from last week.

She stepped out of the walk-in shower and walked over to the counter. She leaned over into the mirror and examined her scalp, noting how much thinner her hair had gotten. She then allowed herself a quick analysis of her body. She cringed at the sight. She looked worse than she felt. Her long-running stretch marks were dark and noticeable. The scar from her C-section was barely visible, but her once flat tight stomach was now pudgy. She had expected to have lost all the baby weight by now, but it hadn't been as easy as she had hoped it would be.

Nadine reluctantly stepped on the digital scale behind her. She let out a stricken gasp and reached for her heart once her final weight was revealed. She had gained an additional four pounds since the last time she weighed herself, bringing her to 167 pounds. That was a thirty-six-pound gain prior to her pregnancy. The realization of that was downright depressing. Nadine hated the woman she had become. She didn't recognize this person at all. Not even stripped down naked. She took one long hard look at herself and decided to forgo work today. She had neglected herself long enough.

The time Nadine had taken out to go see the doctor and then treat herself to a full makeover and shopping spree had done her plenty of good. Well almost. While her new pixie cut made her appear young and stunning on the outside, she still felt miserable, broken, and just as torn on the inside. Her doctor had prescribed her blood pressure medication and also suggested she try to do something to alleviate the stress in her life, like work out. "*Stress can kill you*," he had told her. The saddest part to Nadine was that it all had derived from a man. A man who she thought loved her.

In addition to the medicine she now had to take, her doctor had switched her birth control pills. He had informed her that the old pills may have contributed to some of her weight gain and hair shedding, adding to the reasons why Nadine hated taking pills. But now she really didn't have a choice.

"All right, Ms. Collins, I think I got you all covered."

Nadine's eyes had been transfixed on the man's swollen biceps and triceps. He was so ripped that she could practically see every vein running through his body. He could have easily been the poster board for Borden milk with a physique like that, and she was sure there were many women who would have loved to lap that milk right off of him. She could see the advertisement now.

"This here is your temporary membership card. You should receive the original in the mail in the next two weeks."

Before finally settling her eyes back on his face, she sighed. "Well, that wasn't so painful." Nadine accepted the paper and briefly looked it over. She began to fold it in half and then slipped it into her purse.

"Did you have any more questions for me?"

Nadine took a glimpse at his nametag. He didn't really look like a Jeremiah in her eyes, but exactly what did a Jeremiah look like? "No, I think you covered them all." She smiled softly.

"So I'll be seeing you again later, right?" Jeremiah inquired.

"I was thinking about starting tomorrow," Nadine said.

"Tomorrow?" Jeremiah echoed. He drew his neck back and lifted his right brow the same exact way The Rock did it. "I smeeeellll an excuse cooking." He leaned back in the chair, crossed his arms and twisted his lips. "Why not today?"

"I still have so much to do. I don't have time…"

Jeremiah made a disapproving face. He interrupted her before she could say anything more. "Agh huh! Excuses," he murmured.

"Pardon me," Nadine said.

Jeremiah sat further back in his chair and placed his hands firmly on the edge of his desk. "I said you're already coming up with an excuse," he implied half-jokingly.

Nadine's face was transfixed into a half-grin. "I promise you it's not an excuse." She chuckled lightly.

"All right." Jeremiah smiled, lifting his hands in the air as if he were surrendering. "I have no choice but to take your word for it." He began shaking his finger at her. "But if I don't see you in this gym tomorrow, I might have to come looking for you." He laughed.

It was only then that Nadine noticed his deep-set dimples. She tried to keep her eyes from wandering but failed terribly. "You have a deal." She held up her right hand. "Scouts honor," she added. Her smile faded into a blush, but she convinced herself she wasn't flirting. Perhaps it was him that was flirting and she happened to enjoy the attention. She pulled her keys from her purse. "Thanks again for getting me all set up."

"Hey, that's what I'm here for," he said, never losing that customer-friendly smile.

She stood. "So when will I get to meet my personal trainer?" she inquired out of curiosity.

Jeremiah stood as well and outstretched his hand to her. "My clients call me Jay," he said matter-of-factly.

Nadine returned the gesture, noticing his strength, even in his handshake. "Well then, Jay, I'll see you eleven a.m. sharp."

"I look forward to it."

"This should be interesting," she mumbled, turning the corner to leave the gym.

It was exactly 4:59 p.m. when Nadine pulled into the busy retail shopping strip. She had completely lost track of time. She took a chance and parked illegally along the fire lane.

Walking briskly toward Herald Star Cleaners, Nadine prayed that they weren't already closed for the day. When she reached the door, the owner's daughter, a short and petite teenager who always seemed annoyed to be there with her mother at work, was flipping the sign from "open" to "closed."

"Pleeeease," Nadine mouthed through the thick glass, holding her hand in a prayer fold. The girl turned her head and yelled something that Nadine couldn't quite discern. Shortly after she allowed her inside, Nadine apologized profusely as she followed the girl to the pick-up counter.

"May I have your ticket, please?"

Nadine began fishing through her purse for the pink ticket they had given her the previous day. "I'm sure I put it right in here," she said, looking in the pocket. She sighed heavily as she continued to search. "Oh gosh! I swapped purses earlier and I must have—"

"It's okay, I'll look it up by your phone number." She smiled.

Nadine rattled off her digits.

"Nadine Collins?"

"Yes."

The girl left to retrieve her items. When she returned, she handed Nadine the clothing. Nadine didn't even bother looking over the outfits as she would have normally. Instead, she quickly paid the lady and extended her apologies as she left.

When she returned to her car, there was a tall, dark and handsome man standing in front of it. He was on his cell phone and the dirty look on his face was enough to suggest his unhappiness.

"Is this your vehicle?" the man asked Nadine the second she walked toward the car.

Realizing for the first time that she had blocked him in, she responded, "I'm so sorry, I'll move right out of your way." She quickly dumped everything that was in her hands in the passenger seat.

"Thanks, Lucy, I appreciate it. Tell her I deeply apologize and I'll be there as soon as I can." Nadine overheard him talking and hoped that she hadn't been the reason he was being delayed. She reversed her way out of the parking lot. When she finally raised her head to look in the rearview mirror, she noticed he had not gotten in his car yet. He was too busy watching her drive away.

By the time Nadine pulled into her parking space, she was extremely exhausted. She had practically run herself ragged from all the errands and shopping trips. Good thing she'd left Canvas with her neighbor's daughter instead of dropping him off at daycare, which happened to be way on the other side of town. She gathered all her bags from the shopping she had done as well as the clothes she had picked up from the cleaners. She couldn't wait to see how the skirt and slacks fit after having the alterations done. With her new gym membership, she hoped weight gain would be the last reason she would ever have to alter her clothing again.

She inserted her key in the door and surprisingly, it didn't turn. She did it again and again until it finally dawned on her that her handyman, Ricardo, had changed the locks as she had requested. She rang the doorbell. She could hear footsteps on the other side until finally, Casey, Canvas's babysitter, opened the door.

Casey held an index finger to her lip. "He's asleep," she whispered.

Nadine nodded her head and walked inside as quietly as possible. Casey grabbed most of the bags out of Nadine's arms and placed them in the bedroom, while Nadine walked over to her snoring son who was lying there on the couch. She leaned over and gave him a soft peck on the cheek. She spotted one of her throw blankets beside him and as usual, Casey had been buried with her e-reader before Nadine walked in.

"How did he do today?" Nadine asked, walking back over toward the kitchen area.

"He did great. And guess what?"

"What?"

"I taught him how to say my name!" Casey exclaimed, seemingly flashing all thirty-two teeth.

"Wow." Nadine smiled. "That's awesome."

"Very. I tell you that little booger is so smart. He catches on so quickly."

"Tell me about it," Nadine smiled, sliding out of her shoes.

"He ate about an hour ago and he's already had his bath."

"Ooooh, that was nice of you to do that!" Nadine said relieved. That was one less thing she had to do.

"Oh yeah, I almost forgot. His father called to check on him."

"Oh, did he?" Nadine gasped. That caused her to pause. Her thoughts began to cycle back to last night. Had she said the first thing that came to mind, Casey would have probably thought she was losing her *mad* mind.

"He said he would be stopping by sometime later to pick him up."

Nadine picked up toys as she walked through the dining room area. She wasn't going to hold her breath waiting for Jeff to come over. He had already gone a week without calling, what difference was one extra day going to make. She was so tired of shoveling his shit around. Tired of the back and forth, come and go. How he chose to act with her was one thing, but to take it out on their son was unacceptable. Nadine had made up her mind that if this was the type of father he was going to be, she would let it be his regret because she knew her son would see it all for himself later on in life. He would see the difference Jeff made between his sister and him and no matter how many times Nadine had to refrain from confronting Jeff about it, it bothered her to the core that she sat back and watched him do this to their son.

"When did Ricardo come by?"

Casey held up her hands as if a light bulb had gone off in her head. "He came right after you left this morning." She walked over to the coffee table and picked up the two gold keys. "He wanted me to give these to you." She handed the keys to Nadine.

"Thank you," Nadine said, placing them on the bar. She then grabbed her purse and pulled out her checkbook. She began making a check out to Casey.

"Thanks, Ms. Collins," Casey said, accepting the $40 check.

"No, thank *you* for being available at the last minute."

"Anytime." Casey beamed. "Besides, Canvas is like the little brother I always wanted."

Nadine gave her a warm smile and watched her gather her things. "Hey Casey, just in case his father doesn't pick him up tonight, do you think you can sit for just a few hours tomorrow? I perfectly understand if you have prior engagements."

Casey waved the e-reader. "Are you kidding me? I would love to. The only prior engagement I have is this. My life isn't even remotely exciting as the juicy novels I read." She laughed. "Pretty darn pathetic."

Nadine added to her laughter. "Well, honey, I wish I could say the same. My life feels like a book."

"Fantasy or adventure?"

"Try drama with a capital D." Before Casey could say another word, Nadine heard keys jangling on the other side of the door. She concealed her smile. She knew exactly who that was trying to get in.

"You want me to get that?" Casey asked in almost a whisper.

Nadine shook her head, her eyes smiling. The keys jangled against the door for a moment longer before the doorbell rang. Nadine slowly walked over to answer it. "Who is it?" she asked, a smile on her face.

"Me."

"Who?"

"Nadine, it's me! Jeff."

Nadine took her precious time unlocking the door. When she eased it open, Jeff and Deandra walked inside.

Casey took that as her cue to get going. Nadine was sure the sudden change in her tone, her body language, and her facial expression, said more than words alone.

"Just call me if you need me, Ms. Collins," Casey said as she hugged Nadine. She spoke to Jeff and Deandra and excused herself as she walked past them, out the door, and down the hall.

"Why the hell my key tripping?" Jeff complained.

"Well, *hello* to you too!" Nadine said. But what she really wanted to say was, "*Your black ass don't live here anymore. You and your uncommitting dick have both been evicted!*"

7

Jeff chuckled a little after realizing how rude he'd been. His eyes followed Nadine as she walked ahead of him. She didn't even embrace him in a hug or kiss as she would have normally. The vibe she was giving off was so strong that it didn't take a rocket scientist to figure out that something was wrong. All he could wonder was what the hell did he walk himself into now.

"You good?" Jeff asked with caution.

Nadine only stared at him at first. With narrowed cat eyes she shot him a cold and menacing side-glance. The tension in the air was suffocating, but he wasn't going to give into the funk. His day was going good and he intended to keep it that way. He bypassed her, looking around for nothing in particular. On any other day, Nadine's place felt like home. Today, Jeff felt like an unwanted visitor.

He walked farther into the large living area. It was spotless, as always. He found his son asleep on the couch. He walked over to him.

"And how are you little Ms. Lady?" Nadine asked walking over to Deandra. She outstretched her arms and they obliged in a hug, but from where Jeff was standing, it looked more like a simple brush in passing.

"I'm fine," Deandra answered dryly.

Jeff was grateful to see his daughter finally coming around, but he could tell there was still a ways to go. He no longer expected her to accept Nadine as his woman, being how they weren't walking that path anymore, however, he did need her to accept and respect her as the mother of her baby brother. Bottom line. He had drowned out the idea of making Nadine his wife a long time ago. As far as he was concerned, it became a dead issue each day he discovered she had betrayed him. He could never marry a deceitful woman as her. Never! Not even in a million dreams. He refused to allow her the privilege of calling herself his wife, and the closest she would ever come to the title was her role as his baby mama.

Jeff wasn't looking for monogamy, commitment, marriage, or anything that spelled dick-on-lockdown. He was smarter than that. He was going to take his newfound freedom and run like hell without looking back.

Scooping Canvas in his arms like a newborn baby, Jeff leaned in and kissed him on the forehead. "Looks like he's gotten bigger since the last time I saw him," he said, looking over his shoulders. She cut her eyes at him and probably thought he didn't see it. With his son in his arms, Jeff took a seat on the sofa while Deandra parked herself right in front of the television.

Jeff's attention delivered itself back to Nadine. She tried her hardest to act like she was so occupied cleaning up, but he knew that was her way of avoiding him. Either that or her OCD was more serious than he thought.

"You all right over there?" Jeff asked. "You're awfully quiet," he added, trying to spark a conversation. After all, he hadn't seen her and Canvas in a week. Surely there was something new to talk about. Normally she couldn't wait to tell him about a new word Canvas had learned or something new he'd done. That reminded him of the woman he had seen earlier today.

He wanted to tell Nadine how he had spotted that cocky son-of-a-bitch, Greg Adams, leaving Denise's gravesite. He wanted to share with her how he had played cat and mouse with his ass for fun, then painfully watched him have lunch with a woman that looked damn near identical to Denise. He wanted to know what Nadine would have thought of it all as he was still psyched out about it. But what puzzled him most was that the woman had said his name. Or was that a coincidence too?

"So you just gone give me the silent treatment and act like I ain't even here?"

That comment got Nadine's full attention. She walked into the living room and instead of sitting next to Jeff, she took a seat on one of the ottomans. She switched her eyes from the television screen to Jeff. Their eyes locked on each other's and everything that went unsaid could surely be felt. It was a negative vibe that made his stomach churn, yet his face held no emotion. That might have been what pissed her off the most. Where was that man that used to give a damn about the tears hiding behind her swollen brown eyes, the confusion lurking in her clouded mind and the stress strangling her heart? Jeff wondered. It didn't take long before the answer was revealed to him. Shit, he knew exactly where that naïve motherfucker was. Dead and gone!

He still loved and cared for his baby mama; after all she was the mother of his first-born, but Jeff wasn't in love with her anymore. It took him a year to realize that he was probably never completely in love with her to begin with. Their past relationship had been driven by lust, fantasy, and toe-curling sex on top of more sex! That's what had fondled his interest. That's what had kept his dick rocked. But as truths surfaced and ultimatums came crashing down on his party, Jeff had run for the nearest exit he could find. That wasn't what he'd signed up for.

The smug look Nadine held in place was award-winning. He

had never seen her in this foul of a mood. "Something on your mind?"

Nadine let out a gasp. "No complaints here," she simpered.

Jeff could tell it was all a front. He studied her face carefully. Her mouth said one thing, but her body language and attitude said the opposite. "You sure about that?" That fake smile she wore in an attempt to camouflage her true feelings eventually faded. "Because you look like you mad as hell right now."

"What exactly do you want me to say to you, Jeff?" She grimaced. Her butterscotch skin flushed a soft hue of red.

"I'm feeling a little steam coming off that ottoman and evidently it's directed toward me because you ain't even acting like yourself right now. You haven't said five words to me since I've been here. Your lips are pushed out, your makeup's sweating, and you're sitting way over there. Hell, I know *something's* wrong. I'm just trying to figure out what."

"Humph!" Nadine stood and scooped Canvas from Jeff's arms. "Why don't you tell me what's wrong," she said flippantly with piercing eyes. "Since you know me soooo damn well."

Jeff drew his neck back. *Here we go with this shit*, he thought.

Nadine motioned for Deandra to follow her. They walked into Nadine's room where she laid Canvas in the bed. She turned the television on for Deandra to watch and then walked back into the living room with Jeff, closing the sliding glass door behind her.

Jeff let out a deep sigh, already knowing what time it was. He could tell by the scowl on her face now that he had popped open a can of bitch-a-tude.

Nadine stood in front of him. She looked him square in the eyes. "I can't do this anymore."

Jeff allowed the seriousness of her words to register. He knew exactly what she was referring to, but he queried her anyway. He relaxed his shoulders, tightened his jaws, and casually asked, "You can't do what, Nadine?"

Her eyes narrowed into slits and her voluptuous cherry-painted lips parted ways. "I can't keep allowing you to…" Before she could complete her sentence, those hidden tears that played peek-a-boo with Jeff earlier, began to suddenly stroll down her lightly blushed cheeks. She blinked her eyes a few times and more tears slithered down her face.

Jeff stood to his feet. He pulled Nadine into his embrace, but she rejected him. On any other day it would have worked. Him holding her, trying to console her in her time of need would have been enough to calm her down and ease her worries. It would have been enough just to fuck her brains out and tell her whatever she needed to hear to settle her. But today his efforts hardly worked. She wouldn't even let him make it to first base.

Nadine shook her head slowly, all while staring at him as if he had some deadly contagious disease. Her face etched with an unfamiliar pain. "No," she said softly. She took a long deep breath. "I won't keep letting you hurt me!" she reemphasized this time with more pain in her voice, in her eyes, and on her beautiful face.

Jeff's body was as stiff as a board, his heart undoubtedly numb to the agony she was experiencing. Why, he didn't know. Years ago he'd cared about Nadine's feelings more than the feelings of his own wife. He'd cared if she hated or loved him, cared if she was happy or not. Now, all Jeff could allow himself to be, was concerned. "Where is all this coming from?" he asked boldly. As she stood there silent, the louder her tears seemed to pour down her face. He continued on. "I don't know exactly what I've done to hurt you, but—"

"Stop!" She tilted her head sideways. "You really don't get it, do you?"

Jeff tucked in his bottom lip. He wished that he could empathize with her, but the truth was that he couldn't even remotely identify with her right now. It was like a terrible storm had come through and knocked out his converter box, causing him to lose all connection.

He looked over into the next room at his children. Canvas was still asleep and Deandra was sitting Indian style beside him on the bed. Jeff's recollection of pain was indeed right in that room. Deandra was a reminder of the pain, the resentment, and the betrayal he'd felt the day Denise told him that his daughter really wasn't his. *I can't keep letting you hurt me!* He found himself wanting to beg to differ. Nadine wasn't hurt. Because hurt didn't disguise itself well. It didn't look the way she looked now. No...she wasn't hurt, but he could see why she would want to play the victim. Women did it all the time. It was what his boys had warned him about and he be gotdamn, they were right on the money.

Jeff wasn't quite sure how to diagnose Nadine, but one thing for damn sure was that it wasn't hurt! He stood there and played back all the arguments, the demands, the ultimatums, in his mind. And just like that, it hit him all at once. Nadine wasn't hurt, he reasoned. She was simply missing that twisted-ass affair orchestrated by his dead wife.

"It's time we gave each other space. To clear our heads," she continued. Her voice calm the entire time, but uneven. "I think it would also be appropriate for us to work out arrangements...for Canvas. Because this pop-up thing you tend to do is not going to work for me."

"You mean it's not going to work now that you've let your aunt and your friends fill your head up."

"What exactly is that supposed to mean?"

"You know exactly what it means. You didn't have a problem with it before when you were benefiting from it too," he reminded.

"I have a child to think about now. I'm not going to keep letting you walk up in here anytime you damn well feel like it. Those days are over!"

Jeff chuckled loosely. "All right. But as soon as that pussy gets lonely…you know who to call, baby." He grinned sinisterly.

Nadine scrunched her face in disgust. "Listen to you. I don't even know who you are anymore speaking like that. It seems that ever since…Denise died…you've changed." She continued in hesitation. "Are you…still mourning, Jeff? If you are, just say it and stop beating me up for it!"

Jeff remained silent. His entire body grew numb and he felt lightheaded. He stared at her in contempt. "I don't want to argue in front of the kids," Jeff said, finally, trying to nip that conversation in the bud. He could feel an argument brewing, but he wasn't going to give in to it. Not today. Not for a long time.

Nadine held up one finger. "No…see that's what you would like to think this is going to be." She managed a light chuckle even as fresh tears skidded past her mouth. "This *discussion* is simply about where we stand, our son, and what I expect out of you as his father."

Jeff was taken aback and offended. "Wait, so are you trying to say that suddenly I'm not a good father to my son?" His voice unintentionally shot up an octave and he immediately went into defense mode.

"You said it, I didn't," Nadine retorted mockingly taking a seat back on the ottoman.

"Quit cutting corners, Nadine, and get that shit off your mind. What you trying to say to me?"

Nadine looked away and then back at him. The natural glow in her eyes was shielded by his towering muscular frame. "What I'm saying is that," she stammered, "your son could use a little more of your time than what you've been giving him."

"I see my son!" he snapped back.

"When it's convenient for you! Sure you do. I'll give you that," Nadine retorted sarcastically.

Jeff hesitated for only a minute. Had to guide his words in the right direction. "You know what. I'm not going there with you because I know that I do a *damn* good job taking care of my son. I clothe him, I pay for his daycare, I scoop him up every weekend…"

Nadine's eyes widened in confusion. "Are you trying to convince me or yourself?" she asked. "Because you and I both know that you are making a difference between those kids." She pointed toward her bedroom, never taking her eyes off of him. "I understand Deandra needs you because she doesn't have her mother anymore, but Canvas needs you too! I'm not trying to do this alone and you promised me that I wouldn't have to!"

Every piece of Jeff's skin felt so hot and tight it hurt. His facial expression didn't even come close to revealing to her what he was really thinking at that moment. His eyebrows converged, his eyes narrowed to slits and his nostrils puckered up. An acidic taste filled his once cotton-dry mouth as he searched through his thoughts, trying to process everything she'd just said. His lips tingled as he wet them to say what she definitely deserved to hear, especially after spilling out those foul-ass comments. But something inside of him kept his words at bay all while *her* words echoed in his mind. This was the type of shit that made men like him want to stop trying, stop doing, stop giving a fuck. Nothing he did was being acknowledged or appreciated. None of it. Not the $300,000 in trust accounts he had set up for Canvas's college fund, not the clothes and shoes she never had to buy, not the daycare expenses he paid in advance, not even the relief he gave her on the weekends. What more did she want from him?

Jeff read Nadine up and down. He checked out this new look of hers. She had cut her hair shorter than he'd ever seen it. It was then that he concluded that this *Waiting to Exhale* moment wasn't about Canvas as she had wanted him to believe. This was about the two of them. He exhaled deeply, satisfied that he had figured it all out for himself. Yeah, this is exactly what this was about. And this brand-new language she was talking was her way of throwing salt on his still fresh open wounds. But he knew just how to handle her.

"You know what," Jeff said, "I don't need this shit today." He shot her a repulsive look before he walked over to the sliding door to open it. "Deandra, baby, let's go." He turned back to Nadine who was still standing in the exact spot looking dumbfounded. "Where are his bags?"

"So just like that, huh? End of conversation!" She waited for his response, but it never came. She closed her eyes and reopened them. "Why do I even waste my breath?"

"His bags?" Jeff asked again, sounding more impatiently this time. He refused to entertain her miserable madness. No matter how far this conversation went, predictably so, it would end with him being to blame. "You know what, never mind."

"Behind the door," she retorted without so much as looking at him.

Jeff grabbed both of Canvas's bags before walking over to Nadine's bed. He scooped his son up in his arms and as he did so, Canvas slowly began to stir from his nap. He placed his head on Jeff's shoulder and fell right back to sleep. Jeff walked past Nadine with extreme urgency. Deandra was so closely behind her father, one would have thought the building was on fire. Nadine quickly leaned in to hug and kiss Canvas as Jeff stopped to grab his keys off the bar. He saw two gold keys similar to what used to be his house key. Next to it her old lock. He snatched her old key off his key ring and left it on the bar all while thinking how asinine this was. Had she been woman enough to ask for the key, he would have given it back. No questions asked. She chose to make this more difficult than it had to be.

"I'll call and check on him later," she hollered out as he opened the front door to let himself out.

Jeff turned around slowly and shot her the same cold menacing glare. "I take care of my son!" he said once again before turning to leave.

8

"Add forty on pump two with this," Ménage told the slinky, bumpy-faced Arabian man standing behind the cash register. He had been watching her the entire time from the moment she entered the gas station, as he always did when she came in. She had on a pair of black super tight leggings and a fitted graffiti tank that cut off right above her navel. Sandals instead of stilettos. Panties instead of g-strings. No makeup or false eyelashes, only cherry lip gloss, big red hoops, and a pair of black and gold Gucci sunglasses. She was sure he had never seen her this way. Not this plain.

"That'll be $56.98," the clerk said.

Ménage handed him all five and one-dollar bills. He grinned sheepishly as he reached in the register to collect her change. She knew he was judging her just as the others did that walked in and out of the store. But what they failed to realize was that she didn't give a hot damn as none of them were paying her bills.

"You have a boyfriend?" He smiled, revealing a missing tooth.

Ménage kept a straight face. "Yeah, I have a boyfriend," she hauled out, chewing on her spearmint gum. She held out a hand to collect her change, then watched how he slowly bagged her items.

"Well, that's too bad, beautiful. I could have made you a very happy woman."

Ménage was so turned off but tried not to show it. Not because of his comment or the simple fact that she knew he couldn't do anything for her but keep her Honda gassed up. She was turned off by his overall appearance. Instead of being her normal smug self, she squeezed out a light chuckle. "My loss then," she said. She grabbed her bag off the counter and without saying another word, she walked out of the store. No man could ever make her as happy as she was when she was with Slug. He loved her unconditionally and he would do *anything* for her. That was the solace and companionship she missed so much at times. It was the drama she couldn't put up with.

Ménage pumped her gas and got back into her car. She had a mild headache and excruciating cramps that seemed to get worse by the minute. She quickly popped open the bottle of Aleve and downed two pills with a gulp of Evian. Her day was already starting off wrong and because Mother Nature decided to crash down on her, she knew her weekend was going to suck in addition to putting a major dent in her pocket. She couldn't strip on her period. At least she preferred not to. So instead she would have to waitress for the night.

As she drove on the service road headed back home, she passed department stores, restaurants, and eventually the mall. Her plans for the weekend had definitely been crushed, but at this moment, all she wanted to do was lie up in bed with her honey, Jeff. The more time she invested in him, the closer she would be to the money.

She reached for her cell and as she was getting ready to select Jeff's name, her fingers scrolled down some more and then stopped on another name. Instead of putting the woman's real name in, Ménage had programmed Nadine's phone number under "The Bitch." She knew Jeff had gone over to her place last night. She wasn't stupid. Besides, Jeff never hid that he was still very much involved with Nadine.

One time Ménage swore she'd tasted that bitch's pussy on his dick. That's when she let him know that she wasn't going behind another hoe unless she was getting paid to. That night he whipped out an extra $100 for the inconvenience. So as time went on, the easier it became to accept that Nadine wasn't leaving the situation on her own. Not without a good enough reason and Jeff was going to keep screwing the both of them. Luckily for Ménage, she didn't have any feelings whatsoever for him. Her feelings lied with his dick and his money! She had to keep her eyes on the prize, but The Bitch was becoming a major distraction that she had to eliminate from the equation. Until she got her nuts off and her stacks on deck.

Without blocking her number as she had done last night, Ménage called the number and waited for Nadine to answer.

"Hello," Nadine answered on the first ring, catching Ménage completely off-guard this time.

Ménage laced her voice with seduction. She spoke slowly and every other word had a short moan behind it. "May I speak with Jeff?"

"He just left. May I ask who's calling?"

She thought about giving her some bogus name. She thought about hanging up the phone in Nadine's face. But why? That wouldn't accomplish anything, she reasoned. It was time The Bitch knew that there was a new bitch on the scene.

"Ménage."

"I'm sorry. Who?"

"It's Ménage. His…fiancée."

Nadine got eerily quiet on her. Silence was always a good thing in these types of situations. That meant she had her undivided attention. Ménage continued, knowing her next jab would really fuck Nadine's head up.

"I'm leaving the clinic and I just wanted to tell him our good news…"

"How did you get my number?" Nadine interjected.

"This is his mother, right?" Ménage asked cheerfully. "I've been dying to meet you, Mrs. Jackson," she carried on. "Jeff has told me so much about you."

"No, this is *not* Jeff's mother. Listen, I'm not sure how you got my number or why you're even calling my house looking for him, but please don't call here again."

This time Ménage got quiet. "I'm so sorry, please forgive me. "I'll try him on his cell..."

"Wait! How long have you two been..."

Ménage slowly pulled the phone away from her ear and promptly hit END to cancel the call. Her lips broadened into a dirty conniving smile. She felt like she had just won the lotto.

She turned off the AC and opened her sunroof to let the wind inside of her car. She cranked up her music and sang along to the R&B song she had been jamming to on satellite radio, all while laughing inside. "Dumb broad!" she hollered, pulling into her designated parking spot.

She trod up the stairs and as soon as she walked inside of her apartment, she located her laptop to check her email. As she scrolled over her latest email, her face lit up like a Christmas tree. Her homeboy, Reginald, one of the club promoters for X-Rated, had done exactly what he'd promised he would do for her. He got the casting director for an upcoming feature film to review the portfolio that they had put together. They agreed he would shop her as a model and an actress to decorate her resume to make it appear as if she had experience in film. He had some local film students produce several commercials, trailers, and pilots, featuring Ménage to make it appear as though she was more experienced than in reality. So in addition to her exceptional acting skills, it showed her versatility. The idea worked, and now Reginald was emailing her about this fantastic opportunity.

Ménage quickly replied to Reginald's email and waited for him to respond. She needed more details. Hell, she wasn't trying to be no damn extra or supporting character. She wanted a leading role; if not, it wasn't worth any of her time.

While waiting, she Googled *EVICTION NOTICE LETTERS*. There were over a million results. All she needed was one good letter sample so that she could execute the next step in her plan. If she could get Jeff to take her in, she would be that much closer to the megabucks. She would find out where the money from the insurance policy was stashed as well as the other bank accounts, and then squeeze him for every last dime.

After going through pages and pages of uploaded evictions, Ménage copied and pasted, tweaked and inserted, just to get exactly what she needed to create a legitimate-looking eviction notice. After spending over an hour on her letter, it came out perfect. She printed off two copies of her splendid handiwork. She had made up some bogus name to put in the spot designated for the landlord's representative's name. She signed the false name, folded the paper and placed the letter in an envelope with her name scribbled on it. She tucked it inside of her beige and red Gucci tote bag, then called the leasing office, hoping they hadn't already left for the evening.

"It's a lovely day here at Cornerstone Townhomes. This is Cathy, how may I assist you?"

"Cathy, this is Ebony Greer, Apt 2101," Ménage said with a tremble in her voice. She paused for dramatic effect and made a sobbing sound. "My mother has just been diagnosed with terminal cancer." Another pause. "The doctors don't expect her…to live long." She imitated a weep.

"Oh no," Cathy gasped.

"So I'll be moving back home to be with her…for her final days." Ménage sniffed.

"Why of course," Cathy said, sounding so disheartened by the news.

"I understand there are penalties for breaking a lease, but I wanted to see if you could make an exception this one time," she said through sobs.

"Well…we typically…"

Ménage continued with her charade.

"I'll tell you what," Cathy said. "Come on down to the office and I'll see what we can work out."

Ménage muffled an, "Okay, I'll be right down," before hanging up. Ménage knew if things worked out as planned, it would only be a matter of time before she had Jeff right where she wanted him. She went back to check her email.

From: Reginald Scott

Subject: Ebony L. Greer / Film Audition

Message: You funny as hell, Ménage. Hell naw you won't be just walking down the street. You're auditioning for one of the lead roles. Just trust me on this, baby girl. You in this thang! I got you set up for Tuesday at 3pm. You're meeting with a guy named Russ. It's a low-budget feature film as I told you before, but this dude has major connects and he's well on his way in the film biz. This could be your big break so rock it! Also, he's not a fan of arrogance so don't try to outrun this cat with that fly-ass mouthpiece of yours. Just look sexy, nail the audition, and make me proud. I'll text you the address and phone number in a second.

Love,

Reginald

Ménage let out a sigh of relief. She could feel it. She was damn right going to nail this audition and have Russ's ass begging her to take the part. Following that thought, she checked for plane ticket times and booked the first thing leaving out of Dallas to Louisiana. It wasn't Hollywood, but it damn sure was a head start in that direction. Like the saying went, "You gotta crawl before you walk," and Ménage made a living getting on her knees so this was going to be a piece of cake.

Ménage searched through her closet for a shirt less revealing. She threw on a long beige shirt, overlooked herself in the mirror and began to rub her eyes until they turned red.

She hurried to the bathroom, brushed on some mascara, and thought about the most tragic image she could think of in order to get the tears rolling. All she could see clearly in her mind now was Slug's lifeless body lying up in a silver casket lined in chrome. She imagined every detail right down to the color of the pillow his head lay atop of. More tears crowded her face.

Truthfully, she didn't know if her boyfriend was dead or not. But whenever she thought the worst that could have happened to him, tears would immediately flood her face. Ménage walked out the door and headed for the leasing office, teary-eyed, distraught, and full of lies that she couldn't wait to sell. It was the only way out of that damn contract without ruining her perfect credit.

9

It was like looking off into the Pacific Ocean as Greg stared deeply into the depths of Vivian's luminous teal blue eyes. Something he hadn't done in a very long time. She was more gorgeous than he'd liked to remember. Her perfectly shaped nose, lifted cheeks, luscious enhanced lips, and lifted chin, made her a walking billboard for one of the best plastic surgeons in the state of Texas. It was worth every penny she'd invested and even he was incredibly pleased with the outcome. Her warm tanned skin was tight, smooth, and flawless, thanks to the best cosmetic enhancements money could procure.

He thought to himself how undeserving he was of her as his eyes fixated on her posed sensuously with her long silky blonde locks swept to the right side of her neck. Voluminous curls spilled over her bare shoulder and onto the white mink scarf draped around her neck. Her tiny freckles had been concealed with makeup, but Greg knew they were there. He could point them out in a heartbeat because he could see beyond the mirage. He knew Vivian inside and out, but after all these years of being married to her, he didn't understand why it had taken him this long to realize that deep down, he wasn't completely happy.

He had been living in the illusion of happiness. He had adapted to her way of life. A life that was once all a facade to him, on the outside looking in. Greg adored his wife and he still loved her.

But loving her wasn't enough anymore. She had deprived him of children, of a family, and of himself. Causing him to miss out on life's most precious moments and joys. Some days he found himself staring in the mirror, only to be reminded that he was still black, and that no matter how many elite clubs they were in, parties they attended, or how much money they tossed into political buckets, he would never be one of them. And him marrying a white woman wasn't going to change the hue of his skin or this color complex he'd been accused of having. But he had to admit that it felt good being at the top of the food chain and rubbing elbows with some of the same individuals he and his best friend once tried to get to invest in their entrepreneurial ventures.

So many sacrifices had been made to appease his wife, however, Greg couldn't do it anymore. Losing Denise had made him realize how he didn't want to take another second of his life for granted.

"Sorry to keep you holding there, Mr. Adams. Had to catch that call," Dave said, jolting Greg out of his thoughts. "Now where were we? Oh yes, the Sunset Boulevard property. As I was saying before, I truly believe we might have a deal on that one. And with it being a for-sale-by-owner listing, it really increases our chances of snatching it at the price I proposed."

Greg placed the five-by-seven, silver framed photo of his wife back on his desk and sat upright in the chair. "Great! But how soon will we know for sure?"

"I'm going to call the seller first thing in the morning to see how he feels about the offer I submitted."

"Dave, I want that house. I don't have time to waste," Greg said sternly.

"I know, I know. And I'm going to see to it that you get it. I just have to make the numbers work out because what he's asking for is ridiculously above the market value."

"What's the asking price?"

"It's listed at $4.5 mil which quite frankly he's not going to get."

Without hesitation, "Tell him I'll offer him $5 mil," Greg shot.

"What! I thought we said..."

"And I'll pay for his movers," he interjected.

"Greg, that's ludicrous! You sure you don't want to see what the appraisal report looks like?"

"Listen, I want that house. So do whatever you need to do to make it happen," Greg quipped, leaving no room for negotiation. He had loved it when he first laid eyes on it and Naomi did as well. It was the perfect house to start a family and that was all Greg had ever wanted. All he ever dreamt about. The more he thought of the future with Naomi, the more he couldn't wait to surprise her with the news that they were moving to Los Angeles.

"Are you sure about this?" Dave asked. "Because I say we wait a couple of more days and see if he accepts the initial offer. I'm trying to save you a little bit of money here, pal."

"You know as well as I do that money is no object. So...the faster you can facilitate a deal, the sooner you'll be holding your commission check," Greg reminded.

As if without a single second to spare, "All right. Anything you say, Mr. Adams," Dave said, catching Greg's drift. "I'll call him with the new proposal right now and get back to you with his answer."

"You mean his move-out date."

"Indeed, sir. I'll be calling you back with his move-out date," Dave agreed.

Greg checked his Rolex for the time. "Perfect. I'll be waiting for your call," he said lastly, terminating the call.

Greg sat behind his desk a moment longer before finally retiring work. He had other plans in mind. He shut down his computer, locked up his personal files, and switched off the office light. He strolled down the corridor and peeked into his secretary's office. She was nowhere to be found, but her computer was on. He walked around to the file room where she normally was when she wasn't behind her desk. He stuck his head in the door.

"Macy, I'm getting ready to head out for the day," he said, brushing his short beard and goatee with his hand.

Macy jumped, causing one of the manila folders to fly out of her hand. She turned to see Greg standing there and flew one hand over her chest. "Dear God, you scared me!" she said, trying to catch her breath. She pushed her glasses further back on her face and retrieved the fallen folder.

"I'm sorry. I didn't mean to frighten you," Greg said, trying to hold back a laugh. He figured she would have heard him coming down the hall if she didn't always have that headset glued to her ears.

Macy slipped the headset off. "No, it's okay. I've been extremely jumpy today. Shouldn't have stayed up and watched *Insidious* last night. I'm really not a fan of horror movies, but my boyfriend dared me."

Greg couldn't help but to release his laughter. "Well, I bet you won't be doing that again."

"No, sir. Not for a long time." Macy joined him, not seeming to mind that the tittering was at her expense. She pulled her long tresses behind her ears. She was a fabulous brunette and wore a simple bob that framed her oval-shaped face. Her warm and smooth cappuccino complexion was absent of makeup, but her lips were painted mauve with a hint of lip-gloss. Macy looked to be in her twenties and had the most giving heart of all the employees in the building. She never forgot any of the staff's birthdays, and when the holidays rolled around, she always brought her specialty—lemon meringue pie.

Greg was rather surprised to hear she had a boyfriend. Although attractive, he had always thought her to be meekly modest and somewhat of an introvert, considering how she never went to any of the company's happy hour gatherings or holiday functions. Macy didn't socialize much during work either. She simply came to work, did her job, and went home.

"Well, I wanted to give you a heads-up that I'm leaving for the day. I'll see you Monday."

"Oh all right. I'll be here bright and early."

Greg smiled.

"Tell Mrs. Adams I said hello."

"I will do that. Have a great weekend!"

"You too, sir." Macy waved back as Greg turned around, heading for the bank of elevators.

The main downstairs lobby was empty except for the security guard who threw up his hand as Greg strolled by, briefcase in hand. Everyone else was more likely gone for the day or caged in their office. He picked up a magazine that had been on the floor and placed it back on the table. The colossal Addison tower housed the corporate headquarters for his hotel group, Adams Companies. It was where he was finally able to establish his own identity and climb from out of Vivian's shadow.

Greg headed out of the revolving doors and into the parking lot. It was a breezy day out with a thirty percent chance of rainfall. A few clouds in sight. He hated when it rained now as it always forced him to think back to that tragic day.

Remembering that he needed an update on the equitable distribution that his attorney and best friend Leonard had been working on for him, he dialed his number. He needed some good news today and he hoped like hell that Leonard was going to give it to him.

"Hey, man, I was just about to call you!" Leonard exclaimed, sounding like he was in a good mood.

"I hope with some good news."

"Nnnn...not quite, bro."

Greg closed his driver door and turned on the air conditioner. He ditched his jacket in the backseat, loosened his tie, and removed his cuff links.

"Man, please don't tell me we ran into a problem."

"I wish I didn't have to," Leonard said. He braced Greg by dragging out the news. "That prenuptial Vivian had you sign...has a condition clause in there that states if *you* terminate the marriage, you aren't entitled to any of the future profits from Adams Companies Corp. or its shares."

"Wait a damn minute now, that's *our* money. Starting Adams Companies was my idea. You know that. You did the business plan."

"Yes, I know," Leonard vouched. "It was your idea, but she included it in the revised prenuptial agreement as a non-marital asset because it was funded with premarital inheritance money. Inheritance money that *you* also waived the rights to."

"Shit! This is bullshit, man. The company wouldn't be where it's at today if it weren't for me." Greg fell silent and everything else Leonard was saying fell on deaf ears. He was so upset he couldn't think rationally. He cursed himself for signing that damn piece of paper without having Leonard overlook it like he had him review the first one. Leonard wouldn't have let that slide past them. Suddenly, every piece of his skin on his body tightened and his head felt like it was going to explode.

Vivian had told him her parents felt it was necessary. It was only a precaution to protect the family's wealth and heirlooms, she had reassured him. Greg honestly believed that he would be with her for the rest of his life. He loved her genuinely and he wasn't going to allow a piece of paper to stand between that. But now, that piece of paper was standing between his money and business.

"Damn it!" Greg yelled out, hitting his horn with his fist. "I should've known better than to sign that without having you look at it."

"Calm down, man. You're going to pop a damn vessel."

"Leonard, tell me there's a way around this, man? I can't walk away from this empty-handed. I've worked too damn hard." Greg was seemingly gasping for air. He could barely breathe and his chest felt like it was sinking into his stomach. His tie seemed to tighten up again all on its own. As much as he wanted to avoid Vivian's dramatic prima-donna spouts that she tended to exhibit when it came to money, he prepared himself for the worst.

"You agreed to this when you signed that contract. That's exactly what her attorney will argue."

"That would leave me with nothing," Greg replied. "And I am not walking away empty-handed."

"I'll warn you now, this won't be a cakewalk. It's going to get dirty."

"Just tell me what I need to do and I'll do it."

Leonard sighed and after a long streak of silence, he finally spoke. "Listen, swing by the restaurant later so that we can talk this one through some more." Greg felt his armpits beginning to perspire. Vivian had him handcuffed by the dick, but he wasn't going to let her simply take his company away from him. "Do you think you can pull me from under this?"

Leonard exhaled sharply. "I can't promise you anything, but I might have a couple of ideas that can better prepare us for the court battle."

Greg felt his breathing return to normal. Leonard's ideas normally led to brilliant outcomes so this should be well worth his time.

He jetted out of the parking lot and turned on to the service road leading to the toll way. "What time do you want to meet?"

"Meet me in about an hour."

"All right. I need to make a pit stop home and then I'll head that way," Greg said.

"Cool. Bet."

Greg hung up with Leonard and saw that the missed call alert he'd received ten minutes ago had been from Vivian. Her ears must have been on fire. He considered calling her back but instead settled for a text message. He knew she'd detect the frustration in his voice. She replied right back that she was going over to a girlfriend's house and that his dinner was in the fridge. Greg sent her another short text. He switched lanes and seconds later, his phone beeped again. He read her last reply and instantly his heart began to beat for her again. She had told him she loved him. He sighed deeply and waited until he came to another stoplight before sending the next one. How could he do this to her? He felt foolish and ashamed for carrying on as if everything between them was perfectly fine. As if he wasn't conspiring to divorce her and start a family with someone else. Had he behaved otherwise, she would have become suspicious. And the last thing he wanted to do was draw attention to what he was doing. He needed to be ten steps ahead of her on this.

When he came to a red light, he texted back *"I love you."* No sooner than he hit SEND did trickles of rain plummet. Greg knew exactly why. Denise, the woman who had stolen his heart and changed his life forever, was crying.

10

Peaches and strawberries is what Naomi found herself submerged in at the Relache Spa. She was treating herself to a splendid evening that included a few hours of shopping and relaxation, just as Greg had wanted her to do. It was his way of showering her and making her feel like the beautiful deserving woman he believed she was. Greg liked to take care of his woman inside and out, like he did his luxurious vehicles. And there wasn't one thing he wouldn't do or a dollar he wouldn't spend to ensure her happiness.

It was a unique and humbling experience because with all his money at her disposal, Naomi hardly knew what to do with it. There was one time he'd asked her to name her favorite store. She'd said Target. He laughed, assuming she was joking, but she wasn't. Dating a wealthy and handsome businessman was like living in a foreign country and not being able to speak their language. But Naomi was optimistic that if she stayed around long enough, she'd eventually learn the lingo of the affluent lifestyle, maybe even speak it as fluent as the others. Until then, she really didn't fit in. She stuck out like a sore thumb and was sure others noticed it too. On one of her shopping sprees, the cashier had jokingly asked if she'd won the lottery. In a way, she had hit the jackpot.

After her lunch date with Greg, she'd ended up at some high-end fashion boutique in the Galleria mall. She couldn't even pronounce the name of the store, let alone what she had purchased to make the grand total come to $2,459. However, she did recall the sexy scarlet-red nightgown she anticipated wearing tonight with a pair of matching heels that she'd bought last week. She couldn't wait for Greg to see her in it. After that luxurious shopping spree, Naomi's day wouldn't have been complete without the warm bubbling spa bath and massage Greg booked concurrently for her every Friday afternoon. This was special treatment she had grown accustomed to since dating him. In comparison, his life had been filled with the finest things life had to offer. She envied that because he didn't respect the true value of a dollar like she'd been raised to do. Her parents had been poor, but they managed to scrape up every dollar and dime they could to make sure she and her brother didn't end up that way. They were fortunate enough to make it to college, but it was Naomi who'd cut her years short. She got pregnant, married, pregnant two more times, divorced, struggled, struggled some more, and then fell into a deep depression that she couldn't climb out of. That was when one drink turned into two, and then three, and then it was unstoppable from there.

Her ex-husband eventually got full custody of all three of their children after a Child Protective Services (CPS) investigation found her to be unfit. Losing her kids drove her insane. It set off a chain reaction. None of her family wanted anything to do with her. They begged her to get help but she didn't. It was like once she had that bottle in her hand, all her problems got the cease and desist memo. She eventually found herself homeless and bouncing around from alleys, freeway underpasses, and apartment breezeways. She was out there so bad her family and friends started to ostracize her. That bottle took her down. Made her an addict. "A fucking alcoholic bitch who don't deserve to be in their children's life," she quoted her husband saying the day she'd gone over to try to see them.

Greg, on the other hand, wouldn't know a darn thing about struggling to make ends meet. She watched him blow thousands of dollars on frivolous things while she was used to having to hit the streets non-stop, begging and prostituting for money, just to buy a decent spot to lay her head. It was considered to be luck when she finally got accepted into the halfway house after completing a ninety-day stint in rehab. And most times, even that place felt like hell.

She didn't miss those days of living torture at all, and it was a far cry from being a house she could ever say was home. The foul stench of danger and death lurked in that place like a rotting skunk. She recalled how unhappy she was in that environment. How more mentally and physically sick she was becoming from being around all those strangers. Many of the women were recovering drug addicts and the others were ex-offenders, all trying to walk the straight and narrow path to freedom. Not freedom of the body, but freedom of the mind. Her mentor, Wanda, had said, freedom doesn't start with the body. It starts with the mind. So beneath the surface of all that misery and sickness, which was cramped inside that place that she preferred to remember as only a hospital, were actually others like her, hoping to be nourished back to mental stability.

Naomi inhaled sharply. Her memories had jogged a little further than she needed them to. She realized that she could never hide from her past. No one could. It always had a way of hunting you down like a prison escapee.

Nevertheless, she thanked God for sending Maribel to rescue her when she had. They had been facing the same demons, but

Maribel had been blessed and cursed. All Naomi knew was that she must have seen something special in Naomi that she hadn't even seen in herself. She had offered her a second shot at life. A second chance at happiness.

Greg Adams—the assignment—had also been her knight in shining armor. He was everything her heart desired. He was her lover, her friend, her companion. He had introduced her to so many new things and spoiled her in a way that she had never been in her entire life. Greg was responsible for this newfound peace and optimistic outlook she now had. Even so, Naomi knew her pipe dreams would never come to fruition. Not because she didn't believe, but because they weren't part of the deal.

As the masseuse massaged her scalp, neck, and shoulders, Naomi closed her eyes and relished the moment a little longer.

"That's perfect, Miyuki," Naomi said a while later. While she could have, she really didn't want to spend the remainder of her day there. She had plans and she couldn't wait to be back in Greg's arms tonight. If only he truly knew how much she really loved him. He had professed his love for her plenty of times, but Naomi knew it wasn't *her* that he really loved; it was the optical illusion he was infatuated with. His eyes had deceived his mind. Making Naomi twice as guilty as Maribel.

Naomi opened her eyes completely when Miyuki stopped and turned off the jets. "Ms. Brooks, I will meet you in the other room," Miyuki told her.

"Okay, I'll be right in." Naomi smiled as she looked up at her.

Miyuki was a slender, short Japanese woman with thick black hair. Her eyebrows looked like they'd been drawn on with a black crayon by a preschooler. Her paper-thin lips were lacquered in a vermillion hue. She wore all white, down to her shoes. She looked like she should be doing almost anything other than being a masseuse. But the secret weapon had been her hands. They were blessed with the secrets of knowing how to singlehandedly work out the most stubborn neck kinks.

Naomi slowly eased out of the fruit bath. She towel-dried, then slipped on the white bathrobe hanging on the nearby rack next to her clothes.

Beep Beep.

She had a text message alert. She walked over to her purse and retrieved her phone. The message was from Greg telling her that he was going to be late coming over tonight. As she hooked her earpiece over her earlobe and walked into the other room, she sent a text back asking him how late. *Not too late*, he responded. *But I have a surprise for you when I get there.*

She found herself smiling at the thought of what the surprise might possibly be. She folded her robe in half and placed it in a nearby chair. Completely nude, she eased herself onto the table and before placing her face-down into the open space, she sent him a nice and flirty reply.

Well, I'll be nice and ready for whatever this surprise is. I love you! She inserted a smiley heart.

Soon after, Miyuki entered the room, quietly shutting the door behind her. She began to oil and massage Naomi's backside.

"How's the pressure, Ms. Brooks?" Miyuki asked.

"It's perfect."

Miyuki massaged Naomi from head to toe. Once she was done, she poured warm coconut milk over Naomi in preparation for the Swedish Chardonnay sugar scrub. Naomi melted under the soothing combination of warm aromatherapy and coconut oils. She moaned in delight from the pleasant aroma and from how good it felt as Miyuki worked the rich lather into her skin. This had to be what heaven felt like. Naomi couldn't help but wonder as the soft jazz playing in the background, coaxed her into a state of tranquility.

Almost three hours later, Naomi found herself back in her condominium. It wasn't hers exactly, but it was for the duration of the assignment. She couldn't wait to move out of Texas and explore the world like she'd always dreamt of doing when she was younger. She never had the financial means to experience a lot of things, but she would soon. She envisioned that a fresh start up North might be good for her; the South had way too many bad memories. She tried not to think about how gravely devastated she would be if Greg learned the truth about her. But her feelings were immaterial compared to what she knew he would feel if he ever discovered that their entire relationship had been an organized trap.

Naomi forced those tears shaking in her eyes back where they came from. Out of all the shit she'd ever done in her life, this felt like the lowest. But she had to do this. This was her only chance to turn her life completely around, and if she got all sentimental now, she wouldn't be able to pull this off and disappear, which was exactly as she had agreed to do. Maribel was paying her good money too. She owed that woman so much. After Naomi left the halfway house, Maribel had taken her in. She put her in this nice furnished condo. Bought her nice clothes. Food. The whole nine. She had been there for Naomi when her own family turned their back on her. She had no one but Maribel now. And the least she could do was pull this off without a hitch. Besides, opportunities like this only came once in a lifetime. Lucky for her, she was in the right place at the right time when it decided to stop by and pay her a visit.

Naomi had called Maribel earlier today to discuss the new developments. Maribel had reiterated to her the importance of following her instructions carefully. She had told her not to veer from the original plan, reminding her that by the time it was all said and done, Naomi was going to be enjoying her new life with her children. It would be that easy, Maribel had told Naomi.

Naomi curled the last piece of her hair. She glanced over at the picture she'd replicated the hairstyle from and then swooped the bangs with her fingers to the right and pinned them in place with a gold hair claw made out of Swarovski crystals. The style looked exactly like the photo, right down to the unique hair accessory, which had taken her forever to find online. But she had gone out of her way to pull this look off, so a few online browsing hours weren't going to inconvenience her by much.

Admiring her reflection in the mirror, she sprayed a little bit of hairspray to finish off the look. She glanced at the picture one final time, holding it up to the mirror so that she could do a side-by-side comparison. Naomi looked just like the woman in the picture. So much so that even she was spooked by it.

She placed her diamond earring drops in her ears and spritzed on some Chanel perfume. It was Greg's favorite fragrance and she never went without it.

Stealing another glance in the mirror, Naomi couldn't help but to admit that she was quite a catch nowadays. Maribel had polished her look tremendously by sending her to have minor cosmetic surgery. The procedure itself altered her natural appearance slightly, but made her look an even greater degree like the woman whose identity she'd replicated. Two years ago she didn't look this beautiful, this rested, this happy—and now she did. Whoever said beauty was only skin deep must not have had the money or connections Maribel had.

Naomi thought she heard the doorbell ring but wasn't too sure until she heard it a second time. Knowing exactly who it was, she quickly hid the eight-page, full-color obituary of Denise Jackson back in the *Cosmopolitan* magazine. Naomi was jealous of Denise in a way. She'd had the perfect life and had left a legacy behind for all who knew her to remember. Even for those that didn't. The obituary seemingly captured Denise's entire lifetime within those eight pages. It included a collage of full-colored snapshots of Denise, her immediate family, her friends, and a few others that ran in her inner circle. The program listed all her achievements and club associations; right down to the types of music she would often listen to. The information had been extremely valuable to Naomi, and she used every last detail to her advantage.

"Coming," Naomi called out as she placed the magazine back in the rack. She turned off all the lights, leaving only the bedroom illuminated by a sweet peach bellini-scented candle. She rushed over to the wrought-iron stand and hit "play" on the CD player, creating the perfect ambiance.

Her elegant red silk and lace flowing robe swept across the polished ebony wood as she went to answer the door. Not bothering to look out the peephole, she opened it slowly, greeting Greg the only way she knew how.

"Why don't you ever use the key I gave you?" She smiled.

"Because I love the way you greet me," Greg said lustfully. He took in all of her curves as he stepped farther inside, closing the door with his foot. He wore a dark, wheat brown Burberry ribbed shirt, russet brown casual pants, and matching loafers. "You look…incredible," he complimented.

"Thank you," Naomi said, her voice wrapped in seduction. "I did it all for you." She batted her long lashes and smiled. She was hoping he'd taken extra notice to the time invested in perfecting her hair and makeup. But the longer he stood there looking as if he was ready to bend her over, pull out his whip and give her pussy a lashing it never had, Naomi knew her hard work hadn't gone unseen.

Greg perused her body from head to heel. The smile in his eyes and the slight part in his lips suggested that he was enjoying the premiere. She loved how his eyes made love to her. It turned her on.

Ready to feel his touch again, she walked closer to him. She looped her hands loosely around his neck and then leaned in to kiss him. She could taste the bitter traces of Cognac on his breath way before their tongues intertwined.

His incredibly large hands traveled slowly down the center of her back before coasting along her nice and thick childbearing hips where he retained them as he kissed her lips, her chin, and the succulent skin on her neck.

Greg pulled her so closely into his body that she could feel his dick growing by the second. He craved her and she craved him. His playful hands soon began to caress, cuddle, and explore the roundness of her ample behind, forcing an angelic moan to echo off her tongue.

She halted their passionate kiss, took a few steps back and began slowly shedding her robe. It landed at her bare feet. The red and black negligee she donned underneath brought another mysterious smile to his face. She rubbed her hands over the fabric as if teasing him. She then motioned with her finger. "Come get it," she said.

Greg blindly locked the door behind him and met her starving lips once again. She couldn't fully describe the incredible tingling sensation that caused her pussy to pulsate any more than she could the extreme sensitivity in her breasts that had her fleshy double chocolate nipples so hard they could have cut glass.

Greg scooped her up in his big arms and carried her into the bedroom. It was as if she weren't a plus-size figure at all. When she was with him, he made her feel as though she was perfect in every way. And no man had ever made her feel that good. Not even her ex-husband.

"We have all night. Right, baby?" she asked hopeful as he lowered her onto the king-sized bed.

"All night," Greg reassured her as he began to undress, not once taking his eyes off her shimmering body.

As girlish as it sounded, she felt like a princess. Never in a million sunsets would she have pictured herself with a man like Greg Adams. Largely because women like her didn't attract men of Greg's caliber. At least that was what she had thought. Plus, he had told her early on that his wife was white. But that wasn't a surprise as Maribel had already told her that part. In fact she'd said he'd been married for more than six years. Half of those years, adulterous.

Maribel had painted Greg as a very bad man who needed to be exposed. Who needed to feel the pain he brought to others. But Naomi, on the second hand, saw the opposite side of him. She saw a loving and caring side who was willing to give every part of himself to someone. He wasn't a selfish man and she trusted her instincts were right about him. They connected on such a deeper level and she did not want this fairy tale romance they shared to end. So until the assignment was complete, Naomi was going to continue to bask in every moment they shared. So what that it was all a delusion.

Greg lowered his warm hard body onto hers. The musky cologne that had settled under his skin and the liquor straddling his tongue, stirred all of her carnal desires. She longed for his touch and it had only been less than twenty-four hours since the last time she'd had him inside of her. She craved him, and her pussy was going to make sure he knew just how deeply he was missed.

The rise of her cleavage nestled perfectly under his chin as he leaned in to kiss her some more. He then drove his tongue along her earlobe until it rested on her first hot spot. The other had been the inner part of her thighs.

Ostensibly taking mental cliff notes to the way she squirmed underneath him, his tongue stayed put while his right hand moved between her inner thighs and into her crotch-less panties. She spread her legs further apart, feeling her pussy gush the instant he laid hands on it. It was like Niagara Falls down below, but she knew his tongue and dick weren't afraid of getting soaked.

She gasped at the length and thickness of his middle finger as he slowly penetrated her with it, stroking her pussy to the rhythm of the R&B track playing in the background. Before she could get too comfortable, a second finger entered her, warming her up for the main event.

The slow winding of Greg's fingers inside of her warmth nearly brought her to climax. He was just as good with his hands as he was with his magic wand. Looking at him she would have never guessed he made love this good. She had underestimated the wrong man.

"That feels sooo good, baby," Naomi purred. Just a couple of more strokes and she would have climaxed all over his fingers.

"You like that?" He kissed her softly on the lips.

"Oh yes. Make love to me," she begged desperately. She needed to feel him this instant. She began rolling her hips in such a motion that now the music couldn't keep up.

Greg slid his drenched fingers coated with nothing but her warm erotic passion, out of her. He brought them to her lips and began sculpting them with her own caramel drizzle as if it were only lip balm. It was one of his sexual habits that Naomi found so erotic.

"Nothing like a glass of bubbling champagne," Greg said.

Naomi ran her tongue across her bottom and top lip. "I taste better than champagne."

"Ha, ha, ha. You damn right."

Greg separated her legs even more and lowered his entire face into her wetness. He escorted his tongue over and around her nice and tender love button before devouring it whole. She clenched the sheets the second his stiff tongue lifted off the landing strip and propelled into her erogenous zone. The way her body squirmed and neck jerked while she cursed in a pre-orgasmic fit, one would have mistaken her throes of passionate sexual gratification for an exorcism. He was taking her all the way there. After a few laps of riding his tongue all the way to Paris and back, Naomi reached a heavy climax. She came so hard she thought she'd peed on herself, and she was sure he thought the same.

"I love you," Greg said, looking deeply into her eyes before climbing on top of her.

"I love you too, baby."

Greg slowly, but eagerly, entered her temple. He grabbed her by the waist and made a long deep thrust inside of her. She shuddered as his length and thickness filled her to her max, causing her to sink her nails into his flesh with every thrust, backstroke, and dip.

"Awww yeah!" Greg grunted.

Naomi wrapped her long thick legs loosely around his back until she enveloped him. "Have me your way," she said.

Greg increased his speed, making her pussy cry him a river.

"Oooooh yesss..." She moaned nonstop, forgetting she had neighbors. She bit down on her bottom lip so hard it started to bleed. "Aaaaaa yayayayayyayaya..." she seemingly chanted in Chinese as their bodies pounded against one another. Before long Naomi heard her gown rip.

Greg nibbled on her engorged nipples like honeysuckle.

"Awwwww!" he grunted loudly. He swiped the sweat from his forehead, never once breaking his concentration.

"You're almost there, baby!" she encouraged. "I can feel you." Tightening her vaginal muscles, she gripped him tighter than a glove. He placed his lips back against hers. She could feel him expanding inside of her and that in turn promoted her own climax. She came hard. Harder than the first time. Harder than she'd ever because this man was feeding more than her body. He was feeding her soul.

"Ooooh," she moaned. Her heartbeat raced against his and her breasts heaved from a combination of sexual excitement and temporary exhaustion. In the thirty-six years of her life, she hadn't experienced anything close to what she was feeling now.

Half a stroke later, he scribbled his name all over her walls. She didn't resist. She never resisted his attempts to impregnate her. Sadly enough, no matter how many deposits he made, *she* knew she would never be able to have his children, or any more children of her own. Not biologically anyway. She'd had a hysterectomy three months after her last child, leaving her without a uterus, and no hope of ever conceiving again.

11

Greg laid his naked body on top of Naomi's until he emptied himself completely inside of her. And only until then did he pull out. He flipped over on his back and lay beside her. He put a purple accent pillow behind his head and placed his arm over his forehead.

"I'll get you some water, baby," Naomi said, getting up from the bed and heading to the kitchen.

Greg lay there drenched in his own sweat. He was physically drained, but he knew in a few more minutes, he would recuperate.

Naomi returned with a nice and cold bottle of water. She handed it to him and then cuddled right back in bed with him.

Greg took a long thirsty swig, then placed the cap back over the top. He took a look at her lingerie and saw how badly he'd ripped the top. "I'll buy you another one," he said, smiling as he pointed to the ripped lace.

Naomi only smiled and took a sip of water from his bottle.

"What, that's not enough?" he asked.

"Trust me. It's not that." Her perfectly arched eyebrow peaked a bit. She looked around the room and then back at him. "It's just sometimes I wish this didn't have to end."

"What you mean 'end'? I told you, baby, you got me. I'm yours." He chuckled.

She paused. The wrinkle in her forehead made a bold statement.

"You're not mine, Greg." Her emotive reality reminder made him realize how right she was and how wrong he had been. "You still have a wife that you have to go home to every night. And where do you think that leaves me, huh? Alone."

With his arm around her body, Greg pulled her closer. He brushed the hair gently from her face and lifted her chin so that he could look her in the deepest brown of her lonely forgiving eyes. He wished he could tell her about what he and Leonard had discussed, but decided against it. She didn't need to know every single detail about the divorce process with his wife anyhow. He'd deal with all that drama on his own. So instead of boring her with all the legal mumbo jumbo, he warmed her up for the best news he had gotten all year.

"Baby, as soon as this divorce mess is settled, you'll have every part of me. These things take time. Especially when you're dealing with the kind of woman I'm dealing with. There's a lot at stake here so I have to be very smart about this." He made sure she was following his every last word. Made sure she grasped them tightly. She nodded her head, finally. His words seemed to comfort her and her eyes revealed that she believed them to be nothing short of the truth. "And you know what else?"

"What, baby?"

"Your wish is going to come true sooner than you thought."

Naomi looked puzzled. She sat up in the bed slightly and patted down her tousled curls. "What are you saying?"

"You remember that fancy house you liked so much? The one with the fancy architecture and the movie theater?"

Her eyes grew almost as big as saucers. "Yea. What…about it?" she asked with caution.

Greg glided his words. "How much you love me again?" He leaned his ear toward her.

She playfully hit at him. "Stop playing, baby, and tell me!"

"Ha, ha, ha." Greg smiled. Loving to see his woman sweat. "It's ours, baby," he said finally.

Her breaths seemed to echo as she stared at him in disbelief. "You can't be serious?" she said. "I…I…mean you," she stuttered.

He murdered any doubt in her mind. "I'm dead serious, Naomi. I made an offer on it today. And they accepted it."

Naomi got quiet again and that surprised him. He expected her to be ecstatic about the news. Expected her to jump up from the bed and run around the place like a cheerleader with pom-poms. Instead, she looked disappointed. He sat up in the bed. "I thought you would be happy?" Greg said. "Talk to me."

"Oh no. I am. It's just that…"

"Just what?"

"I didn't expect we'd be moving so soon. That's all," she said dismissively. Greg could feel there was something more. He measured the look in her eyes as she pursed her lips. "I couldn't be happier." She stood up from the bed and walked over to the CD player. She changed out the music: Maxwell, her next choice. She turned the volume down. "When should I start packing?" she asked, her back turned to him.

"Right away. I told my real estate agent that I'm sending you ahead of me."

"Aaaaa…head of you?" she murmured. It was evident how completely off-guard she'd been caught. "Wow! I can't believe you didn't bother to tell me." She started walking out of the room. Her voice trailed behind her. "So I'm just supposed to pack up… and leave…I would have liked to had a choice in your decision," he heard her say.

After realizing she wasn't returning to the room so soon, he rose from the bed, slipped on his briefs and followed her. She was in the kitchen getting ready to make them both a toasted pastrami sandwich.

"Baby, I plan to fly out every single weekend to see you until I'm there permanently. Besides, that'll give you time to fix up the house the way you like. You know how y'all women like to do." She didn't respond. He walked up behind her, grabbed her by the waist and turned her toward him. "Hey. What's bothering you?"

She shook her head. "Nothing."

He could read her face better than she might have given him credit for. "Don't lie to me."

She relaxed her shoulders and their connection was restored. "I'm worried about the outcome. That's all. Worried something's going to happen and screw everything up."

He cradled both sides of her angelic face and placed his forehead slightly against hers until the tips of their noses touched. They melted into one. "Hey. You let me do all the worrying. All right. That's why my head is bigger than yours." He grinned. "I have extra room to worry."

She smiled and her face lit up like a Christmas tree. He took his index finger and slid it along the right side of her face. "We were meant for each other. It's a reason God sent you to me…and I can't afford to lose you..." He doubted she heard him when he whispered, "Again," just before wrapping his lips around hers. Without notice he lifted her onto the black marble kitchen island. He was so damn good at this, their kisses went undisturbed.

"Close your eyes," Greg said, between amorous kisses. Naomi did as told. On that cue, he reached deep into his pocket and pulled out the small silver box. He opened it, inspected what was inside, and took a deep breath. Against his best friend's advice, Greg lowered himself to the floor. He wasn't going to hold out anymore. It had been long enough. She didn't deserve to have to wait another minute for him to put a ring on it. He was going to show her, right here, right now, how ready he was to take their relationship to the next level.

Tears began to well in his eyes as he thought about the last time he saw Denise. He knew deep down how much she had loved him. How much she had cared. He didn't feel those tears skate down his cheek, but he knew they would soon. Greg believed that what he was about to do would make everything feel right again. And if not, it would at least be an attempt to calm the guilt tearing at his soul and the bedlam tormenting his mind.

Engraved in that platinum five-karat engagement ring was today's date. It was the date he'd lost the love of his life. The woman of his sweet dreams. That date marked the one-year anniversary of Denise's death. Her body was gone, but her spirit had found its way back to him through Naomi. How else could one explain the happenstance? They resembled each other considerably. Could have even passed as twins. Naomi also had Denise's personality. Being with Naomi sometimes felt too good to be true. It was like she had been an angel sent straight from heaven. And perhaps that's exactly what she was. But no matter how Greg viewed it, there was no doubt in his mind that she was meant for him. And today marked the day he would vow to always be there for her. He would make sure that Denise's memory lived on through Naomi. It was his way of making amends.

With the ring in his right hand, Greg stared up at his future wife. "Open your eyes now, baby."

Naomi's eyes lifted in utter amazement. Her mouth hung agape and she appeared as nervous as he was. Her bottom lip trembled, as did her hands. Her swelling eyes darted from him to the ring.

With his eyes transfixed on hers, Greg pinned back his shoulders and swallowed whatever bit of doubt that crept up his throat.

He drowned out Leonard's voice. The one telling him to wait until after the finalization of the divorce. But as he held those voices at bay, another worry presented itself. What if she said no? What if she felt the way Leonard had when he told him? Maybe it was too soon. Marriage was a big step and six months hadn't been a long enough courtship, many would say. Greg also worried that she'd bring up his wife *again*, and ruin their moment. So many things flooded his mind, but he was ready to go all in and give it a shot anyway. He needed her to say yes. Needed her to make him feel complete so that he could right all his wrongs and pick up where he and Denise had left off. Needed her to say yes so that he could repurpose those old and worn ways of his.

Tears began to roll down Naomi's face as her eyes slowly began to settle back on his. "What are you doing, baby?"

Greg raised his head more, wanting and needing to appear as confident as he could. "Naomi Brooks. Will you marry me?"

Naomi sucked in her bottom lip. Tears rounded her cinnamon blushed cheeks. Her eyes smiled at him and her lips began to move again. "Yes! Yes, I'll marry you!" More tears showered her face.

Greg sighed in relief and a megawatt smile widened his face. He slipped the ring onto her left finger, then stood back on his feet. He embraced her with a hug, a kiss, and then carried her back to bed. They made love over and over again all through the night. Greg came inside of her every time, praying each time he released his love seeds, that one of them would make him a father.

12

Nadine exited 24 Hour Fitness sweating from head to toe. She sweated out her curls so bad that her hair didn't look anything like it had this morning. She had never had a workout like that in her entire life, and it reminded her of how out of shape she really was. She could barely keep up with her personal trainer and for a minute there, she thought he was trying to kill her on that Stairmaster machine.

She walked slowly to her car feeling physically drained and out of breath. She stopped, took a gulp of her bottled water and started back up, all while thinking that she wouldn't care if she never saw Jay or that damn gym again.

It was barely 11 a.m. and the temperature was nice out, but Nadine couldn't wait to get home out of those sticky clothes. Getting into her car, she thought about the party she had to go home and get ready for. Her soror, Kelli, had invited her to a barbecue at her lakefront house. Not only did Nadine find it as a good time to catch up on old times, she thought it'd be refreshing to get out and enjoy a much needed break to escape the drama in her own backyard.

Nadine thought venting to her Aunt Mickey last night would have helped. It hadn't. Nadine felt the same as she did before she made the call. Her feelings for Jeff were mixed and unforgiving. No matter how hard she tried to let it go, she couldn't help but think about the audacity of some folks. Did he hate her that much? Her frustration and anger toward him was at a ten. This was the final straw, she'd decided. Jeff giving his fiancée her number was way out of line. She didn't understand where they'd gone wrong and it bothered her that he couldn't come right out and tell her. Why this *Ménage* person and not her? What did she have that Nadine didn't?

Turning on to her street, she smiled halfheartedly. This was God's way of punishing her. She was certain of it. How else would one explain all this bad luck? She regrettably hadn't been back to her church in at least a year, and this had to be his way of getting her attention.

As the Mary Mary CD thumped in the background, Nadine began to hum the words as she reflected on her own life. Past and present. She thought about what her horoscope said this morning. She had only been checking her Facebook messages when she clicked on the advertisement pop-up. Nadine didn't believe in astrology, but out of curiosity, she wanted to know what it would reveal about her life. Once she entered the necessary information, her reading came back within seconds. Only if life really were that simple she had thought.

Her horoscope told her to confront her biggest fear, and that doing so would open her heart to new experiences. She reread that particular sentence until she memorized it, and she still didn't know exactly what that was supposed to mean. Nadine's only true fear was that she would never find the man worthy of having her heart again. That meant, that she may never marry or have the family she so deeply desired. She had entrusted Jeff with so much, only to be deeply hurt. And because of that, she refused to ever fall in love again. Not because she was bitter, or maybe she was. But she'd lost faith. She didn't believe love existed for her and she didn't want to continue to take herself through the motions, only to set herself up for failure. She had to protect herself; if she didn't look out for her, no one else would.

Nadine and love were not on speaking terms, but she'd experienced enough of its wrath to accept that if she opened her mind and heart to love again, the possibility of getting burned was even greater than the last time. She was good with numbers and the odds were stacked against her. Nadine had also learned the symptoms, the side effects, and the proper diagnosis for the different types of pain love takes you through. Her experiences with Jeff had been quite the joyride. She now understood that at times, love might fuck her brains out, then leave her to go crawl back into another woman's bed. That it might play mind games or have other women playing on her phone all times of night. It might neglect her, abandon her, or simply dismiss her when she tried to have a simple adult conversation concerning their child.

Nadine knew the bad side of love all too well. Even its shady characteristics, its MO. Humph, the son of a bitch had a method to its operation, she mused. Once things got heavy, love's alter ego would tear its ass and...well...leave her holding the short end of the stick. And she'd be damned if she gave it the satisfaction of taking her through hell and back all over again.

She parked her car and walked into her building. Instead of taking the elevator up to her floor like she would have normally, she took the stairs. She could still feel the burn in her calves, thighs and legs as she climbed each step slowly.

Once inside her cozy apartment, she headed into the kitchen to ditch the empty bottle of water in the trash and to grab another one out the fridge. She glanced at the clock. She had two hours to shower, get ready, and make it to Kelli's house. She was excited about seeing her old running buddy, whom she hadn't seen in a while. While they often communicated online, it wasn't the same as seeing each other in person.

She went into her room and opened the closet. She pulled out her outfit. Solid mint-green leggings and a poncho-style top with muted floral print. It was a cool, befitting, yet simple look for the occasion. She figured she'd pair it with a nude Jimmy Choo open-toe pump and then embellish her look with vanilla pearls. A look that would exude confidence, class, and a dose of sexiness.

It took Nadine hardly any time to get dressed and she loved how sexy she felt in her clothes, despite her previous worries of weight gain. Her makeup was subtle. Still it enhanced her natural beauty. She fingered her hair until every single strand was where she wanted it. She loved the new look and after all these years, she couldn't believe it took a breakup to inspire her to switch up her style. Her new short cropped hairdo framed her face perfectly and highlighted her high cheekbones. It made her face look fuller and her eyes seemed more pronounced. She felt entirely more phlegmatic than she had yesterday. She didn't know where this energy and confidence boost had come from.

Nadine checked the time again and rushed into the kitchen to grab a protein bar. She took a couple of bites, downed her blood pressure medication with a full glass of water, and headed out the door looking simply magnificent. She called Jeff to check on Canvas on her way down to the car.

"Hello," Jeff answered dryly.

"Hey. I was just calling to check on Canvas. How's he doing?"

"We're watching a movie."

"Oh yeah? Sounds like fun! What are you guys watching?"

"*Cars*," Jeff answered flatly.

"Again?" Nadine chuckled.

"His choice."

Nadine picked up on how short he was being. But she wasn't at all surprised; after all, their last conversation hadn't ended so well.

"Well, tell him Mommy loves him. And give him a big hug and a kiss for me."

"Yeah."

Nadine stopped talking but there was more she wanted to say. She wanted to ask him about Ménage. Wanted to know how long he had been seeing her. She started to bring it up, but clearly it wasn't the right time. Lately, it seemed it was never the right time to discuss them anymore.

"Well, I guess I'll let you all get back to your movie."

Jeff was silent.

"I'll check on him when I get back in tonight. If it's too late, I'll wait and call back in the morning." She waited for him to question her whereabouts.

Silence.

"Okay. Later," Nadine squeezed out just before hanging up. She didn't wait for a reply as she would never get one.

13

Nadine pulled into the private gated Frisco community approximately fifteen minutes earlier than she had expected to arrive. Thankfully she remembered the way as she had forgotten to print off the map Kelli had emailed her. She gave her name to the security guard sitting in the booth and seconds after notifying Kelli, he allowed her entrance onto the property.

The wind could be heard whistling through the glass and as soon as Nadine rolled the windows down, the fresh and gentle breeze greeted her. There was nothing like a good kick of wind that bounced off the cool lake.

As she drove five miles per hour through the row of multimillion-dollar mansions surrounded by huge acres of land and water, she took in the breathtaking scenery of the tropical landscape. She took a long minute to savor the lush living. Beautiful seventy-degree weather like this always made her miss her hometown Atlanta. Nadine had only come to Texas to attend college. She never thought she would pursue her career here, fall in love with a married man, bear his child, then wind up another unwed baby mama. She felt like she had become a statistic. Felt like she'd been dealt an unfair hand.

Nadine recognized Kelli's house right away. It was the cornered property with the huge ranch-sized lot. Life had been good to her.

Well, marrying a pro football player had been good to her. She was living every woman's dream and Nadine envied her in a way, because unlike Nadine, Kelli didn't have to lift a finger or work for anything she had. Had been that way since Herald had swept her off her feet back in college.

Parking beside a fiery candy-apple red Corvette, Nadine looked around to see if she recognized any of the other three vehicles. She didn't. She checked herself in the mirror one final time and then applied a fresh coat of nude lipstick.

She was determined to have a good time this evening, and to ensure that happened, she placed her phone in the glove compartment. Her world had been a living hell lately and she was going to leave all her problems and worries right inside of that car. Yes, she was going to relax, relate, and release.

She grabbed her purse, pushed her shades further back on her face, and walked up the maroon cobblestone pathway leading to the house The closer she got to the door, the faint smell of smoked barbecue and brisket lifted her nostrils. It smelled delicious, but she had to remind herself of her diet. She rang the doorbell once.

"It's open, Nadine!" Kelli called out through the intercom, apparently watching her on the surveillance camera. Nadine let herself in. She closed the door behind her and followed the music coming from the back of the house. She marveled over the colossal living room and its fancy décor. The vaulted ceilings, massive white columns, and swath of custom drapery made her think twice about buying another condominium. She might have needed to invest her monies into a house. Of course she could never afford a mansion on her income, but a three-bedroom house in the suburbs was definitely feasible.

As she walked even further into the house, she began to admire the travertine floors, the fourteen-foot-high stone fireplace, and the equally huge formal dining area, which was tastefully decorated in the finest of crystal. Nadine noted the panoramic floor-to-ceiling windows throughout with open waterfront views from every room. The home reeked of elegance and grandeur. Kelli and Herald were definitely living it up. It was no wonder *MTV Cribs* came out to get a peek of their lavish living.

Before Nadine made it all the way into the spacious chef kitchen where the music was coming from, Kelli was removing her apron and wobbling over to her.

"Nadine, you made it!" Kelli exclaimed, hugging her.

Nadine removed her shades and stared at Kelli's protruding belly in astonishment. She couldn't get the words out fast enough. "You didn't...tell...me you were expecting!" She beamed.

Kelli conveyed a girlish blush. "I know." She smiled. "No one knew before today. I wanted it to be a surprise," she said as she rubbed her stomach excitedly. "That's why I've been avoiding the media. You know how they like to get all up in your business."

"Well, mission accomplished." Nadine laughed.

Kelli brushed her long black luscious strands out of her face. She was a gorgeous biracial. The type you'd see modeling on a fashion magazine. She had perfect facial features. Her father was African American and her mother Swedish. Kelli was slightly taller than Herald, slender, and curvaceous. Let her tell it, she had gotten her derriere from her grandmother on her father's side who ate a lot of cornbread. She had smooth, tight olive skin, silky tresses, slanted emerald green eyes, and a convivial personality. She had majored in marketing, but when she'd met Herald, she'd pushed her ideas of working in corporate America aside.

Nadine's face was still lifted with happiness. "So how far along are you?"

"Twenty-one weeks as of yesterday."

Nadine's mouth was still hung and her eyes the size of walnuts. Her shock stemmed from knowing how difficult it had been for Kelli to conceive. She had gone through a battery of draining tests and a series of fertility treatments in an effort to conceive. And she'd finally done it, Nadine thought, refusing to inquire further.

"Well, congratulations, sis!" she said once the words came to mind. "You and Herald are going to make great parents. You really are," she added. As they embraced in another hug, Nadine gave her a reassuring rub on the back. She hoped Kelli noticed the sincerity in her gesture.

Kelli took a deep breath and while she may have tried to conceal the tears blanketing her bright green eyes, Nadine saw them. "Thank you!" Kelli smiled warmly, shifting her body a little as if to disguise any uncertainty. "I really needed to hear that," she said, her voice falling flat. She looked out the window at the beautiful view of the lake. She blinked back any other tears before they could surface. "Just nervous about being someone's mommy, ya know," she admitted suddenly.

Nadine nodded her head slowly in agreement "I know the feeling all too well. It's perfectly normal." There was a quiet pause between them. "Kelli, stop worrying," she said softly. "Everything's going to be just fine."

Kelli pressed her lips together and sighed deeply. This time when she looked at Nadine, she held a confidence in her face that hadn't been there five minutes ago. "You're right. Everything's going to work out just the way God intended," she said. "Now," she exhaled. "Enough about me!" She rounded the commodious island and sat on one of the leather wingback bar stools. She patted the seat of the stool beside her. "Sooooo, what's been going on with you? Unlike some of us, your business isn't being aired on

Facebook, Twitter, and every damn gossip website out there," she mused, referring to Herald's recent suspension from the Atlanta Falcons.

Nadine didn't volunteer that she had heard about the DWI violation. Instead she feigned surprised by the news. "Oh no, Kelli."

"Yeah, it's quite unfortunate, but he's taking it pretty well."

"Well, that's good to know."

"So how have things been for you since...Denise died?" Kelli inquired.

Nadine pulled her lips in. She was quiet for a long moment. This time *she* looked out of the window at the lake.

"If you don't want to talk about her, I understand," Kelli said. Her words were gentle and respectful, causing Nadine to feel warm inside. The truth was that she needed to talk about Denise. She needed to get her feelings out and find some sort of closure. And Kelli would have been the ideal person to talk to because unlike many, she never judged her. But today wasn't the day.

"No...it's not that. I'm just still dealing with it, you know?"

Kelli nodded her head. "Yeah." She paused. "I surely do miss her."

A soft smile swept Nadine's lips. "Me, too. Very much."

When the buzzer went off, Kelli walked over to the stove to turn off the pot.

"So where is everyone?" Nadine finally asked, ditching the subject of Denise altogether.

"A few of them are out back. Everyone else is en route." Kelli removed the tea bags and then poured the fresh pot of tea into a pitcher.

"And I thought you were really over there cooking something." Nadine laughed.

Kelli shot her a playful look. "Now you know I can't cook!" She laughed.

"Ha, ha, ha. Oh…I do remember now. It's all coming back to me. I remember how you burned all the cookies you were supposed to make for the Christmas event we volunteered for at the Senior Living Center."

"Hey, I thought they looked pretty good. Ha, ha, ha."

"Remember one of the residents claimed you were trying to poison her." They both laughed hysterically.

"How can I forget? She called the police and everything. Had me thinking I was going to the pen. Ha, ha, ha!"

Nadine could barely contain herself she was laughing so hard. Remembering that day brought joyful tears to her eyes. "Poor Herald."

"Poor Herald nothing!" Kelli turned her nose up and did a playful wind of the hips. "As they say, he didn't marry me for my cooking, honey. Ha, ha, ha!"

"Awwww shuckey now!" Nadine clapped, laughing uncontrollably at the dance Kelli was imitating from Beyoncé's "Dance for You" video that happened to be playing on the flat screen hanging above the kitchen nook.

"What the hell are you over there doing, girl!" someone called out from behind. "The Funky Chicken?" Kelli and Nadine both turned around to find Janeesha walking into the kitchen. Neither of them had heard her come in before now. Janeesha's wide-toothed grin vanished when she looked toward Nadine. She acted as though she wasn't as happy to see her.

Janeesha was a thick sistah with skin the shades of maple and orange. She was at least a size twenty, according to Nadine's guesstimate. The blue dress she wore was fitted to celebrate her voluptuous curves, and a silver sequined belt accentuated her waistline while her matching sequined flats depreciated her true leg value. She had a baby face, full lips, and a roundabout waist.

She wore her hair the same way she had in college. Hard and skinny tight curls with a fade at the back.

"Hey girl!" Kelli said. "Come right on over here and get comfortable."

Janeesha's face contorted into a scowl as her eyes shifted from Kelli and then back to Nadine.

"Well hello, Janeesha," Nadine said. She wasn't going to be rude and disrespectful in Kelli's house. She was bigger than that. It was no secret that she and Janeesha weren't the best of buddies, but damn, Janeesha had a serious eye problem and whatever her issues were with her, Nadine wished she'd get over it, because she sure had.

Janeesha rolled her eyes at Nadine and then looked back to Kelli. "Who the hell invited her?"

Nadine was taken aback and she sat there stiffer than a tree stump.

"I did!" Kelli said, obviously seeing where this was headed. The tension in the room had changed and the camaraderie had been killed the moment Janeesha had walked in.

Nadine's incredulous eyes darted from Kelli to Janeesha. "Janeesha, is there a problem?"

With scolding eyes, Janeesha pursed her lips. "The problem is the nerve you have showing your face here after what you did to Denise."

"What *I* did to Denise?"

"You run around and act like you Miss Goody Two-Shoes, but word gets around and you ain't as holy as you pretend to be! You had an affair with that woman's husband and then procreated with him," Janeesha spat with conviction, cutting Nadine a look of disdain.

Nadine stood up and grabbed her purse from the counter. "You don't know what the hell you're talking about!"

"Really? So everybody at church is a liar!"

"Stop this!" Kelli said, stepping in between them. "Janeesha, if you have a problem with my friend, *you* can leave." She pointed in the direction of the door. "This is *my* house and Nadine is *my* guest!"

Janeesha cut her eyes and wore a conniving smirk. "Fine! I'll leave," she huffed. "I refuse to be in the same room as this jezebel." She hooked her purse strap all the way up on her arm. "Just keep your enemies close, and your sorors closer!" she admonished nastily before turning to leave.

Kelli shook her head at the perpetual rubbish that had just transpired. "I'm sorry that happened, Nadine. Her ass was completely out of line for that."

The color in Nadine's face was nearly gone. Janeesha's words had been so cutting that Nadine didn't deny the tears that jetted down her face. Her perfectly arched brows folded in at the innuendo. "Oh my God." She sniffed. "So is this how everyone really feels about me?" she asked Kelli, her voice barely audible.

Kelli quickly shook her head. "Not at all. We all know that Janeesha can be garrulous. And she can even be a bitch sometimes, but that right there was totally uncalled for." She shook her head despicably as she turned to retrieve a paper towel. Nadine accepted it and blotted both her burning eyes.

She gave Kelli a pained look. "If I could take back my part in all of it, I would. If I could...see her one last time..." She paused. "I would tell her that I'm sorry!" Her voice cracked along the way as a despairing look settled in every crease of her skin. Her eyes pleaded for empathy. "I would tell her I never meant for any of it to happen." She stopped as more tears piled on her face. This was a sore subject for her and she hated when it came up. "But what no one understands is that I didn't do anything to hurt Denise," she tried to explain. "She knew about Jeff and I all along," she sniffed. "For three years."

Kelli's hand flew to her mouth. She appeared completely shocked by the revelation.

Nadine continued. "And she never said a word. Do you care to know why?"

Kelli was speechless.

Nadine really didn't care if Kelli wanted to know or not but someone was going to hear this. "She never said a word because it was what she wanted. We were the perfect diversion for her to commit her own affair."

Kelli placed her left hand over Nadine's shoulder. "It's okay, honey," she murmured. "I believe you. You don't have to say…"

Nadine shook her head. "It's not okay and…" Her words dragged out of her mouth, but the heavy weight of her burdens was finally being lifted. "I am so damn sick and tired of people judging and criticizing me on what they think they know. Assuming that I'm the one to blame for all of this!" Traces of her mascara skidded down her warm butterscotch skin. "When the truth of the matter is, they don't know a fucking thing!" She snatched her keys up. When she looked over her shoulder, she saw that two of her sorors were standing right behind her in utter disbelief of what they'd overheard. "Great! Now the whole world will know how bad of a friend I am."

"Nadine, please don't leave," Kelli pleaded. "You just got here."

"Congratulations again." Nadine leaned in and gave Kelli a kiss on the cheek. "I'll call you," she said, dismissing Kelli's request to hang around. "Hello, ladies," she acknowledged. She found herself leaving before anyone else could get the chance to humiliate her.

Barely out of the estates, Nadine found herself being flagged down by a jogger. Nadine slowly reversed to see what the woman could have wanted. She was in a hurry to get home and the last thing she wanted to do was talk. She stuck her head slightly out of the window. The pale white woman with long sandy-blonde hair pulled back into a ponytail, jogged over to her.

"You're not going to get very far with that bad tire," the woman said, pointing to her rear tire.

Nadine's eyes bucked. "Are you serious?" Her head started to pound. She stuck her head out of the window further to see that her rear tire was practically on flat. "Oh God. Not now." She cursed Janeesha under her breath, suspecting she'd done it on her way out.

"Do you happen to have a spare in your trunk?" the woman asked. Her accent was subtle and distinctive of a true Texan's.

Nadine placed her car in "park" and turned on her hazards. She couldn't believe this was happening. "I do. I'll call my friend," she said finally, referring to AAA. There was no way in hell she was calling Jeff's ass. She would have had it towed to her house before she did that. And she would have called Kelli, but she didn't want to interrupt her party.

The woman shook her head. "Don't trouble yourself. My husband can fix it for you. Let me go grab him. You stay right there." She smiled.

"Thank you," Nadine said. Relieved.

The woman began jogging up to the grandiose house on the left. It was immaculate on the outside and Nadine couldn't help but wonder how it looked on the inside. She bet it was twice as nice as Kelli's because it was twice as big.

Nadine laid her weary head against the headrest as she waited.

"My wife said you needed your spare..." The resonant voice stopped mid-sentence.

Nadine literally froze. She couldn't understand how she managed to find herself in yet another tight fix. "Greg Adams," she gasped, acknowledging him as a former client of Denise's, but in the back of her mind, she played out the version she remembered him best. It was the night she'd caught him and Denise having sex on the conference room table at Platinum Crest. The night Denise confessed to her that she was having an affair with him. The night Denise admitted to knowing all about Nadine and Jeff. Seeing Greg stirred horrible memories. And no matter how bad she wanted to push that night out of her mind, she couldn't.

"Here's the flashlight, honey," his wife said, walking back up.

"Thanks, baby," Greg said, shifting his gaze from Nadine to the deflating tire. "I need to get to your spare," he said, walking to the back of her vehicle.

Nadine popped her trunk and got out of the car. It was going to be a long night after all.

14

"What I need you to understand, Tyrone, is that I'm looking for more than just sex! I need a man who can satisfy me on a deeper level. Intellectually, emotionally, and physically. So until you can handle all that, I need you to lose my number." Ménage's eyes were mixed with seriousness and sadness. She didn't miss a beat as she stared straight ahead, imagining something like the size of the Dallas convention center, where the Mavericks sometimes played, being filled to its capacity. The scripted lines she had memorized for the audition flowed out of her mouth like smooth wine. The easygoing tone of her voice and the confidence in her posture made her appear like a seasoned veteran opposed to the neophyte she really was.

She remained in the exact position, waiting for Russ to completely assess her. She had taken Reginald's advice of not wanting to come across aggressive, so instead of talking herself up to him on why she was the one for this role, she kept a tight lip. After all, actions spoke a hell of a lot louder than words.

While Ménage had dreamt of her first audition being in a Hollywood studio complete with a stage and big bright lights, today's audition didn't measure up to those expectations by a long shot. She found herself in a cramped hot-ass studio apartment. She knew it was a low-budget film, but damn, could he at least afford a decent spot to bring her, she complained in her mind.

"I have to say I love your energy," Russ said, revealing a full top row of gold teeth. "You bring life to that character."

Ménage warmed her face with a humble smile, all while praying that he was getting ready to tell her that she got the part.

"Where you from again? You have an accent," Russ asked in his deep Southern drawl.

"Detroit. But I live in Dallas for the moment."

"Aghhh...for the moment, huh?"

Ménage blushed a schoolgirl grin. She faked an innocence that Stevie Wonder himself could see right through. But it was all in the act. The performance. This is what she did for a living.

"Yeah, just for the moment," she said, warming up to Russ. Her shoulders relaxed slightly. "I'm still trying to find work so that I can further my acting career," she continued.

Russ nodded his head with every word that exited her mouth. "I can dig it. Well, I'll tell you what. Because I'm feeling you. I mean really really feeling you. I'm gon' turn you on to something big that I happen to be working on behind the scenes. Something that's gonna get you hella paid, ya heard me. And put you in the Hollywood spotlight in no time."

Ménage's eyes lit up in excitement. "Really? How big and behind the scenes we talking?" The seductive way she licked her lips should have told him she was more than interested. She just needed to hear those dollar figures.

"Ten grand!"

Ménage's pussy started to tremor and all she could see was green money and big bright lights. She was on her way to superstardom.

"One scene," Russ added, as if she needed more convincing.

"One scene?" Ménage had already made up in her mind she was doing it, but she didn't need him to think she was that easy.

"Trust me on this. I'll make you a celebrity overnight."

"You got it like that, huh?"

Russ nodded. "I know people that know people." He simpered. "Don't let this little studio gig fool you?"

Ménage stuck her hands in her back pockets. "Well I'm all about getting money so…let's get money. When do I start?"

Russ smiled wickedly. "Let me make a couple of phone calls. In the meantime, there's a few outfits upstairs to choose from."

"All right," Ménage said, heading upstairs.

Ménage couldn't wait for Tiffany to pick her back up from the airport so that she could tell her all about her business meeting with Russ.

Tiffany pulled up in his sparkling blue Toyota Solara drop-top convertible right as Ménage was coming out of the airport. Although Ménage had seen Tiffany roll up, he honked twice, just as Ménage knew that he would. Tiffany loved attention and he sure was getting it. Everybody was looking as if trying to figure out who was this Nicki Minaj look-alike in drag. He had on his neon pink wig, Barbie pink lipstick, and matching nail polish. His tight black tank exposed his large breasts and his electric blue tights showed off his shapely legs and new ass shots. But he wouldn't be the glamorous diva he was without rocking his Versace shades.

"Soooo…how did it go, diva?" Tiffany probed before Ménage could get both feet in the car. She tossed her carry-on case in the backseat and strapped on her seatbelt. Tiffany stared at her in anticipation.

"You're looking at a movie star in the making," Ménage exclaimed, firing up a cigarette.

"Bitch, I told you you were going to get the part!" Tiffany rejoiced, high-fiving Ménage in the process. He pulled off into the moving lane, occasionally looking over at Ménage as she spilled all the goods.

"Girl, I got several parts!" Ménage confessed. "And one of them was a big-ass dick!" she bragged. "And that shit was so good I can still feel it slithering up my spine," she said, shimmying in her seat for emphasis as she occasionally took a pull off the cigarette.

"Say what! Bitch, you done went down there and snagged you some of that New Orleans grocery meat."

"Baby yes. And I made a chunk of change out of it."

"You lucky bitch!"

"Don't hate! Congratulate. Ha, ha, ha. I put it on his ass so good he thought Hurricane Katrina was up in that bitch."

"Ewww-weee. Ha, ha, ha! I ain't mad atcha. But was he fine though? That's all I want to know."

Ménage gave Tiffany the look. "Girl, he look like Lil Wayne on steroids. Tats, dreads, and every damn thing! He looked like something out of the wilderness."

Tiffany scrunched his face. "Sound like he belong on aww hell naw dot com."

They both fell into hearty laughter and maintained that energy all the way home.

When Ménage walked inside her dark apartment, the pungent fish odor caused her nose to turn up. She had forgotten to take out the trash before she'd left. "Got damn!" she cursed under her breath, realizing that the smell was coming from the leftover sushi she had thrown in the trash two days ago. She located a bottle of air freshener, aired the place out, then hurried to take out the garbage.

When she returned, she checked the time before rushing to the bathroom to shower. She had at least three hours to freshen up, get changed, and get to work. Tonight was Big Titty Tuesday and she was scheduled to perform.

Dripping wet, Ménage grabbed a towel from the closet and dried off. She quickly dressed into a pair of white sheer booty-strangling boy shorts, and a matching sheer tank. She slipped on some sandals and grabbed her traveling case, which held her outfit for tonight's show. Also inside was a change of clothes, several pairs of g-strings, toiletries and makeup. She was going to rock the stage like she never rocked it before.

Half an hour later Ménage entered through the backdoor of the infamous nightclub, X-Rated. Judging by the parking lot, it was a full house tonight. The energy was high, the music was bumping, and Ménage would bet that there were at least 200 rock-hard dicks upstairs, waiting to get close and personal with her. Everyone knew she was the HBIC (Head Bitch In Charge) up in there. She made the most money, had the most return customers, and all the strippers respected her hustle. In fact, those that weren't clocking it like she was sat back and took notes.

Ménage spoke to a few of the other girls in passing. She made it a point to be extra friendly with the waitresses. They were like her agents in a way. They found the goldmines and led her right to them. Cindy, also known as Chocolate Butter, was a white girl trapped in a black girl's body. Ménage thought the girl was a ding bat at times, but the men loved her. She was built like a stallion and had a real pretty face, and in this game, that's all it took to get by.

"Hey, Ménage!" Cindy said as she walked up. "Girl, you're going to make some money tonight. Most of them brothers up there looking for you."

"Already. Definitely what I wanted to hear. How'd you do?"

"Not so good. But, hey, the night is still young."

Ménage nodded, knowing that was wishful thinking because once she hit the stage, she was going to suck the blood out of every dick in there while milking their pockets. So there wasn't going to be any leftovers.

As she began to transform, she looked up at the wall clock. It was almost time. When she was finished, she double-checked herself in the mirror, then anxiously headed upstairs to get that money.

She waited behind the pink velvet curtain for the current slow jam that was playing to come to an end.

"Now fellas, I got something real nice and nasty in store for you tonight," Ménage heard the DJ announce. She peeked from behind the curtain to see that the club was jam-packed all the way from the bar to the main stage. There wasn't an empty seat in sight and the men, and women that looked like men, began clapping and yelling for him to bring it on.

"You already know what time it is. I know it's Big Titty Tuesday, but this fine hot thang is what I call a double shot!" The crowd roared in excitement as they waved and flashed the money in their hands. "X-Rated, get your money together so we can pay some bills in this bitch!" the DJ hollered as he turned the pink light on over the stage. "Now show some Big Titty love for my girl, Ménage!" he sang as her theme music started to play.

Ménage came from behind the curtain donned in a super sexy sheer leopard print bra and skirt trimmed with black fur. Her matching garter straps and seven-inch stilettos added to the wicked fantasy she hoped would fulfill her regulars and prospective regulars tonight. She swayed her hips to the song's prelude.

Her oiled skin was dusted in a shimmering gold glitter, and her sixteen-inch hair weave draped past her shoulders and down her back. She surveyed the club, making eye contact with every eye in the room as she moved her body to the beat beginning to fuse in.

She began mouthing her heavily glossed lips to the lyrics of the Weeknd's "Wicked Games" as she danced, translating the words sexually.

"*Bring your love baby I can bring my shame...*" Ménage slowly began to shed her bra. As she did so, money began to fly from every direction of the room. She moved her body in a sexy rhythm as she slid out her long ornamented tongue. She squeezed her oiled luscious breasts together and flicked the leopard spiked ball across both her swollen pierced nipples, causing the crowd to go wild. She could feel all eyes on her, and that was enough to get her pussy leaking with excitement.

"*...give me all for this, I need confidence in myself.*"

She teasingly danced out of her skirt, then slid to the floor. She crawled across the stage, collecting money with her mouth and breasts. When she found her biggest tipper, she did her signature move. She scooted to the edge of the stage, spread her legs in a V-shape, and made her pussy blow bubbles. He started popping bands and began dealing out a full stack. She counted at least a grand and was positive there was more where that came from. She couldn't see his face due to the darkness of the club, but she could see the green flying out of his hands. She found a money train and she wasn't getting off of it.

She lay all the way back, then jiggled her legs and thighs in the air, making her ass clap like crazy. Ménage stretched her legs into an upside-down split and motioned for her big spender to come closer. She grabbed one of the bills he'd just thrown on her, laid it across her pussy, and seconds later, the bill went twirling in the air, landing right on her stomach. She did it a second time for the non-believers. And again she blew air out of her pussy, converting Benjamin Franklin into a sexy-ass ballerina.

Her new best friend leaned in to place his face closer between her thighs. He ran his long fingers across her pubic area and she could feel his fingers tracing her tattoo. Without a break in her performance, she began to grind on his entire arm. Money continued to pour from every direction, but the big spender whose left hand was still palming her pussy, had all of her attention right now.

As the song came to an end, Ménage leaned forward to offer him a VIP service. "We can go to the back if you want a *real* private dance."

He removed his black Gucci shades.

"I knew the second I walked through that door that that was my pussy on this stage."

"Oh my God. Slug!" Ménage uttered, barely able to catch her breath.

"Get your shit and let's bust a move."

Ménage quickly hopped up, collected all her money, and rushed off the stage. Her past had come to visit her, but she hoped like hell that it didn't plan on staying.

15

Nadine peered out at the spectacular view of downtown Dallas. Her corner office suite jutted thirty-two floors above ground level and it overlooked the plentiful array of some of the finest architectural office buildings, eateries, and nightclubs in the city. Nadine appreciated the fact that she still had an office to sit in and a window to look out of in this political and economic climate, and even more after being penalized $200,000 by SEC (Securities and Exchange Commission) for Denise's role in the accounting violations that overstated the company's income by a long shot. Nadine was positively certain they would shut the doors to Platinum Crest Investments forever. And maybe if they had, she wouldn't be under the pressure she was now.

The past year had been challenging and every day that rolled by seemed tougher to get through. Since Barack Obama had made it through to a second term, she hoped he'd finish what he started and turn things around. Fast! Her clients, mostly wealthy Republicans, were not so easy to appease these days.

Nadine remembered when she enjoyed coming to work every day. Now as she sat sulking in Denise's old office, immersed in worldly problems while trying to recover from the news her partner had just laid on her, that love Nadine once had for her job seemed as distant as a childhood memory.

She tried relaxing some by taking short deep breaths as she gazed out of the window, but that simple technique took all the energy and strength that she could muster. She had just lost another one of her large accounts, and to make matters more depressing, the volatile market wasn't showing any signs of an early turnaround. The stock market had slumped again resulting in the Dow and S&P closing out at an all-time low yesterday. Even the annual percentage yield on the ten-year Treasury note wasn't looking pretty. Nadine sighed deeply, terrified to see what today's numbers were going to look like.

Ring!

Nadine picked up the call on the first ring. "Nadine speaking," she answered, seeing that it was Belinda, her new office assistant.

"There's a Mr. Adams here to see you," Belinda said.

"Who?" Nadine asked more in disbelief.

"Greg Adams," Belinda repeated.

Nadine rolled her eyes at the mention of the name. She cleared her throat. "Go ahead and send him back, please." *What in the hell does he want?*

"Will do."

Nadine sat up straight in her chair. She lowered the soft jazz music coming from her computer and waited for him to enter her door. The door slowly opened and in walked the man she'd hoped she'd never have to see again. "What do you want?" Nadine unloaded without so much as a greeting.

Greg walked slowly toward her spotless glass desk, but not before checking out her office as if he were searching for something.

"Excuse me." Nadine waved her hand. "I'm over here."

Greg finally made himself comfortable in the chair directly across from her before even being offered a seat. "Is this how you greet all of your clients?" he asked, eyeing her strangely. "Or am I just special?"

Nadine's face twisted into a disgusting frown. "Why are you here, Mr. Adams?"

"The last time I checked, I *still* have money here," Greg replied. "So I have every right to be here."

He smiled, but Nadine wanted to slap the taste right out of his mouth. Everything about him had her on edge and she hated that eerie feeling she got whenever he were in the same space as her. She pressed her lips tightly together and looked at him.

"In fact, how is the market treating me?"

She inhaled sharply. "If you don't mind, I will have Veronica go over your financials with you." Nadine reached for the phone to call the other broker, but before she could pick it up to dial Veronica's extension, Greg put his hand on top of hers to stop her.

"I didn't only come here for that," Greg said finally.

Nadine placed the phone back on its hook. She pulled her hands in and with her back to the chair, she fixed her eyes on his. "Well, then what exactly did you come for?"

"I came to apologize."

"Humph! Apologize?" she questioned dubiously. Her menacing stare could burn coal.

Greg nodded his head. He began to look around the office once again before resting his sights back on her. "This office reminds me of her so much."

Nadine sighed and looked away. She wasn't interested in hearing this. She shifted in her seat, clearly uncomfortable and annoyed.

"Nadine, I'm sorry for making you hate me so much."

Nadine was rendered speechless. Her hard fixation seemed to soften on its own as his apology left his lips. She had to ask herself if she really did hate Greg or if she was only acting this way toward him because she knew what type of dog he was. He hadn't done anything to Nadine personally, but he had done a whole hell of a lot to Denise. She had sacrificed her entire life for him. Her husband for him. Her friendship for him. Nadine had asked herself many times if she and Jeff would have ever given in to each other if he had not felt that Denise was cheating on him. The answer always made itself crystal clear. No! He wouldn't have come on to her if his marriage was intact and Nadine wouldn't have felt she needed to be his emotional pillow. None of it would have happened if it weren't for Greg, she made herself believe.

Her eyes followed Greg's as he stared at an old photo of her and Denise. It was a picture of the two of them in Hawaii four years ago. Nadine had come across the picture cleaning Denise's office. She pulled it out and kept it on the table stand next to her so that even at work, Denise's presence would be there.

"And I'm sorry for whatever stress or discomfort my involvement with Denise might have caused everyone," Greg continued.

"I don't hate you, Mr. Adams," Nadine interjected. "I…wish I didn't have to live with the fact that I knew about the two of you."

Greg kept a straight face as he tried to complete her thought. "Like she knew about the two of you?"

Nadine grimaced. "Humph. Excuse me?"

"You and her husband that is," he added matter-of-factly.

Nadine felt her stomach sink to the bottom as her entire body tensed. She couldn't believe Denise had told him about her and Jeff. How could she do that? Nadine wondered what else this man knew about her.

"I'm afraid I don't know what you're talking about," she lied, trying to play it off as best she could. And she thought they were getting somewhere.

"Look, Nadine. I'm not here to point fingers, air dirty mattresses, or to place judgment. Everyone makes mistakes and we *all* have our secrets that we have to protect," he said smugly. "And at the end of the day, I would hope we can let bygones be bygones so we can put the past behind us, once and for all."

Nadine couldn't stomach much more of this. Is this what this bastard called an apology? Because it sure as hell didn't feel like one anymore.

"Look, can we just skip all the punctilious incidentals of *my* life, and get to the bottom line of why you're really here?" Nadine asked sternly.

The amused look on Greg's face vanished as time ticked away. He brushed his salt-and-peppered beard with his broad palm then leaned further back in the chair. "I need a favor," he admitted finally. "The securities that I have with you. I would like to gift them."

Nadine thought she had lost all of her senses. "You would like to gift them?" she repeated for clarification.

"Yes. And I would like to expedite the process as much as possible."

"I must make you aware of the tax..."

"Please. I'm pressed for time on this," he said. "I appreciate your concern, but I've already consulted with my tax adviser regarding this matter. So the quicker I can get this handled, the better off I'll be."

Nadine saw the desperation in his face and hoped like hell this wasn't any funny business he had going. She began typing away on her keyboard to pull up his account information. He was already under the microscope.

"I can start the process now, but I will need the brokerage account information of the recipient so that I can initiate the transfer."

"I have everything you need."

Nadine's fingers pecked feverishly across the keyboard. "What's the name of the organization, Mr. Adams?"

"Please, just call me Greg."

Nadine took her eyes off the screen to address him as so. "*Greg*," she enunciated sarcastically.

Greg chortled to himself. He flattened his tie over his chest. "It's not an organization," he elucidated. "It's a...personal friend."

Judging by the smile in his dark cavernous eyes, the projection in his forehead, and his furtive nature, Nadine suspected that this personal friend was more than that. She wondered if his wife knew about this, or if she *ever* knew that her husband was a two-timing low-life. *Too bad the poor thing would have to find out the hard way*, Nadine thought.

"Well, I'm saddened to be losing your business," she lied.

"Ha, ha, ha." Greg's eyes were locked on hers. "No you're not. You and I both know damn well that I'm the last person you wanted to see in your office today." He chuckled again.

Nadine diverted her eyes and began typing again. She couldn't argue with that. She liked to think that if he disappeared, the past secrets surrounding her and Jeff's relationship would somehow disappear too. "Mr. Adams, who...I'm sorry, Greg. Who will the stocks and bonds be transferred to?"

"Naomi Brooks," he said, pulling out his wallet. He pulled out a folded piece of paper that had all the information Nadine would need to complete his transaction.

"Are you sure you don't want to preserve some of your shares in..."

"No," Greg said adamantly, cutting her off before she could finish her sentence. "I would like to transfer all of it."

There was a moment of pause.

Nadine continued to take down all the necessary information to complete his request. She willed herself to let it go, but the words were dying to come out. "Oh yeah, and how's the missus?" An inconspicuous grin spread across her lips, matching the one he had held earlier. She looked up at him. "She seems like a very lovely woman." Nadine smiled while Greg only stared at her stone-faced, and in stony silence. That was enough to let Nadine know his wife was not up for discussion.

After feeling like the Dallas Cowboys in a major comeback game, she stood up to grab the paperwork off the printer.

As she strolled past him, he grabbed her by the wrist.

"My wife cannot find out about this!" His posture changed, his skin felt clammy, and his voice was shaky from nerves, or sheer desperation.

Nadine roughly jerked her arm away from him and shot him a blistering look. "Don't worry. I'm not in the business of spilling people's secrets," she said in a hushed tone. "Now if you don't mind, I'd like to wrap this up so that I may prepare for my next appointment."

16

"I try not to pry or meddle in folks' personal or business affairs," Nadine said, taking another bite of the Healthy Choice grilled chicken and linguine frozen entree. "But I had to throw him under that bus with me. His arrogant ass deserved it," she chortled. She had been on the call with her Aunt Mickey for the entire lunch hour. She had only called to check up on her, but the call turned into her filling her in on her crazy weekend, leading up to today.

"I can't help but wonder who that negro in cahoots with?" Aunt Mickey said.

"Not sure and I couldn't care less about who he's doing and screwing. It's just seeing him brought back a lot of bad memories." She took a deep breath as if in deeper thought. "And then to see him twice in one week. I don't know, it's just so weird." She got quiet. "I could be overanalyzing this. You know how I am sometimes."

"I would bet that he's cheating on his wife again," her Aunt Mickey speculated further. She had landed at that assumption right away.

"He's such a slime bag. He makes my skin crawl every time I see him," Nadine said. "And it makes me wonder what Denise ever saw in him." After Nadine realized what she had just said, she closed her eyes in contempt.

"Hell, I can answer you that. Money, honey!" Aunt Mickey

blurted, followed by a hearty laugh. "But whatever the old sneaky rat has up his sleeve, know that it won't be long before it hits the fan. Because what's done in the dark, always comes to the light," she mused. "And I'll put that on a Don King haircut."

They both laughed and then Nadine grew so quiet she could hear her Aunt Mickey's television in the background. She was watching her favorite game show, *Family Feud.* While discussing Greg's business transaction was totally against her company's practices, Nadine felt as though she had to tell her aunt about this one.

"I've decided I'm never getting married," she blurted. "I'm not putting myself through that."

"Get off my phone with that nonsense!"

"No, I'm serious, Aunt Mickey. It seems that every man I meet turns out to be either unavailable, gayer than a snapping turtle, afraid of commitment, or just a plain old dirty dog. And that's dog with a capital *D!*"

"You just haven't met the right one that's all. Not all men are like that so don't go putting them in the same box. I think you should try that harmony dating service. You never know, your husband might be a mouse click away."

"Heck no! I'm definitely not that desperate."

"Suit yourself. I met my new beau online," her aunt teased.

"What. Are you serious?"

"Ha, ha, ha. No. But I sure did think about it."

"Humph. Well, I'm glad you came to your senses because the last thing I need you calling to tell me is that your online beau turned out to be a psychopath."

"You worry too damn much. You're young. Live your life and stop worrying so much!"

"That's easier said than done."

"So you're going to let one man keep you from finding happiness, Nadine. We've all been hurt before. It's how you deal with it and where you go from there."

"I didn't expect for my life to turn out like this." She paused for thought as her emotions began to surge.

"What is it about your life that is so bad? You have the job of your dreams, your health is good, and you've been blessed with one of God's most precious gifts. You have so much to be thankful for, baby."

"And I am thankful."

"Well, what is it that's really bothering you?"

Nadine stopped altogether. She told herself she wouldn't do this time and time again. That she would just move on with her life and accept things for what they were. She laughed to keep from crying.

"What's so funny?"

"Even in pain, I still love him. I think that's what bothers me the most."

They both got quiet.

"Did you go see that lady I told you about?"

Nadine had hoped her aunt wouldn't bring up the woman she'd been begging her to go see.

"Nadine, are you there?"

"I'm here, Aunt Mickey."

"Did you go see the woman?"

"I really don't think a psychic is what I need right now."

"She's not a psychic. She's a prophet," Aunt Mickey said. "This woman told me things that nobody knew, but me and God. She revealed something to me that…"

"Oh wow, look at the time," Nadine said, cutting her aunt short. "I better get going. I have a two o'clock conference call that I absolutely cannot be late for."

"Well, all right, honey. Thanks for calling and give my grand-nephew a huge kiss for me!"

"I will. I love you."

"I love you too, baby."

Nadine disconnected the call, finished off her black tea, and retreated back to her office. She considered calling the woman her Aunt Mickey had told her about but couldn't help wondering what this woman could possibly tell her about her own life that she didn't already know. Her aunt had insisted she call for clarity, telling her the woman was spiritually gifted. But Nadine never believed in psychics and fortunetellers. To her belief, they weren't real and were only out to deceive people by taking advantage of their vulnerabilities. It was merely entertaining to think of someone trying to read someone's mind or predict their future. Impossible, she thought. It was as comical as the daily horoscopes she received on Facebook that hardly ever applied to her own life.

The complexities of life in general was enough to sink anyone into a state of mental tyranny, but add a spiraling twisted affair, a baby, and an unforeseen heartbreak to the mix and you had Nadine's life in a nutshell. It was the not so cookie-cutter version.

Nadine would admit at the drop of a dime that she was still very much in love with her child's father, but he didn't reciprocate her feelings. She knew this woman was only going to remind her that she was creating more pain for herself by entertaining these toxic feelings that she subconsciously disguised as hope. While a part of her wanted to stop chasing Jeff, quit cold turkey and move on with her life, her forlorn heart pleaded for more time, patience, and faith. Something she was losing more of by the minute.

After her conference call, Nadine carefully scrolled through the numbers in her cell phone. When she found the woman's number her aunt had given her, she dialed it. *What harm could it do?* she thought. Figuring she could use some uplifting news after her hellacious weekend, even if it was all a lie.

"This is Zeola," the woman answered in a singsong-like voice that made her Jamaican English extremely pleasant to hear.

"Hi, Ms. Zeola," Nadine began, oblivious of the woman's last name. "My name is Nadine and I was given your number by my aunt, Mickey Collins."

Zeola didn't respond right away which started Nadine to worrying. "Mickey? Hmmm...the name...doesn't...really...ring...a...bell."

Nadine could tell Zeola was cycling through her memory.

"Wait! I do believe I remember her. Yessss!" She started laughing. "We met at a gospel convention I attended a few months ago in Atlanta," she stated. "I remember her quite well now actually. She's the one that sat on the front row. Ha, ha, ha. She wore a big fancy purple hat that day."

Nadine laughed softly. "Yes. That would be Aunt Mickey." All of Georgia should have known and recognized her aunt from a mile away. She had a very eclectic style for fashion and it was all designed and created by Mickey Clothiers, a home-based clothing and accessory boutique that she'd started shortly after her late husband had died. But even before, Aunt Mickey was acknowledged by many as the best seamstress in Atlanta. She was even called if anyone needed extra help.

"Nice woman, your aunt is," Zeola said.

"Thank you," Nadine grinned. "I called because I was hoping I could meet with you this evening."

"For a session?"

Nadine hesitated. She had to remind herself to have an open mind about all of this. Even as wild and extreme as it might have seemed, she believed she would enjoy this.

"Yes, ma'am."

"Now I must warn you that I don't share my gift with everybody," Zeola said. "Many believe it's a hoax and therefore do not take my readings seriously."

Nadine was dead silent. Maybe the woman was trying to read her right now, she thought.

"But...I'm sensing some confusion with you. You're searching for clarity of your life." Zeola paused. "Is this true, Nadine?"

Nadine blinked her eyes a couple of times and looked around her spacious office. She was obviously all alone, but she felt like the woman was sitting right there in the room with her. A twinge of doubt washed over her, but she couldn't resist the urge to hear what this woman had to say. "Yes," she replied, hoping Zeola didn't detect her skepticism.

"You're already very interesting, but I look forward to meeting you in person," Zeola said, just before rattling off her address.

Consumed with jitters, Nadine looked down at the woman's address, then tucked the piece of paper in her purse. She looked forward to the meeting even more now. She thought about the first question she would ask Zeola. Wondered if it made any sense at all to keep entertaining that tiny seed of hope that she and Jeff could rekindle the love they once shared.

Her eyes reverted to the computer screen, although her mind was elsewhere. The more she tried to suppress what was really bothering her, the more she made herself out to be delusional. She grabbed a Kleenex off her credenza and blotted the corners of her eyes. *He deserves to be happy*, she thought. But why wasn't *she* the woman he was marrying? What was so special about this Ménage? Nadine's soul ached for his love and her body longed for his touch. She blotted her eyes again, careful to not ruin her makeup. She still had another client to see. Just as she tossed her tissue in the wastebasket, Belinda walked through the door carrying a huge bouquet of lavender roses, a gift bag, and a smile as wide as a Cheshire cat.

"Looks like somebody's been holding out on me," Belinda said, a serious swing in her gait as she carried the large clear vase and bag over to Nadine's desk.

Nadine shot her a perplexed look. "Is this for me?" she asked as Belinda positioned the bag and bouquet directly in front of her.

"Has your name all over it." Belinda smiled. As she stood there in anticipation, she began chanting, "Open, open, open!"

Nadine stood up and took a seat on the edge of the front of her desk. She pulled out a single rose and sniffed it. "Does it say who they're from?"

Belinda shrugged her shoulders. "I didn't check, but I'm sure he has his name right…in there," she said anxiously, pointing to the red envelope affixed on top.

Nadine's forehead crinkled as she pulled the envelope off the clip and tore it open.

"Soooo…who do I give these brownie points to?" Belinda inquired.

Nadine began reading the card silently at first. She then read it again for Belinda to hear:

"It's very rare that I find a woman that makes my heart stop with just one glance. Since the moment I laid eyes on you, I haven't been able to get you out of my mind. I have to see you again. If you are available, and I sure as hell pray that you are, please do me the honor and join me for dinner."

Belinda smiled and pumped her fists in excitement. "She has a winner!"

"Ha, ha, ha!"

Below the note were the meeting details but no name. "I'm not sure who it's from," Nadine said. "There's no name."

"Hmm. Must be somebody very special to not leave his name. Unless…" She raised an arched brow and tilted her head. "You have an admirer."

Nadine blushed mischievously. "I strongly doubt that," she said, waving off the thought of it. She peeked inside the bag and pulled out a bottle of red wine.

"You never know," Belinda said in her pleasantly light voice. She leaned in to inhale the roses once again. "I'm jealous!" She laughed. Nadine laughed along with her. "There seems to be a shortage of good men and judging by this guy's chivalry, I'd go out on a limb and say he might be a keeper." She stretched her neck out some in an effort to get a glimpse of the name on the bottle. "Definitely worth putting on the books. And if he looks as good as *that* tastes, you've struck gold, baby!"

Nadine fingered the rose as she sifted through her thoughts. Outside of her clients, she couldn't think of one person her gifts could have come from. Not one. She couldn't help but crack a smile as her eyes shot back up at Belinda. "Do you think Mr. McCormick sent it?"

Belinda's eyes practically popped out of their sockets. "Seventy-three-year-old Mr. McCormick?" she asked, frowning as if having to repeat it sounded more worse than the thought.

"Well, he's always felt the need to express to me that he has a thing for beautiful brown women. He's the first person that came to mind."

Belinda looked as if she had a bad case of bubble guts.

"Maybe it's time I broadened my horizons," Nadine said.

Belinda looked on unbelievingly at Nadine. "Can somebody say Geritol and Viagra! Ha, ha, ha…"

"Ha, ha, ha! You are so crazy!"

Belinda struggled to catch her breath. "Would you seriously date a white man that old?" she asked.

Nadine stood up and rounded her desk to sit back in the chair. "A white man, yes. An old man, I highly doubt it."

"Afraid he'll croak on you?"

Nadine gave her a frivolous grin. "I'm more afraid his little blue pill will stop working." They both burst into an inconspicuous fit of hilarity, but little did Belinda know, Nadine was serious as a heart attack. "Just kidding girl," she lied dismissingly, realizing how big of an undercover freak it made her sound. The last thing she needed was to be exposing herself.

Belinda's laughter continued as she fanned the tears from her eyes. "You are a trip!" she exclaimed.

Nadine returned a warm smile. While Belinda was only with the firm part-time until Tonya returned from leave, Nadine really enjoyed having her around. She had only been with the company for a couple of months, but the two of them got along like old girlfriends.

"Well, I better get back up front before the phones start going crazy again," Belinda said, regaining her composure.

"All right. I think I'm going to wrap it up in about another hour or so. I have an appointment outside of the office."

"Oh, all right. I'll hold all your calls."

"Thank you." Nadine smiled, as Belinda turned to leave. She could hear the clacking of her Miu Miu plum suede peep-toe pumps, receding down the corridor. Staring at the bottle, Nadine could almost taste the wine on her tongue. She reflected back on what had taken place the last time she'd had one too many glasses. She permitted her spinning untamed thoughts to escort her down memory lane once again. She missed the smell of Jeff's cologne, the warm sensual caress of his hands, the glide of his tongue, and the ride of his dick. She was going through withdrawal and with a sex drive as high as hers, her celibacy vow now seemed more like a self-deprecating joke. She had gone a full three weeks to date without engaging in any sexual act whatsoever. Not even the fine art of masturbation. It sure as hell wasn't easy, but she recalled what she had heard someone say: *"It's hard as hell going cold turkey. You have to wean yourself off good dick."* But the weaning part was still a challenge for Nadine because she didn't know how to detach her feelings from sex. In the beginning she could, but it didn't seem to work the same way anymore.

Nadine flirted with temptation but didn't want to renege on her promise. Although in the back of her horny mind, she couldn't help but think that all it would take is one call to turn things around and put her out of her sexual frustration.

She looked over at her cell phone. Her fingers impatiently tapped at the desk while her pussy remained eagerly on standby. For one night of passion she felt she could look over their petty arguments and disagreements, and maybe even the idea of him being engaged to someone else. That's if it were even true since she had yet to hear it from the horse's mouth. She needed one last time for old time's sake. One last time…for closure.

She picked up the phone and placed the call. She looked back over at the roses and the wine. *Am I really ready to move on?* she asked herself.

The phone rang several times before he finally answered.

"Jeff speaking."

Nadine took in a short breath. "Good afternoon. I was calling… to…ask you to help me with something," she began. Just one quick and simple plea for closure and her pussy could be back in the Kentucky Derby. She searched for the right words, feeling somewhat ashamed for betraying her personal commitment.

"After sitting here thinking, I've come to realize that I need some type of clo—"

Jeff cut her smack off. "What's up, Nadine, because you caught me at a really bad time?" In only a matter of seconds, he killed the little bit of sexual energy she still had left. The contemplation of going back down that road with Jeff had been short-lived as she quickly got a grip on her common sense. She cleared her throat. "I apologize for disturbing you. I wanted to see if you could pick up Canvas from the daycare. I have a late appointment and I don't believe I'll make it in time."

"Sure. I can do that. I'll go get him and you can pick him up at the house."

"Great, I'll be there as soon as I'm done. Thank you for doing this at the last minute."

"You don't have to thank me, Nadine. He's my son," Jeff said lastly before ending the call with nothing more or less to say.

17

Ménage lay there for a minute. Her head was throbbing and spinning. She definitely had a hangover. She wondered if it was even possible to get carpal tunnel in the neck; if so, she had that too. She'd never felt so damn bad in her life.

She eased up, careful to not wake Slug.

As she scanned the room, she saw liquor bottles, cigarillos, and a bag of weed sitting on the stand below the wall-mounted flat screen. And it smelled like a concoction of sweaty butt-naked sex, weed, and alcohol, with a hint of her sweet perfume. She began to recall most of what took place last night, causing her throbbing head to pound even more. Ménage slowly climbed out of bed feeling so lightheaded she thought she was going to faint.

Clad in only her birthday suit, she walked around the king-sized bed in search of her heels. She eased into them and staggered toward the bathroom. The liquor hadn't quite worn off so every step was a balancing act.

Spending time with Slug last night felt like old times. Instead of bringing her back to his hotel, he wanted to crash at her spot for the night, but Ménage refused to show him where she lived. There was no way in hell that was going down. She didn't know what new situation he had going on and she wasn't about to put her life or freedom in jeopardy. So the less he knew, the better off she was.

She returned from the bathroom and walked around to the sink. It wasn't a pretty sight. She had bags under her eyes, no makeup, and her hair was all over the place. She began fixing the pieces of hair that were out of place because even after oversleeping for most of the day, a bad bitch like her had to look good. She washed up and then powdered on some makeup and lipstick.

"Ummm..." Slug moaned.

Ménage looked up in the mirror to see him staring at her.

"I see somebody getting ready for another round," Slug said as he got up from the bed and headed over to her.

The first thing she pointed to was the huge hickey on the left side of her neck. "You just getting reacquainted with this and you already trying to mark your territory?"

"Damn right. And I'm about to mark it again," Slug said, pointing to his hard-on. He slapped her on the ass, then headed for the bathroom. After he was all done, he walked back over to her and started kissing her.

He kissed her as if they had never left each other's side. It felt like they were picking up right where they'd left off, but in the back of Ménage's mind, she knew differently. A lot had changed over the years and although Slug was the love of her life, they belonged to two entirely different worlds. She yearned for Slug's touch for so long, and now that he was here, in the flesh, giving her body what it wanted, what it had been missing, she didn't know what to do other than fuck him in memory of lost time.

She could feel her pot of honey being stirred as Slug slipped his hands between her legs to wake up her pussy.

"Ummm," she moaned. Her round swollen nipples poked at his chest.

Slug was hovering at six feet four. He was medium build, wide chest, with pure solid muscle—at least in his arms. He still had the beer belly pudge she always teased him about. Slug also had incredibly smooth high-yellow skin and money-green eyes. Where he used to rock Allen Iverson braids back in the day, he now wore a shadow fade with neatly trimmed sideburns and mustache. Physically, nothing much about him had changed. He had a few new sleeve tattoos. But the one she admired most was his neck tattoo with her name on it. He'd gotten it the same day she'd gotten hers. Those were the conditions she'd laid out. And she made him go first.

All in all, Slug was still that pretty boy from the hood that she fell in love with when she was sixteen.

Slug picked her up and sat her on the edge of the counter. As he gradually spread her eagle, he kissed and tongued the top of her legs, then worked his way to the middle. Ménage panted and moaned in satisfaction as her pussy began to melt from his touch. Her nipples hardened as she braced herself for another Omni Hotel adventure. She'd been there so many times she knew the night crew by name. Her head fell back against the mirror and that cold glass up against her shoulders and back sent a surge of energy below. Her hands were at either side, giving him the leverage that he needed to eat her pussy properly.

"Now this is how I like my coffee," Slug said, diving his tongue in and out of her.

Ménage purred like a kitten as he gave her some serious head. *He hasn't lost his touch one bit*, she thought, as she watched his head bobble with every stroke. She extended her legs further until her ankles were hooked over her shoulders. The pointy heel of her stilettos jabbed the mirror with every tongue thrust. It felt so good and she couldn't help how wet she was for him. If she never told him she missed it, he knew now.

"Get that shit!" Ménage egged him on as he swallowed her yoni whole. She could feel her nut getting ready to crack. She was right there. She could see the finish line and in just a couple of more licks, she knew she'd be creeping across it. But right then, Slug changed it up. He must not have been ready for her to release. He pushed her knees toward her chest as if she were getting ready to give birth, then slowly prepared to lay his pipe down sideways.

"Oh yessss!" Ménage gasped as he entered her. Her entire body stiffened at first and she tried to clench something, but there was nothing next to her to grab. "Oh my God!" she panted as the back of her head occasionally bounced against the glass.

"Whose pussy is this?" Slug asked.

"It's yours, baby!"

He gripped her hips and gave it to her full throttle. Ménage's breasts flopped around as he pounded into her. Slug slapped her on the ass, remembering how she liked it. His pace quickened as he drove farther into her tunnel. He tightened his grip around her waist and held on like a NASCAR driver as he hit every single corner of her pussy. When he managed to find her g-spot, Ménage began screaming in pure ecstasy. As if that was all the encouragement he needed, Slug raised her legs well above her head once again and gave her one final swerve. Once again her heels beat against the mirror. This time she heard it crack.

"Arrggghhh!" Slug grunted. His face contorted as he exploded so deeply inside of Ménage that her body jerked. She had arrived with him.

A smile swept across Slug's face as he leaned in to kiss her. He slowly slid out of her and Ménage sat up.

"Let's hit this shower," Slug said.

"You go ahead. I'll take mine at home. I know my roommate is probably worried sick about me so I better roll out."

"Roommate?" Slug questioned.

"Yeah. I have a roommate," Ménage lied. "That's the reason we couldn't go back to my place last night. We have a no-man-in-the-apartment policy."

"Well, it shouldn't be no other niggas period, now that I'm back in the picture." Slug didn't crack a smile.

"Yeah, well for how long, considering how you just up and shot ghost on me."

"I tried reaching out to you, Ebony. I called your moms, your sister, everybody that fucking knew you and they told me you moved across state somewhere because you got a new job."

"I did. But that doesn't change the fact that you left me hanging out there. I thought you were dead!" She paused. Genuine tears immediately filled her eyes. "I didn't know what happened to you. First, I'm hearing you owed somebody and you skipped town, the next I'm hearing that you might be dead. I didn't know what the fuck to believe! I had to bounce because I thought my life was in danger too!"

Slug wiped the tears from her eyes. "Look, baby. Yo nigga ain't dead. He right here!" He took her hands in his. "I had to lay low because the laws were rolling in on us. I paid a youngblood to catch a case for me so that I wouldn't go down." Slug stared deeply into her eyes.

"What kind of case?"

"Doesn't matter."

"But you still left me, Slug! I had no money, no car, no food. I couldn't fucking survive without you!"

"Baby, I had to lay low until the smoke cleared. But as soon as I came out, you were the first person I came looking for."

Ménage shook her head sideways as tears continued to stream down her unmade face. "So much has changed."

"Ain't shit changed between *us*. This right here been real."

The way he looked at her was if there was no doubt in his mind that things couldn't be the way they were before. But that was the problem. She didn't want things to be as before. She wanted a life with a promising future. She didn't want to have to worry about all that extra madness that came with being Slug's woman. It was too much then so she knew it would be too much now. She wasn't built to be a dopeman's girl. She wanted more than that out of life.

"Been real, huh?"

Slug drew his neck back. "You doubting us now?"

Ménage paused for a minute. "Answer me one question. Are you still dealing? That's all I want to know." She didn't have to ask because she could see it with her own two eyes. In fact his three homeboys that he had been with at the club last night all looked like drug dealers too.

Slug looked away.

"That's what I figured."

Ménage looked around the suite. It was all nice and dandy, but she couldn't see herself ever going back down that road again. "This ain't for me," she said finally.

Slug gave her a smug look. "Well, this dope money is what put your ass through school so don't forget that."

She cut her eyes up at him, then fell silent.

"Listen, Ebony, I understand you done got down here and found yourself and everything…but, I can take care of you. Always have, always will."

"No. See, you're not even listening. I'm not trying to be on the run every time we look around. That's not what I want for myself. I want more out of life." Her eyes seemed to widen as she mentally searched for a better way to tell him that she wasn't going back. “Slug, I never stopped loving you. Even when you left me,” she said. “But I’ve moved on with my life.”

“You call shakin’ your ass in that strip club moving on?” He chuckled.

“You know what,” Ménage said, climbing down from the counter. “It was good seeing you again, but I gotta bounce.”

“Wait a minute!” Slug said, grabbing her by the elbow. “You ain’t going no motherfucking where! We still talking.”

Ménage tried pulling her arm back, but Slug’s grip was too tight.

“Owww, you’re hurting me!” she said, trying her best to wiggle her arm away from him. He finally let her go and she quickly hurried over to the chair to throw on her clothes. She didn’t care this time about anything except for getting the hell out of there as fast as she could. She grabbed her keys off the end table and jetted for the door.

“Ebony!” Slug called after her as she hurried down the hall, passing an elderly white couple who looked like they’d just come from Bible study. “Ma’am I think he’s trying to get your attention,” the man called out to her. But she kept on walking until she reached the elevators. She scurried through the lobby, her skinny gold heels seemingly like cat claws across the marble floor. She was pissed and from the stares she received, it was obvious.

Ménage jumped into her car and sped out of the parking garage. She didn’t look in her rearview until she was back on the freeway. The visual of the Omni became smaller and smaller by the distance. As for Slug, he was another long-lost memory. And that’s exactly where she planned on keeping him.

18

As soon as Ménage walked through her door, she headed straight for the shower. She towel-dried her hair, threw on her Juicy Couture tracksuit, and styled her hair. While in the mirror putting on her makeup, it hit her that she hadn't heard from Jeff. She didn't want to come off too strong, as that would only scare him or draw suspicion. Instead, she gave him a little space to get his mind right, figuring that eventually he would call her when he needed a good fuck. She knew for a fact that he wasn't getting any from his baby momma. She'd made sure of it. Ménage wanted to be his only supplier, but it'd been five days and she hadn't heard one single word from him.

Ménage walked into the living room and began looking for her purse. "Fuck!" she cursed out loud. She had left it back at the hotel. Her wallet, her cell...everything was in that purse. As much as she didn't want to, she had to go back.

She slipped into some flip-flops, ready to head across the hall to ask Tiffany to roll with her in case she needed some backup. She flung open the door and her entire body froze.

"You got a nigga driving all the way out here with all these white folks," Slug complained as he handed Ménage her purse. "Better be glad a nigga love your ass," he said, pushing his way past her. He walked inside and began looking around her small, but lavish apartment.

Ménage clenched her jaws and gritted her teeth. She did not need him knowing where she lived. "Thanks for bringing it," she said, looking through it to make sure everything was there.

Slug made himself comfortable on the couch.

"What are you doing?" Ménage asked, her face frowned.

Slug stretched his size thirteen shoes on her coffee table. "I'm making myself at home, baby." He leaned back and folded his hands behind his head. "I can get used to this."

"Get your dirty shoes off my good shit!" She walked over to the table and pushed his feet off of it.

"What's your problem, ma? A few hours ago we were all over each other and now you trying to flip the script like you don't know a nigga."

Ménage crossed her arms. "My problem is that you think I'm supposed to drop everything I've built for myself here, and go back to that shit you're doing."

She looked over his attire. Starched blue jeans, crisp long white tee, and a white baseball cap. The look was pretty simple, but the gold diamond-encrusted chain hanging around his neck, the shoes on his feet, and the four permanent teardrops on the right side of his face would give anyone reason to believe that he was slanging or banging.

"So all of a sudden, you too good for me?" Slug stared at Ménage wide-eyed. "Is that what you saying?" He got up and slowly walked closer to where she stood. He lifted her chin and turned her attention back to him. "I want you back. And I'm going to do everything in my power to get you back."

Ménage gave him a straight face. "Are you going to stop selling drugs?" she asked blatantly.

"I can. After this shipment comes through this week, I'll unload it, and go legit for you, baby," he said persuasively.

Ménage twisted her lips and cut her eyes at him. "You're lying."

Slug managed a humorous chuckle, only Ménage wasn't laughing. "Look. I'ma keep it one hundred with you. I can't promise you that I'll change overnight. But I can, and I will promise you, that I will never leave you again. And you can put that on everything I love."

Ménage looked him in his eyes and she knew he was telling her the truth. She could feel it in her bones. He leaned in and kissed her and she embraced him. She loved Slug with all of her might, but her mind had been made up. They were clearly on two different paths in life. She was headed north and he was headed south. Ménage refused to sacrifice her dreams for him. She wasn't that little girl anymore and his charming manipulation wasn't going to work. Not this time.

Her cell phone started ringing. It was Jeff's ringtone. "I have to get that," Ménage said, pulling away.

"Ugh-uh. Whoever it is can wait," Slug said as he kept kissing her, gripping her ass.

"It could be my roommate."

He finally released her and before she could get her phone out of her purse, it stopped ringing. Seconds later, a text came through. It was from Jeff. She texted him back before returning her attention to Slug.

"Where are you going to be later?" she asked. "I have to get ready for work."

"You mean you going back to that hoe spot?"

Ménage drew her neck back and put one hand on her hip. "That *hoe spot*," she shot with attitude, "is what pays my bills."

Slug dug his hand in his pocket and peeled off a grand. "Here. That should hold you down for the week. I don't want you back in there."

Ménage scanned the money with her eyes and started laughing hysterically. "Did you just say a week? Please, I make this in an hour," she quipped, still laughing.

Slug walked closer to her. "Ebony, I ain't playing with you. Don't let me catch your ass back in there."

Ménage turned her lips up all while measuring the seriousness in his eyes. "Whatever you say, Boss," she retorted sarcastically as she stuffed the money in her bra.

Slug shook his head.

"Now, pretty boy, if you don't mind. I have places to go and people to see."

"Still hard-headed-ass Ebony." Slug smirked. "I told you ain't shit changed."

Ménage followed him out the door and down the stairs. "Yeah, yeah, yeah!"

"I'm leaving in two days and I want you to come with me."

"Go with you where?"

"Home."

She stopped as they came to the end of the stairs. "You mean back to Detroit?"

Slug turned around to face her. "Yeah."

Ménage grew quiet as if she were giving it some thought.

"We can start over fresh. You don't have to worry about a thing. I got you!"

"Let me sleep on it, okay."

"All right. I'll call you tonight."

"I don't recall giving you my number."

"Ha, ha, ha. You didn't. I took it upon myself to call my cell from your phone."

She nodded her head slowly. "Okay, sneaky ass," she said, forcing a smile. She gave him one last kiss on the lips. "I love you."

"I love you too."

As he walked off, Ménage turned to hurry back up the stairs. Once back in the apartment, she called X-Rated to let one of the girls know that she would be out for the rest of the week. Family emergency, she had told her.

"Okay," the girl on the other end of the line said. "I'll pass it on to Marvin."

"Thanks, Bree." Ménage knew she would be getting a call from Marvin, the night manager, later. He hated when she called in as she was the main clocker in that place. After the call, Ménage dialed Tiffany.

"What's up, mamacita?"

"Girl, I need you. Bad!"

"Oooh diva, what's wrong?"

"I need you to come over here and help me pack."

"Pack? Bitch, you didn't tell me that you were moving this soon!"

"I'm not. I have to put my shit in storage *today*. Long story, but we'll talk when you get over here."

"All right. Me and Ms. Prada on our way."

Ménage hung up the phone and began pulling out the few empty boxes she did have. She would have to make a quick run to get more. She went into the closet and began pulling down her clothes until she heard Tiffany and Ms. Prada knocking at her door. When she went to open it, Ms. Prada, Tiffany's white Shitzu, greeted her as always.

"Diva, you sounded so stressed on the phone," Tiffany said the second she laid eyes on Ménage. "What's wrong?"

"I've had a crazy-ass night and an even crazier day."

Tiffany set Ms. Prada down and followed Ménage to the bedroom. "Do tell!" Tiffany said as she overlooked the room.

Ménage handed Tiffany a box. "Let's just say, my convict ex-boyfriend, has risen from the dead. And now he knows where I live."

Tiffany placed a hand over his chest. "Did you just say convict?" he shuddered. Ménage nodded her head. "Ewww-weee! That sounds like major trouble, boo."

"Believe me. It is!"

"So what are you going to do? I mean, you can't let that get in the way of your plans with Jeff. Nuh-uh, honey, you are on the stairway to riches and we can't allow such a setback." Tiffany upturned his lips.

"I don't plan to neither. Trust me. I have a plan. Ménage always has a plan," she stated confidently. "For now, I need us to pack as much as we can so that I can put all of it in storage tonight."

"All right, Ms. Thang. Hand me that box." Tiffany pointed. "I better be getting something out of this, why you got me over here working like a slave on my day off. I'm supposed to be resting up for my sugar daddy tonight."

Ménage only laughed.

"Hee-hee nothing. I want a purse, some shoes, and some MAC makeup out of this."

Ménage walked over to the radio system half-listening and half-ignoring Tiffany. She popped in a rap CD and turned the volume up a notch. She knew just the thing to eliminate Tiffany's ranting.

Bitches ain't shit and they ain't saying nothing...

Tiffany began waving his hand in the air and tooting his ass to the lyrics of his rap idol while Ménage took more clothes and placed them on the bed. It was going to be a long week, but now was just as good a time as any to position herself for the *real* move to Hollywood.

19

There was no place Naomi would have rather been right now. This was heaven on earth and she felt like Michelle Obama as she walked hand in hand with Greg throughout the two-story mansion. The house had everything she could have imagined. Even more. It was perfect and like a dream that had finally come true.

"The cleaners will be here first thing tomorrow," Dave said, leading the way. "But I'd say this place is in phenomenal shape as is."

"I agree," Greg said. "They did a wonderful job getting it ready for us."

Naomi was still in awe. She couldn't believe this was happening. It felt so surreal.

"Thanks for moving this along so quickly," Greg said. "I'm sure my fiancée here can't wait to get settled in so that she can start decorating the place," he said, lifting Naomi's left hand to kiss her ring finger where the engagement ring lay.

Naomi returned a soft smile.

With his hands stuffed in the pockets of his brown slacks, "Anything for you, sir," Dave said, a broad smile lifting his otherwise sagging cheeks. The balding white man appeared to be in his early to mid-fifties, and from the way the conversation was spinning, Naomi could tell that the two had known each other for quite some time. Much of the conversation on the drive over to do the walk-thru of the property, had been about tax hikes on the wealthy, solar energy investments, and then golf. She simply sat there in silence and let the men engage while she soaked up the beautiful California scenery all the way from the airport.

Greg turned to Naomi. "So what do you think?"

Naomi was breathless. Everything was happening so fast. First the proposal, the stock transfers, and now this. She surveyed the area of the house they were in and then turned to Greg. This man really did love her. And he was doing everything he could to prove it.

"I love it. It's… perfect." She hoped that the pain etched in her face went undetected. That the indecisiveness in her voice, overlooked. She didn't want to hurt the only man that she had ever loved and cared so much about. She told herself that if she put an end to this now, maybe, just maybe, she could save him from the pain that would ensue from this twisted premeditated plot Maribel had devised against him. If Greg could find it in his heart to forgive her for this deceptive guise she used to seduce him into loving her, there was still hope that they could salvage their relationship and follow through with marriage. If it all worked out that way, none of this would have to be in vain.

"That's music to my ears, baby," Greg said before turning back to Dave. "Did you bring the paperwork?"

Dave tapped his briefcase, smiling. "I never leave home without it. If you'll follow me to the kitchen, we can finish everything in there." They walked down the right side of the double stairwell that dropped them off back in front of the house. They walked through the foyer and down in the direction of the kitchen.

"If the two of you could please excuse me for a moment. I'm going to go to the ladies room," Naomi said.

Greg must have noticed the nauseous look on her face that she'd failed to hide. "You all right, honey?" he asked concerned.

Forcing a smile, Naomi nodded. She let her hand slip out of Greg's and walked quickly toward the left wing of the house where she'd recalled seeing one of the five bathrooms. When she finally found it, she shut the door, and began panicking.

"I can't do this...I can't do it..." she panted. She looked in the mirror and staring back at her was a woman she had only known for six months. A woman's whose life and identity she had stolen, for her own self gain.

She dug inside of her purse and pulled out her cell phone to call Maribel. She couldn't do this and she wouldn't do this. It just wasn't right. Her conscience wouldn't allow her to keep leading Greg on the way that she had. She had to make this right before it was too late.

"Where are you?" Maribel answered on the first ring. "I've been calling all morning."

"We're in Los Angeles?" Naomi answered, speaking as quietly as possible.

"Why are you in Los Angeles? What the hell is he up to now?"

"Maribel, I can't do this anymore. It's not right."

"Listen to me," Maribel said in a calming tone. "It's almost over."

"I can't do this anymore."

"You can and you will!" Maribel snapped. The evil tone in Maribel's voice caused Naomi to pause. Tears raced down her cheeks and she fell apart right before her very own eyes.

"He will pay for *everything* he's done to me, and you're going to help me see to it that he does!"

Naomi fell silent once again.

"What exactly did he do to you to deserve this?" Naomi asked for the first time ever. She had assumed the woman was an obsessive jealous ex-girlfriend out to get even, but the longer this went on, the more Naomi wanted to know if that were the case at all.

Who would go to the extreme that she'd gone through and spend the kind of money that she had spent, concocting this type of plan for revenge?

Maribel had told her all about Denise, his former lover. She'd even told her about his wife, Vivian. She had given Naomi much detail about the two women, claiming that Greg had used them both, and that she would make him pay for his philandering, even if it killed her. But she never, ever, told Naomi how she had been involved with him, and why watching him suffer, meant so much to her.

"The less you know, the better off you are," Maribel stated. "So just do the job that I hired you for."

Naomi took a deep long breath as a terrible pang stabbed her right in the center of her chest. "What if I don't want the money anymore?"

Maribel fell into laughter. "Sure you do. I'm all you have. Without me, you would be back on the streets or in that hell hole I rescued you from! I'm giving you a way out and you're not acting very grateful."

Naomi's throat was clogged with tears. She was swept with so much emotion that she couldn't think clearly.

"And one more thing, just in case you might have forgotten. He doesn't love you. He loves *her*. So when he looks at you and tells you you're the only woman in the world for him, it's Denise he's talking to. You're merely a clone, but you'll *never* be able to compete with a dead woman!" Maribel added with much disdain.

Naomi opened her tear-filled eyes completely.

"So now that we've settled our differences, I suggest you continue to play by my rules if you plan on getting compensated for your troubles, at all."

Naomi thought about her life before all of this. If she pulled out now, she would end up back with nothing. She would be back to square one. Maribel had been right about many things, but Naomi wondered if she was right about Greg not loving her. She might have looked like Denise Jackson on the outside, but underneath all that cosmetic surgery and the extra weight she had gained for this obscure role Maribel had her playing, was Naomi Brooks. Part of her wanted to believe that nothing would change between them if she came right out and told Greg the truth about her. About everything. But in the back of her mind, she knew that line of thinking was impractical.

"Are we on the same page?" Maribel asked.

She had to force herself to answer. "Yes," Naomi said. "But I have to go now. He's calling my name." She clicked the call off before Maribel could get another word in. She opened the door just as Greg appeared out of nowhere. She jumped when she saw him. "You scared me, baby." She chuckled.

"I thought you might have gotten lost."

Naomi cleared her throat. "No. I was freshening up a little." She rubbed the back of her neck and turned her head to the side, barely able to look him in the eye now.

"Well, Dave and I have some paperwork for you to sign."

Naomi's brows converged as her eyes shot back to him. "Papers for me to sign?" she repeated. It was obvious that she didn't have the slightest clue to what he was talking about.

"Yes. It's the sales agreement for the house."

"So why do *I* need to sign?" she asked, unclear as to what was going on.

"Honey, I'm putting our house in your name."

Naomi stood there stunned. "My name? But why?"

"It's the only way I can do this without my wife finding out. Trust me on this."

Naomi sighed, her stomach still in knots. "Okay." She followed Greg to the kitchen. Dave had the papers and ink pen aligned on the counter, awaiting her signature.

"All yours, Madam," he said, handing her the blue ink pen. The same wide cheesy grin was still planted on his face.

Naomi looked at Greg and then down at the agreement. Her full name had been listed in several places. Feeling as if she were preparing to sign her life away, she began signing each designated spot.

Dave looked all the paperwork over carefully. "Perfect! Here are your copies, sir," he said, giving Greg the second set.

Naomi's breathing was labored. Her head spinning.

"I need you to sign one last thing before we pop this cork to celebrate," Dave said. He pulled out three certified checks. Each of them was dated for today's date. The payee line read: *Naomi Cathryn Brooks.* The memo line—*GIFT.*

Naomi gasped when she read the dollar amounts. She looked back over at her future husband. His expression said it all.

"If you will," Dave said, flipping the checks over and indicating exactly where he needed her signature.

Naomi signed her name and Dave signed underneath her. He then reached back into his briefcase, pulled out an endorsement stamp, and stamped each check.

"I'll wash these through my Swiss accounts and then wire the money to the title company," Dave said confidently. "You don't have to worry about your wife trying to trace these babies."

Greg leaned in to kiss Naomi. "I did this for us. You know that, right?" Greg said.

Naomi nodded and laid her forehead against his. "Yes. I know," she said, believing every word of it.

"Here are the keys to your new house," Dave said in his happy-go-lucky voice as he handed each of them a set.

Naomi held the keys in her palm. She realized at that very moment that this was actually happening. It wasn't a dream. She owned this million-dollar mansion, free and clear.

"Now this calls for celebration!" Dave exclaimed. He walked over to the champagne that had been chilling on ice, apparently reserved for the new homeowners. He poured three glasses and passed one to Greg and then Naomi. Naomi refused hers politely.

"My 'fiancée'...," Greg smiled at Naomi, "doesn't drink." Greg took a healthy sip from his glass. He then walked behind her and put his arm around her waist, pulling her into his groin. "I love you," he whispered in her ear, planting a kiss on her jaw line.

Hearing that brought a reassured smile to her face. That's what she needed to hear, and that's what would give her the valor to do what she knew undoubtedly had to be done.

20

"Did you file a police report?" Jeff asked as he shuffled papers on his desk, searching for a file he had misplaced.

"Yes," Ménage said painfully.

Jeff could hear her sniffling through the phone and he could only imagine how upset she really was after coming home to find her door kicked in, her apartment ransacked, and the majority of her belongings stolen. She had been robbed in broad daylight and from his understanding, nobody saw a damn thing. Jeff expected that kind of thing in the hood, but not in the modest suburban community she lived in. The other thing that puzzled him was how they managed to clean her out all in one swoop, especially since she lived on the second floor.

"Well, what did the police have to say?" Jeff queried further, finally locating the missing folder. He removed his glasses, then rubbed his itchy eyes. Allergies were kicking his ass something serious today.

"They gave me a number to call, but you know they're not going to do shit! They don't care about nobody but their own," Ménage retorted. "They may never recover my things and I wouldn't be surprised if my shit was sitting up in the pawn shop by now."

"Well, try to calm down. I know you're mad, but everything's going to be okay. Besides, all that was materialistic shit. Thank God you weren't home when they broke in," Jeff said, hoping to make her feel a little better about the situation.

"But that was everything I had," Ménage said, crying once again. "I don't know what I'm going to do now," she murmured.

"Listen—"

"Ughm! I'm interested in buying a car," a voice called out to Jeff.

Jeff quickly turned around and his face lit up in utter disbelief, causing him to pause instantaneously. "Baby, I'm going to have to call you right back." He stood up from the chair. "But don't worry. I'll be there to pick you up. Go ahead and pack what you need for the next few days until we can figure something out."

"Okay, baby," Ménage said, sounding as if she were scared for her dear life. "I'll be at Tiffany's."

"All right. Talk to you soon." Jeff slipped his cell phone in his pocket and rushed over to the young man he hadn't seen in over a year. "Canvas Green. What's been up with you, man?" he said, embracing in a half-shoulder hug and slap of the hands.

"Nothing much. Out here grinding. Trying to get it, ya know."

Jeff shot him a disapproving look.

"Naw, not like that." Canvas chuckled loosely. "I'm a barber now. I cut hair in Oak Cliff at Precisionz Cuts."

Jeff drew his neck back and gave Canvas a onceover. That's when he noticed Canvas was no longer rocking the long braids. His hair was cut in a bald fade. "Precisionz Cuts, huh?"

"Yep. Matter fact, I got something for you." Canvas reached in his knapsack and handed Jeff a flyer and a CD. One side of the flyer promoted Canvas as a barber, but when Jeff flipped it over, it was a picture of Canvas with a mic in his hand. He was promoting his single, *Better Days.*

"Singer, barber…man, tell me something you don't do." Jeff chuckled.

"I do it all. Like I told you before, I'm a hustler and entrepreneur by blood. This shit is engrained in me." He laughed, poking his chest out. "Can't help that I was the chosen one," he said cockily.

Jeff laughed as well, all while thinking he hadn't changed a bit. Still the same cocky son-of-a-gun he'd hired a year ago. "Man, that's good. I'm really proud of you."

"Thanks," Canvas said.

He shifted his attention to the young lady standing beside Canvas. She looked no older than Deandra. He stuck his hand out to shake hers. "And what's your name?"

"Anaya," the little girl answered.

"Nice meeting you, Anaya."

"You too, sir." She smiled.

"This my little sister I always talked about."

Jeff nodded his head, feeling more prouder of Canvas. "You did good, man."

"Thank you." Canvas looked around the office. "I ain't gon' hold you up. I just wanted to stop by to check on you. And to thank you. For everything, bro."

"Don't even sweat it. We all slip off the right track sometimes. As long as we get back on it, is all that matters," Jeff told him. "But now I might have to come through some time to check out your skills."

"Do that, man. The first cut on me."

Jeff chuckled. "All right. Count on it then."

"Well, we're about to go out to dinner. Anaya made all A's on her report card."

"All A's?" Jeff smiled at Anaya who gave him a wide-toothed grin as she nodded vigorously. "That means you're super smart."

"And I made perfect attendance!" she added, lavishing in the attention.

Canvas chortled to himself. "Oh yeah, I forgot to mention that one."

"You're doing a fine job, man. Keep it up."

"Thanks, Mr. Jackson. I will." Canvas looked down at his sister. "All right, Anaya, let's let Mr. Jackson get back to work."

Jeff rounded his desk and grabbed his suit jacket. He spotted the green folder underneath a pile of paperwork and pulled it out. "Actually, I was getting ready to head out myself. I'll walk out with you." Before leaving, he popped his head into Christie's cubicle.

Christie lowered her eyes and a sinister grin played on her lips. "Back for seconds already?"

Jeff eyed her hungrily. He looked around him and then back at her. "Actually my head is still spinning from two hours ago, but I'd love to get a rain check."

"Your wish is my command. You know where I live and you know where I work."

Jeff's dick began to swell all on its own. He almost forgot the reason he'd stopped by. "Oh. If you don't mind, could you give this to Robby, please? He was looking for it earlier."

"No problem."

"Thanks." Jeff winked at her. He turned around and headed out. Canvas and Anaya were hanging by the door. "I'm heading north if you need me to drop you guys off anywhere," Jeff said as they walked out of the doors.

"Actually, we rolling now," Canvas beamed, pointing to the lemon candy-painted box Chevy Caprice.

"Nice ride you got there."

"And check out her twenty-inch silver stilettos," Canvas said, referring to his car as a woman.

"You showing out, ain't you?"

"Got the ladies breaking their necks, man!" Canvas laughed.

"Ha, ha, ha. I can believe it. Well, y'all be careful and I'll come through Saturday and let you tighten me up. Maybe we can hit the court and catch up some more afterwards."

"Bet that!"

They parted ways and Jeff got in his car and headed straight to Grace's house, Denise's mom, to pick up Deandra before going to pick up Ménage. Since Nadine had called him back to tell him that she had made it out of her appointment in time to pick up Canvas, that was one less thing he had to do. However, he couldn't believe that he was about to do something he'd told himself he'd never do—bring a woman into his house. But he couldn't leave her hanging, he thought to himself. She had no family here. No real friends, besides Tiffany, whom she had refused to ask. Jeff was all she had. He hoped and prayed Deandra would be okay with it. Besides, it was only temporary. A couple of weeks couldn't hurt.

21

The apartment really did look like she had been robbed. She had sold her white leather furniture and bedroom set to Tiffany for $800 on the spot cash money, and everything else was basically boxed up and taken to the storage.

Ménage had decided on purchasing the unit simply for this exact reason. She never knew when the point and time would come for her to have to bounce, but she was aware beyond a shadow of a doubt that it would come. And with Slug popping up in her life and trying to convert her back to his thugged-out lifestyle, the warning signs couldn't have been more heedful. This had to be a sign from God that it was time to set sail. She was going to leave everything behind so that she could pursue her dreams of becoming one of the best actresses alive. She'd had her fun, made her money, and left her mark. Now it was time to explore new things, new people, and new opportunities, in Hollywood.

She placed her suitcase and purse by the door. That was all she was taking with her tonight. She eagerly waited for Jeff's call so when her phone rang, she jumped to answer it, hoping it was him. When she saw the number she had programmed for Slug pop up, she shot the call straight to voicemail. A minute or two later, he called right back. Again, she forwarded the call. This time she received a message alert.

She played back the voicemail he had left.

"Sup, Ebony. You know who it is. Get back at me." She deleted it and went to the next one. "This me, Slug. Call a nigga back, girl. I'm trying to come scoop you tonight." Ménage froze and her fingers moved in a panic before she could even hit the delete option. She began calling Jeff to see where he was. The last thing she needed was for them to both show up at the same damn time.

"Hello," Jeff answered.

"Hey baby, where are you?" Ménage managed to disguise her hysteria.

"I'm actually pulling up now. Go ahead and come down."

"All right, baby."

Ménage grabbed the suitcase and her purse as she opened the door. When she saw Jeff's BMW pull up to the curb, she headed down. He got out of the car and rushed over to get the suitcase. He loaded it into the trunk and she started for the front seat. Her eyes bucked wide when she saw the little girl in her spot.

"I forgot to mention that I was bringing my daughter with me."

Ménage forced a smile as she climbed in the backseat. *You damn right you did.* "It's okay," she mustered once Jeff got in the car. "I love children."

"Deandra, this is Ms. Men—"

"Ebony," Ménage interjected. She reached her hand out to Deandra who smiled as they exchanged handshakes.

"You're really pretty," Deandra complimented.

Ménage batted her eyes. "Why thank you. You're very pretty too."

Jeff began driving off, occasionally looking back at Ménage in the mirror. She could tell he was pleased with how the two of them had warmed up to each other so quickly. This was going to be easy, she thought, as she smiled at Deandra. What the little girl failed to realize was that she wasn't going to steal her daddy from her, she was going to steal his money.

"I can't wait to play in your pretty long hair," Ménage said.

Deandra's face lit up in excitement. "I want long curls like you, Ms. Ebony. I'm tired of ponytails, but that's all my daddy knows how to do."

"Hey, I tried the curling thing and it didn't work out." Jeff chuckled.

Ménage laughed along.

"And I burned myself," Jeff continued. "Ten times."

"My…my…Daddy's afraid of a little *heat*," Ménage teased. Jeff caught on as he gave her a look that said everything his mouth couldn't. "Well, I will do your hair for school in the morning in some really pretty long curls."

Deandra's smile was broad. "I can't wait!"

Ménage kept her smile locked and her seductive gaze fixated on Jeff so that every time he looked in the mirror, he knew what she was thinking. She had given herself a period of three weeks to find what she needed. But from the way things were going, she doubted it would take that long.

Her phone started ringing and once again, it was Slug. She sent the call straight to voicemail. And like all the other times, he left a voice message. She pulled the phone closely to her ear to listen to it.

"Where are you? I've called you like a hundred times. You better not be at that damn strip club. You know what, I'm on my way."

That last voicemail had Ménage scared shitless. She didn't know exactly what Slug was capable of and she wasn't trying to find out. But she did know that his ass was crazy and that he couldn't take no for an answer. He was also very much still the jealous type. He couldn't stand for another guy to look at her. That was always the reason for unnecessary altercations. Dealing with him always came with chaos. She didn't miss any of that drama and she sure as hell wasn't going back to it. So she couldn't wait for him to go over to her place like she knew that he would. She had a surprise waiting for him—she wouldn't be there.

"Daddy, I'm hungry."

"What about you, Ménage? I'm sorry, Ebony," Jeff corrected.

"Starving," she said.

"All right. What are you ladies in the mood for?"

"Spaghetti," Deandra shot.

"I was thinking the same thing," Ménage said.

"Olive Garden it is then," Jeff said.

Deandra and Ménage slipped each other a victorious grin.

Ménage then leaned back in her seat to strategize her plot even more. She couldn't afford to mess this up. She looked back down at her phone, which she had placed on silent. There were seven more missed calls from Slug. Yep, she had to pull this off. Her money, her career, and her life were on the line.

Hours later they were pulling into a posh suburban neighborhood. Ménage looked around at all the nice houses on the street, wondering which house might be Jeff's. As they came to the last house, Jeff slowed down. Ménage expected nothing less as her eyes marveled over the big house. After all, his former wife had been an investment broker and with a salary as hers, they'd better be living nice.

"We're here," Jeff said, throwing the car in "park." He popped the trunk and got out to retrieve Ménage's suitcase as she and Deandra got it.

Jeff led the way up the well-lit sidewalk as she and Deandra followed. Once inside, Ménage began to scan the house as if she had come only to stake out the place.

"All right, young lady, it's time for you to take your shower and hit the sack. You have school in the morning."

"Aww, man, but Daddy, I'm not even sleepy."

Jeff gave Deandra a look that she must have been all too familiar with. She pulled in her pout, said goodnight to both of them, and headed straight to her room.

Ménage was going to finally be able to get in some alone time. "You have a beautiful home," she complimented.

"Thank you, but my wife gets all the credit for this. Interior decorating was like a secret hobby for her so she spent a lot of time and attention on this house."

"Wow! I can definitely tell."

"I'll show you around later. You've had a rough day and I'm sure after everything you've been through, the last thing you're in the mood for is a tour."

"Yeah. I'm pretty beat," she lied as she stifled a yawn. "Where should I put my things?"

"There's a guest bedroom down the hall. Or...you can sleep... in the den." He smiled. "I've camped out in there myself plenty of nights so the couch is already broken in."

Ménage lavished in his attention for a moment, then took a step closer to him. On one hand, she was willing to respect the boundaries that might have applied to the home front, but on second hand, she had to shower him with affection and tender loving care. That was her recipe in the beginning, and ain't shit changed, she thought. She leaned in for a generous hug. "I appreciate you letting me stay here." Artificial tears welled in her eyes, but Jeff wouldn't have known the difference if his life depended on it. "I feel safe here with you." She was laying it on extremely thick. She laid her head on his shoulder.

Jeff rubbed her back. "It's okay. I'm here. And you can stay as long as you need to." She hadn't expected him to say that.

Ménage raised her head and placed both her hands on either side of his face. "You are a perfect man. You know that."

He shook his head. "I'm far from perfect. I'm just doing what I can to help out a friend in need."

Friend, Ménage thought. They were more than friends and the sooner he accepted her as so, the sooner he would let his guard down. It was time he got over his dead ex-wife and his stuck-up baby mama anyhow, so in actuality, she was doing him a favor by coming there. And as long as she played her position safely, yet strategically, she would get the financial blessing she had come for.

"Well, will you be so kind to show this *friend* to her room?"

"Sure. Follow me."

She reluctantly followed him to the guest room. He showed her where things were and where he'd be if she needed anything. He closed the door and disappeared back down the hall. Ménage's mind raced 100 miles per hour. She wondered if this was the room his wife had slept in. If this was the bed. A perturbed feeling swept over her and suddenly she was creeped out. She turned on the television and lowered the volume.

She put her suitcase on the bed and began unpacking and hanging up her clothes.

After her shower, Ménage oiled herself all over and slipped on a raspberry-colored lace cami. She had every intention of going straight to bed, but she began to miss Jeff's warm, hard body. It had been five days since she'd had him inside of her, and she doubted if she could go another night without it.

She turned off all the lights, then quietly opened her door. She passed by Deandra's room to find the little girl knocked out. Ménage's bare feet padded across the polished hardwood floors as she followed the musky trail of Jeff's cologne.

The rest of the house was pitch-black, but Ménage managed to find her way through just fine. She was on a dick mission and she could snort out dick like a crackhead could crack.

The door to his room was open just enough for her to slip through without making a peep. She closed it as quietly as she could behind her, then locked it. Her eyes roamed the room before focusing on Jeff. She moved toward the bed, excitement rising all the way from her hips to her lips. She pulled the clip out of her hair and her long black curls fell over her shoulders. Jeff lay there on his back, asleep. His fine dark skin looked like Godiva chocolate up against the white linens and she definitely had a sweet tooth tonight.

She slipped off her thongs and cami, climbed on the bed, and crawled over to him. As she began to straddle him, he woke up.

"Ménage. What are you doing?"

"I came to take care of you, like you've taken care of me." She lowered her pussy to the curve of his mouth. He knew the routine so there was no need for her to walk him through what was about to go down. She opened up her feverish pussy and practically fed it to him.

"Ummm," Jeff moaned, surrendering without a fight.

"I've missed you, daddy," Ménage whispered, loving the way his tongue stretched the folds of her yoni. In between licks, Jeff told her he missed her too. She reached behind and stroked his dick as he ate her out. He had definitely missed her.

Jeff feasted on her pussy a while longer before she decided that she wanted to return the favor. She turned around and their bodies molded into the sixty-nine position. She delivered just what the doctor ordered, and when she could taste and feel his sweet banana pudding filling the back of her throat, she opened her gates of ecstasy, and climaxed.

22

She couldn't believe she had come here tonight. More so because she knew in her heart that she wasn't completely over Jeff. They hadn't even officially broken up either. Nadine really didn't know where their relationship stood. He wasn't even man enough to tell her that he was interested in seeing other women. She had to hear it from his woman herself. The woman he was engaged to marry. Now *that* is what upset her the most.

The least Jeff could have done was talked to her. Maybe she wouldn't have understood why he'd chosen the other woman over her, but maybe she would have. He would have never known how she would have reacted to the news because he couldn't be a man and face her with the truth. Instead, he had some other woman that she knew nothing about, doing his dirty work. Nadine had given him way too much credit. She thought they were better than that. Boy, was she wrong.

"Right this way, Madam," the host said to Nadine as he led the way toward the back of the upscale restaurant. She was dressed to impress in a black vintage, elegant flowing gown that revealed her new workout body. The dress highlighted her curves in a tasteful fashion, yet it still left room for the imagination to wander. The twelve-pound shed was a result of the switch in birth control pills and the extensive workout regimen with Jay. While she still had another goal to reach, she looked and felt amazing.

As they came to the VIP section of the restaurant, the host pulled out her chair and motioned with his hand for her to take a seat.

"Mr. Dupree will join you shortly."

"Thank you." Nadine graciously smiled.

She took a look around and smiled at the trouble this Mr. Dupree must have gone through to reserve this space. Nonetheless, it definitely made quite an impression. The entire room was romantically lit by low hanging chandeliers. The décor—hues of brown, peach, and gold. But what delighted her the most was the beautifully dressed Asian woman in front of the room, playing a harp.

Her thoughts one-tracked to this mystery man who had sent her a bottle of wine and roses as an invitation to dinner. She couldn't help but wonder what he looked like and the waiting was killing her. The second she took her eyes off the harpist and turned slightly to the left, a tall, bald, debonair man dressed in the finest of linen approached her.

"Nadine." He gently kissed the top of her left hand before taking a seat across from her. "I prayed to God that you would show up tonight."

"Well, good thing he was listening." Nadine smiled, somewhat baffled because she couldn't place his face. And that face was one she could never forget. He had skin the color of maple, brown almond-shaped eyes, and perfect teeth. She always took notice of a man's teeth. If he took care of his teeth, he took care of every other part of his body, she'd grown to believe. His voice was deep and harmonic. As rich as that kiss that sent a surge of tingles down her spine.

"I bet you probably thought you had a stalker on your hands." He laughed, eliminating any awkwardness.

Nadine let out a loose chuckle as she nodded her head in agreement. "Your guess would be correct."

"I knew it. Ha, ha, ha. Well, let me assure you that I'm not a stalker. But…"

Nadine paused and held her breath, hoping he wasn't about to confess anything crazy. He started out as a ten and she needed him to stay there.

"When I see something that I want…I don't stop until I get it." His eyes never wavered.

Nadine cleared her throat. Suddenly, it had gotten very hot in there. It was evident that he had caught her completely off-guard with that last comment. She casually reached for the glass of water in front of her and took a sip, feigning shyness. Although she couldn't help but whip out her mental travel guide and see what the trip would be like on that thing. He had big feet, large hands, long fingers, and a huge Adam's apple and according to one of her sorors, that equated to a really nice and long yacht. Nadine felt a twinge in her pussy and she had to remind herself of the vow.

"I admire your persistence," she said. She placed her glass back on the table. "Forgive me in advance, but I really don't remember you. I'll admit that I'm terrible with names, but I never forget a face. And for some odd reason, I can't recall ever meeting you."

"Parking lot."

Nadine's brows furrowed. "Parking lot?" She shook her head.

He nodded. "I was on my way to meet with a client that day, but when I came out to get in my car, I was blocked in by an Audi."

"Oh my God." Nadine's eyes lit up the room. "It's you." She was embarrassed to say the least. She recalled that day very well. She had gone to pick up her clothes from the cleaners and remembered parking illegally in the fire lane.

"Needless to say I was late for that appointment and…let's just say I lost a client."

Nadine's eyes widened. "I am so sorry."

He smiled as he buried his eyes within hers. "Please don't apologize. I'm a firm believer that everything happens for a reason."

Nadine was falling under his spell and she knew it was obvious. "Hmmm. I wonder what that reason could be."

"In time we will both know. But for now, I say let's eat."

When Nadine looked up, the waiter was rolling their food over.

"I didn't know exactly what you might have wanted. So I had my chef make one of everything."

Nadine smiled as her eyes savored all the food being placed on their table.

"Oh, wow." She gasped. She picked up one of the napkins and placed it across her lap. "You're awfully thoughtful."

"I try to be."

Nadine lowered her head to pray.

He reached for both her hands. "Allow me." He bowed his head and she followed his lead as he commenced to saying grace.

Was this really happening? Was she really on a date? She then thought about what the psychic had told her. She said she would find love and happiness. Said if she opened her heart and be willing to overlook flaws, that her husband would find her. But she also told her something that Nadine had found quite disturbing. She told her she would marry twice. That was something Nadine didn't want to hear and she refused to believe it. Besides, psychics didn't know the future. Only God knew that. She had decided to push everything that woman had said out of her mind.

"Amen," she said, raising her head.

"Dig in and don't be bashful now. I know how sisters like to throw down."

"Ha, ha, ha." Nadine picked up her fork and knife to sample the steak first. "May I ask you a question?"

"Anything you'd like."

"How did you know where I work?"

"Tsk. Lucy. The young girl that works in the cleaners."

Figures, Nadine thought.

"She charged me one hundred dollars for your name, and another hundred for your phone number."

Nadine's daintiness didn't go unseen as she swapped plates to taste the Mahi-mahi. "Are you serious?"

He nodded. "You had your office number on file so when I found out where you worked, I realized that this really was meant to be."

Nadine scrunched her face. He didn't waste any time predicting their future together. "How so?" she wondered.

"Well. You're going to laugh at this one, but that building you work in, I used to work in as well three years ago." He reached over to dab the left corner of Nadine's mouth. "You had a little honey sauce right there."

His touch was so sensual and romantic that it ignited a fire all through her body. She licked her lips. "Thank you." She stopped to tame her naughty thoughts. Damn, it sure was hard being a virgin all over again. "I'm surprised we've never met before now. So what floor did you work on?"

"I actually worked on the seventeenth floor for the Richards and Crads Agency."

"Oh, okay. So you're a lawyer."

He nodded. "Lawyer and restaurateur."

"You practice criminal law?"

"Why all the brothers gotta be associated with criminal law?" He laughed.

"I'm sorry. I really didn't mean anything by it."

He erupted in laughter. "Ha, ha, ha. No, I'm only kidding. Giving you a hard time, that's all. I get it all the time. I actually practice family law."

Nadine was doubly impressed. "Soooo let me guess. This is your spot."

"Bingo." He smiled. "This is home away from home when I'm not in the courtroom. A buddy of mine helped me get started and the rest is history in the making."

"It's exquisite and the food is delicious."

"Thank you."

"Now may I ask you a question?"

Nadine smiled. "Yes, you may."

"I don't see a ring on *that* finger." He placed his manicured pointer on her ring finger. "So I'm going to presume you're single."

Nadine sighed. "Unfortunately, yes."

"And you have a son. A small son."

Nadine's brows raised a notch and she pursed her lips. "Are you sure you haven't been stalking me?"

"I noticed a blue car seat in the back of your car that day."

"You're very observant. And detailed."

"I'm a lawyer. We pay attention to all the details." He grinned.

Another smile washed over her face. "I do have a son. He's eleven months." This time he paused and Nadine took notice. "His father and I are no longer together. We…couldn't seem to make it work." She shrugged. "So yes, I'm in the single department…and I have a small baby." Her face relaxed a little, but she couldn't help but wonder if her honesty would qualify her any more or less. She wondered what he was thinking of her now.

As if reading her mind, he said, "Well, that's a bonus for me. Because if you give me a chance to prove that I'm not like him," he looked deeply within her eyes and spoke directly to that pain and hurt she still bottled inside, "I'll make up for *everything* that he failed to do right."

Damn! Nadine thought. She allowed his words to soak in.

She couldn't help but wonder if she had been wearing her emotions on her sleeve as she thought she'd covered up those love scars. Apparently, she hadn't done a good enough job.

"Everything?" she asked with reservation.

Leonard nodded confidently.

"How do you know I'll even call you after this date? I mean…I don't even know your name."

"Leonard. Last name Dupree." He whipped out one of his business cards. "And you're right. I don't know if you'll call me. But you being here tonight tells me I have a chance. And I'm a patient man, Nadine. So I don't mind waiting."

She didn't know Leonard from a can of paint, but she could feel that everything he was saying tonight was real. But she still had to pinch herself to make sure that this fine, suave, charming gentleman in front of her was the real deal, and not simply making a cameo appearance in another one of her dreams.

She exhaled sharply. Lord knows, she wasn't ready to dive back into a relationship so quickly. But they were only conversing, she reminded herself. She was still recovering from an unofficial breakup with Jeff. And on top of being emotionally disconnected, she doubted she could ever fully trust a man with her feelings again. Jeff had left her wounded and discouraged, not to mention swarming in self-doubt. If she weren't good enough for him, who would she be good for? But Leonard's words were like Hershey's Kisses for her soul. They were comforting in her time of need. Her time of mourning. And the more he kissed her deepest wound of all, the more she wanted to kiss back.

23

It had been a little over two weeks since her date with Leonard and they had practically spoken on the phone or chatted on Skype every day since then. She tried her best to avoid Facebook at all cost. Janeesha's lunatic ass was as nosey and crazy as they came, and Nadine didn't need her all in her business. The woman was trying to ruin Nadine's reputation. It had gotten back to her days after Kelli's party that Janeesha had spread all types of nasty rumors about Nadine having a thing for married men. She had been apparently warning women to keep their man away from her. She had posted that memo on several of their mutual friends' Facebook walls, which happened to be considerably more than half of their graduating class from Prairie View University. Even with Nadine unfriending her, Janeesha still managed to harass her by direct messaging her Bible scriptures. It had gotten to the point where Nadine didn't even care to log in anymore. She refused to put up with that childish nonsense, and reporting it would only add fire to the entire ordeal.

That was why Nadine found a much-needed peace with Leonard. He was her serenity when things were chaotic and he always had the right words. He was also the perfect distraction, seeing how she really didn't think about Jeff at all. She no longer cared about him breaking her heart, being engaged, and moving on to someone new. Not that she forgave him for it, but at this particular point, she only cared about *her* moving on and finding the true love and happiness that she deserved. While it was still way too early to tell how things would pan out with Leonard, she believed a future with him was looking brighter by the day.

As she finished getting dressed, she double-checked herself in the mirror, loving the way those jeans hugged her body. She put on her shoes and threw on her chunky gold accessories. Lastly, she applied her makeup.

"How does Mommy look?" she asked her son who was too busy rolling off all the toilet tissue. "No, no, no." Nadine hurried over to Canvas and started to pick up the mess until her doorbell rang. She picked him up in her arms and kissed his chubby cheeks. "I know who that is," she said, tickling her son as he hung off her hip. "Coming," she called out, tickling Canvas all the way to the door.

She looked out the peephole and surprisingly so, he was right on time. She opened the door and Jeff and Deandra walked inside.

"Hey, how you doing?" Jeff spoke as he walked in.

"I'm good. You?" Nadine replied casually.

"I'm here to see another day so that's good enough for me," he retorted. "Hey, son!" Canvas instantly reached for his father and Jeff tossed the boy in the air. "What my lil man been up to? Give Daddy some love." He kissed Canvas on his cheeks, then playfully hung him in the air.

"Your hair is really pretty," Nadine said to Deandra. "I see your father finally got the hang of the curling iron."

Jeff casually walked off and farther into the living room, playing with Canvas.

"Daddy didn't do my hair," Deandra said. "My new Mommy did it."

Nadine nearly doubled over.

"We're not going to stay too long," Jeff said, grabbing Canvas's bags off the dinner table.

Nadine pretended not to hear him. "Well, that's nice to hear," she told Deandra, disguising her true feelings so well.

Deandra had a wide smile spread across her face. "Yeah, she does my hair every morning for school."

Nadine then looked up at Jeff as Deandra continued on her own. "Humph. Every morning, huh?"

"Yep. She lives with us," Deandra added in a mighty chipper voice. "And they're getting married real soon. I'm going to be the flower girl."

"Wow." Deandra was unloading so much on her so quickly, Nadine couldn't recover as fast from the news.

"Deandra!" Jeff shot her a look and the girl's face nearly melted. "I'm sorry, Daddy."

Nadine took a much needed deep breath and tried to stomach all of it. Her head felt tight and the room seemed as if it were spinning. She could hardly think straight now. She tapped her forehead until her thoughts came back to her. "Ummm...you have all his things there..." She paused. "There's Motrin in there too... just in case...the fever comes back." She shook her head as all her thoughts seemed to derail, making her tense. "I'm going to step out for a while, but I'll have my cell on me if you need me for anything."

"We'll be fine," Jeff assured her.

Finally, she looked at him as if trying to figure out the toughest Sudoku puzzle. There were no words left to say.

"May I use your bathroom for a minute?" Jeff asked.

She rolled her eyes. "You know where it is."

Jeff handed Canvas to her and she took a seat as he walked off.

Deandra was quiet, but Nadine could sense that her goddaughter wanted to tell her so much more. What she didn't understand was if Deandra was volunteering all her father's business out of spite. It was obvious their relationship hadn't been the same since her mother had died. And she knew Deandra had even blamed her for her parents' divorce. But she never wanted their relationship to come to this.

"Look like you running a florist shop up in here," Jeff said when he returned. "You got purple roses all up in here, in your room, and in the bathroom." He laughed, looked at her and licked his lips. "Tell the brotha I said he doing way too much." He laughed again.

"They're not purple," Nadine shot with attitude. Nadine got up and handed Canvas back to Jeff.

"They sure look purple to me."

Nadine could tell he was trying to switch the subject from what Deandra had brought up earlier. And that was perfectly fine. She didn't want to hear about him and his newfound love any more than he probably wanted to hear about the actual symbolism behind the color of the roses that Leonard had sent to her every day following their first date.

"They're lavender," she enlightened him.

Jeff stood, looking as clueless as all get out.

"Again, call me if you need me. I have to finish getting ready." She felt Jeff's eyes roam her new body and that was the cue to get him the hell up out of there. She picked up the bags and handed them to him. Catching the hint, he turned to walk toward the door.

"One more thing," she said before Jeff was completely out of her sight. "I don't know this woman you're taking my son around..." Jeff tried to interrupt, but she held up her hand and continued with what she had to say. "So please. Please don't make me regret this."

Jeff's face scrunched all on its own. "Don't ever think that I would put my son in harm's way. He'll be fine. He'll be with his father."

Nadine tried her best to not show her ugly side. If Deandra had not said anything, she wouldn't have known Jeff was even taking their son around another woman. She almost regretted letting him leave, but she tried to ease her worry in knowing that Jeff wouldn't dare let anything happen to Canvas.

"Okay," she said, leaning in to kiss her son. She looked over at Deandra who seemed to be impatiently waiting. "See you later, Deandra."

Deandra didn't wave back, only snarled. But of course, Nadine couldn't make out what she had said and Jeff had been too busy catching the call on his cell. She slowly closed the door, then treaded over to the dining room table where one of the many flower arrangements in her home served as a centerpiece. She took one of the roses out and as soon as she sniffed it, Leonard's sweet words came rushing back to her. *"I'll make up for everything that he failed to do right."* That alone gave her the reassurance she would need to make her date with Leonard worthwhile and truly unforgettable.

24

After hours of rummaging through Jeff's office, his bedroom, closets, and even the kitchen drawers, Ménage found what she had been looking for. Not only did she find recent bank statements for his trust accounts, CD's, and IRA's, she found the letter from the insurance company with the exact dollar amount of Denise's life insurance policy. Jeff had not only collected over $1 million on his wife's policy, but he had received an extra $500,000 because her death had been accidental.

Ménage's eyes bucked at the paperwork that she held in her shaky hands.

"Girl, I am not lying. I'm looking at it right now. This nigga is loaded," Ménage rattled off.

"But didn't you say he was a car salesman," Tiffany interjected, sounding as if that was the worst type of job anybody could have.

"Yes!" They both started laughing. "I don't know why in the hell he still working." She allowed her words to linger in the air. "On second thought, he gon' need his day job after I hit his ass up."

"Bitch, did you find the checkbook, is all I'm waiting for?"

"Do you think I would be calling you if I didn't? Hell yes, I got it!" She ran her fingers over the sleek black leather. "Me and this little black book have become bosom buddies."

"So when you want to do this?"

Ménage started thinking. "Monday! Yeah, let's do it Monday," she reconfirmed.

"All right. I'll be ready."

"Oh shit, Tiffany, I hear them coming up. I'll call you first thing Monday morning to come get me."

"Okay. See you Monday, chile."

Ménage hung up the phone and stuck the folder with all the paperwork in it into her suitcase. She checked herself in the mirror and walked out of the room.

"We're here!" Jeff called out.

"Ooohh, something smells good, Daddy," Deandra said.

Ménage appeared from around the corner with a smile on her perfectly made-up face. She had on Denise's apron that said *MOMMY CAN THROW DOWN* in big and bold orange letters. "I made you and your dad's favorite." Ménage smiled.

"My favorite?" Jeff questioned, as he put Canvas down. "I didn't know I had a favorite."

"Don't be silly, baby. You have a favorite."

"I know what it is, Daddy!" Deandra said, turning to her father.

"You do?"

Deandra nodded. "Pizza!"

"Oooo yeah! That is my favorite," Jeff said, giving Ménage the eye that told her he was going along with Deandra on this one. Ménage knew that Deandra loved cheese pizza so that's what she'd made for dinner. And she had done it all by scratch.

Ménage walked over to Jeff, kissed him on the cheek, then took the bags out of his hands. "You had a long day at work, honey. Time to relax." She looked down at Jeff junior and saw how much the boy resembled his father. "He looks just like you," she said, watching Canvas walk around.

Jeff nodded. "Thanks." He looked around the house and saw how much she had cleaned since he'd been gone all day. She hoped she hadn't left anything out of place. "The house looks great!"

Ménage laughed. "Thank you, but when is the last time you vacuumed those rugs?"

Jeff closed his eyes as if trying to remember.

"Never mind." She laughed. "That look just gave you away," she said accusingly. "I also cleaned your room and reorganized your office. I hope you don't mind."

"You didn't have to go through all that trouble."

"It wasn't any trouble at all. I actually enjoyed it."

Jeff gave her a peculiar smirk. "Sure you did." He walked farther through the house. "Well, I'm going to go shower and change into something more comfortable. Do you mind looking after Canvas for me?"

"Sure," Ménage said. "I'll have your plate ready when you get out." She walked over to Canvas and picked him up. "Hey, handsome boy you," she sang.

Jeff watched her a short while longer before leaving her alone. She looked at Canvas again and turned her nose up. Babysitting was the last damn thing she wanted to be doing this weekend. "Fuck," she hissed. And was his nose running? *Yuck*, she thought, searching through his bag for a wipe. "You stink," she said, frowning. She pulled out the wipes, powder, and a diaper. Her lips upturned and she tried to hold her breath.

Deandra walked back into the room and over to Ménage.

"Hey, pretty girl," Ménage said.

Deandra smiled. "I did what you told me to do."

Ménage looked around to make sure Jeff wasn't around. "You did?" she asked excitedly.

Deandra nodded profusely, pleasure in her eyes.

"What did she say when you told her?"

"She didn't say anything. But she looked sad," Deandra reported.

Ménage smiled. It was low of her to play the little girl for information like she had, but it was the only way she saw fit. "Well, I didn't want her to be sad," Ménage lied, further manipulating her.

Deandra looked confused. "You didn't?"

"Of course not," Ménage said. "I only wanted you to tell her so that I could make her an invitation to the wedding."

Deandra looked as if she didn't understand. "Oh," she said. The thrill she had in her voice earlier was completely gone.

"Don't worry. You couldn't have known, because I forgot to tell you that part." Ménage put Canvas back on the floor and he ran around the living room. "You want to help me make the salad?"

"Yes." Deandra smiled.

"Okay, grab your brother and follow me." She turned back around to face Deandra. "I can't wait to be your new mommy." She reached down to hug Deandra and just then Canvas started screaming. She realized at that moment that she never wanted kids.

25

As they walked hand in hand to her car, Nadine almost didn't want to leave. She'd had so much fun with Leonard tonight and out of all the places she could have imagined their second date being, she never expected it to be on the rooftop of one of the most beautiful hotels in downtown Dallas. She couldn't help but wonder how much trouble he might have gone through to make this night extra special. Nonetheless, the view was spectacular. His thoughtfulness amazed her because he would go over and beyond to bring a smile to her face. This is what made him different and worth getting to know even better.

Leonard had wined and dined her all night under the stars with a romantic dinner, rooftop salsa dancing, and his charming personality that she couldn't seem to get enough of. She hated their night had to end, but it was now a little past eleven and she had to get home.

"I had a wonderful time tonight," Nadine said once they reached her car.

Leonard kissed the top of her hand. "I'm glad to hear that. I did as well."

She looked around her. They were on the seventh level in the hotel's parking garage and there was nothing but space and opportunity between them. Oh how she would have loved to get to know him on an intimate level. Her mind needed the relief and her body needed the release. As if cosigning her latest thoughts, her pussy began to speak in such a language that only she could interpret.

Leonard slipped his arm around her to open her door and the brush of his body up against hers started her fire engine to roaring. She hadn't been this close to a man other than Jeff, in years. But the signals her body was giving off suggested to her that it didn't know the difference.

"I'll call you." She smiled, leaning in to kiss him.

His lips felt smoother than oil and softer than cotton. Nadine reopened her eyes. The way he looked at her made her feel like the most beautiful woman in the world. He cupped her face. Apparently, one kiss hadn't been enough. He leaned in to her and passionately kissed along her neck. Before she knew it, their lips were having intercourse.

It felt so good and it felt more than right. *That* Nadine couldn't deny. And the smallest of climax building inside of her was so forceful it could have shut down every last one of her vital organs. She needed to be held, needed to be loved, and needed to be taken care of more than anything in this world. But she couldn't allow this man to blindside her by sweeping her off her feet in the first couple of dates. It was going to take a hell of a lot more in order for that to happen. She slowly pulled back.

"I..."

Leonard placed his finger against her lips as if knowing what she was going to say. "I'll wait for as long as you need me to."

An easy fulfilling smile crossed her lips. "Thank you." She got into her car, placed the key in the ignition, and drove off. Her pussy was terribly disappointed, but Nadine felt so good that she'd respected and honored the commitment she had made to herself by keeping sex out of the equation. If it really was meant to be like he had proclaimed so many times before, when that time did finally come, it was going to be magical.

26

He should have known in advance that he'd fucked up big time when he'd decided to stay the entire weekend with Naomi. Something he had never done before. They had flown back to L.A. to get more acquainted with the new house. They'd even started decorating and family planning. Everything was going perfect and he couldn't be happier with his decision to move out of state. But with every day that went by, the messier he was becoming. He'd stopped wearing his wedding ring weeks ago, stopped checking in long before that, but now… he wasn't even taking his ass home anymore. Part of him worried that his wife would discover he was having another affair, and the other part of him would be relieved. Then he wouldn't have to hide and pretend all the damn time. It was wearing him out. Giving him more grays than what he already had.

Since Greg hadn't called to tell his wife where he'd been, he figured she'd called everyone they knew, including his best friend, worried sick. So now as he rushed to his best friend's house, Greg hoped like hell he hadn't screwed up too badly.

He pulled into Leonard's driveway. When he didn't see his car right away, he pulled out his phone to call him.

"Hello?"

"Hey, man. You home?"

"Yeah, I'm here."

"Well, your car's not."

"Oh yeah, I parked out back last night. Come on up, I'll buzz you in."

"All right, I'm heading up now."

Greg parked on the side of the building and walked toward the gate. He pressed Leonard's loft number and seconds later, the gate unlocked.

"Damn, you look like shit. What the hell happened to you?" Leonard said when Greg walked in.

Greg almost didn't want to answer that. He looked like shit because he hadn't slept much lately and preparing to file this divorce had put a lot on his mind. Especially with the financial setback he might take. But at least he prepared himself for the worst.

Leonard scratched his head, clearly bewildered by the fact that Greg had shown up so early on a Sunday morning. "What'd you do man?" he asked finally.

Greg looked at him without any remorse in his eyes. "I didn't go home."

Leonard sighed heavily. "Damn, man."

Greg seemingly stared into thin air.

"I thought you were going to give yourself some more time to figure out if this is really what you wanted to do." Leonard walked into the kitchen and pulled down a bowl from the cabinet. He made himself some Honey Nut Cheerios as they talked.

"That's what *you* wanted me to do. I made up my mind a long damn time ago. I want out! I'm not happy."

Leonard looked at him oddly and Greg didn't appreciate that look. He knew what he must have been thinking. "Don't judge me, man."

Leonard shook his head. "I'm trying hard not to judge you. But I can't help but be worried because you haven't even known this woman that long! I mean, what, six…seven…eight months or something like that?"

"I've known her long enough to know that she's more of the woman for me than my wife has ever been."

Leonard shook his head. "It's all in your head, man." Leonard walked over to the sofa. He turned on the television and sat on the couch eating his cereal.

"Damn, I came over here to clear my head. Not be lectured. If I wanted that, I could have kept heading east," Greg said. He grabbed a Coke from the fridge. "Hell, man. We've known each other since elementary, but I think I've been in the game long enough to know what I'm doing."

Leonard turned back around. "I never said you didn't. I'm just trying to keep you from making a huge mistake that you'll regret later."

Greg walked over to the other couch. "Listen. I love her."

Leonard finished off his cereal and placed his bowl on the table. "Love." He chuckled. "That's a strong and scary word." He sat there nearly in a daze.

"Hey, man. If it doesn't work out between Naomi and me, you have my permission to rub it in my face for the rest of my life."

"That'll be the day I live for. Ha, ha, ha!"

They both laughed.

"By the way, how'd the date go with your new lady friend?"

Leonard turned to him and a wide smile spread over his face. "Romantic," Leonard summed up in one word.

Greg took a sip of his drink. "Ha, ha, ha. I knew you were holding out." He shook his finger at Leonard. "Hell, I think I'm worried about *you*. What's it been?"

"Just a few weeks. Nothing too serious."

"Yet." Greg laughed.

Leonard laughed along with him.

"But how in the hell do you do it?"

"Do what?" Leonard asked.

"You know." Greg didn't want to come out and say it because it always made him uncomfortable. But this was his best friend. "Do you tell them about your…situation….when you first meet them?"

Leonard sucked his teeth, his expression changing a little. "Naw, man."

Greg gave him an unsure look.

"Because every woman that I ever told right in the beginning… left me. And it's not fair, man. I didn't ask for this shit. You know what I'm saying?"

Greg nodded.

Leonard's voice fell to a whisper. "I didn't ask for it."

"So you think not telling this woman is a good idea?"

"I'm going to tell her when the time is right. But first I have to make sure it's real."

Greg stared at him.

"Now I know damn well you're not sitting over there judging *me?*" Leonard asked.

Greg shook his head and sighed. "You're a good dude. I just wish that shit never happened to you."

"It's life, bro. It happens to the best of us," Leonard said, a pained look in his eyes. He cleared his throat. "Besides, I take a cocktail for this shit." He stood up. "Do I look like I'm HIV positive?"

Greg shook his head. "You would have fooled me."

"Exactly!" He walked around to his library shelf and pulled down a thick folder. "As long as I take care of myself, doctors say I will live just as long as someone without it." Leonard handed the folder to Greg.

"What's this?"

"Copies of all of your and Vivian's assets. I need you to look everything through carefully to ensure I've included everything."

"What's the next step?"

"We file a petition with the court stating the grounds for divorce. Separation and abandonment," Leonard said. "We'll make that stick with how she left you for three years to move to Connecticut. Her failure to complete the rehab program should work in our favor as well."

There was stony silence. Greg shifted in his seat and took a deep breath. He flipped through the folder. Leonard had included everything, right down to the money Vivian had stashed in her bra sock. It was definitely going to get ugly.

"Care if I hang out and look through it here?"

"Not at all, man. You'll have the place to yourself because I'm taking my lady to church with me this morning. So I'm going to go get ready."

"Go do your thing," Greg said. He made himself comfortable while Leonard headed upstairs.

"Oh yeah," Leonard hollered from the stairwell. "Call your wife, man! She called me looking for you."

Greg gave it some thought. In fact he gave it a lot of thought. When he finally made up his mind to call her, she didn't answer. He looked at the clock. By now she was in the mirror patting foundation on her face as she got ready for church.

"Leonard, I'ma go ahead and go home, man."

Leonard peered from the stairwell. He was looping his tie.

"Everything in this folder looks sufficient. I'm ready to get this over with."

"No problem. I'll file it first thing tomorrow morning."

Greg walked to the door and let himself out. He made it home in thirty minutes flat, without speeding. He unlocked the door and walked inside what now seemed more like a tourist spot. It didn't feel much like home anymore. His home was now in Los Angeles. As he walked through the great room, he hadn't noticed the new draperies until now as the sunlight lit up the usually dark house. The smell of roasted coffee beans gave her away. She was still home. Damn, he thought she'd be at church by now. She came out of the kitchen, a fresh cup of coffee in her right hand and no clear evidence that she was going anywhere.

"My, my, my. Look at who decided to come home," Vivian said sarcastically.

Greg cleared his throat, obviously surprised to see her. "I just left Leonard's place. Stayed out pretty late last night," he said shortly as he headed toward the bedroom, hoping to avoid the interrogation. He didn't mean for Leonard to be his alibi; it just sort of came out that way.

"And the night before. Where were you?"

"Look, I really don't feel like having this discussion. Can it at least wait?"

"I called you at least a hundred times, Greg! I was worried sick about you and you couldn't at least call once? That's so fucking inconsiderate of you!"

"I'm sorry," was all Greg could say as he undressed, headed for the shower, his wife right on his tail.

"You're sorry every time you can't think of a good enough lie to shut me up," she clamored.

Greg cut through every corner of the house to try to escape her madness but couldn't.

"Are you involved with someone else?" she asked finally.

Greg stopped in his tracks. He turned to her and the air in the room seemed to dissipate.

She sniffed. "Just be honest with me for a fucking chance," she said, with pleading eyes. "That's all I ask."

This was the moment he knew would soon come. He was forced to face her with the truth. She looked down at his left hand. His wedding ring was missing. She tucked in her lips and tears began to fall from her bright blue eyes. "You haven't worn your ring in nearly eight months," she said, acknowledging how long she'd known about his latest affair.

"I never meant to hurt you, Vivian," he said.

She splashed the hot coffee in his face. "Bullshit!"

"Aghhh! What the hell is wrong with you!" he screamed.

"You will pay for this," she said. "Mark...my...word."

27

She lay there in bed, missing everything there was to miss about him. She missed his conversation, his friendship, and his warm hard body in her bed. Naomi wanted that feeling she had when she was with Greg to last for a lifetime, but she knew that it wouldn't. She had kept so much from him and had deceived him in a way that she couldn't bear to bring herself to tell him the truth now. It would be too difficult to do. So all she could do now was accept things as they were. He would probably hate her for the rest of his life, and she wouldn't blame him, because she'd brought it all on herself.

As she got up to finish packing what little belongings she would take with her, she started to cry. She didn't know where she was going, but she was going. She couldn't do this anymore.

She stopped when she heard the doorbell. *It was him*, she thought. The last thing she wanted was to see him right now. It would make this that much harder. She had wanted their last moment together to be her last memory of him. She had wanted to hold on to that.

She hurried to the door to answer it and as soon as she did, Maribel barged inside.

"Maribel!" Naomi said surprised. She tried to hide the tears misted in her eyes as Maribel walked right past her without uttering a word. The woman reeked of alcohol and cigarettes. Naomi had known she wouldn't give up the bottle. She knew it the day she'd dropped out of the rehab program they had been in together. It was where they had first met. Where they voluntarily shared their battles and addiction with alcohol. Where they traded stories about how it had ruined their lives and the lives of their families. Naomi remembered thinking the first time she saw her, *What's a pretty white woman like that doing in a place like this?* She'd found out very soon that like drugs, alcohol didn't discriminate. The counselor had told them all as they sat there waiting for the secret cure, that the first step was admitting that there was a problem. Maribel had been in denial, Naomi remembered. She was addicted to alcohol and prescription pills. And looking at her now, nothing hadn't changed.

"I wasn't expecting you," Naomi said, watching Maribel's eyes scope the place.

Maribel finally turned to her and it was only then that she noticed the woman's mascara-streaked face. "Are you okay, Maribel?"

If looks could kill, Naomi would have taken her last breath right then, right there.

"You know, Naomi, it breaks my heart that you haven't been completely honest with me. After all I've done to try to help you." Maribel allowed her words to register fully. "Did you think I wouldn't find out?"

Naomi was completely caught off-guard. "I don't believe I know what this is about."

"Sure you don't." Maribel walked over to where Naomi stood and flipped over her left hand. "*That*, is what the hell this is about!" She clearly pointed to the diamond ring.

Naomi took a deep breath and tried to quickly gather her thoughts. "I can explain—"

"Too late! I have all I need. That's why I've come to tell you I don't need your help anymore. My husband and I have decided to reconcile. We're going to work on our marriage," she said without a break in her voice.

A distressed look caused every part of Naomi's face to crumple. "What do you mean, *your* husband?"

"You seem like a pretty bright woman, Naomi. Figure it out."

At that moment, Naomi realized that she had been deceived by Greg's own wife.

"How could you do this to him?" Naomi managed as she glared at Vivian incredulously.

Ignoring Naomi, Vivian snatched her purse wide open and whipped out a mustard-colored envelope. "Your plane ticket is in here."

"Plane ticket? Whaa—" Naomi gasped.

"Yes. To Canada."

Naomi was speechless. Everything felt like a whirlwind. Her eyes were fixed on the woman who had led her to believe that her name had been, Maribel, when all along she was Greg's wife. She had even gone by the alias in rehab. Maribel Strutters.

"Call me when you arrive," Vivian added.

Naomi had completely become undone. She could hardly think straight.

"Are you listening?"

"I don't know about this!" Her tone changed unexpectedly. "This is all so sudden." She tried to catch her breath. It felt like she was drowning.

"Here!" Vivian practically shoved the envelope into Naomi's hand as if there were no other options to consider. "Your plane leaves out Friday morning."

Naomi kept her words at bay all while contemplating how she

had unknowingly made a deal with the devil himself. Vivian had used her and she was too blind to see through all the lies. She had been plotting on her since day one. Everything Naomi had told her, everything she had confessed, Vivian used to her advantage. Her thoughts were scrambled and her heart ached for Greg. He needed to know the truth. He needed to know what this woman was capable of.

"And give me the phone. You won't be needing it any longer."

Naomi reluctantly walked over to the table and handed Vivian the phone she had loaned her.

"Leave the keys under the mat. I'll pick them up Friday," Vivian said matter-of-factly. She headed for the door then stopped in her tracks once again. "It'll hurt much less if you make yourself forget that it ever happened," Vivian suggested. "So…I'll warn you now. Stay the fuck away from *my* husband," she threatened, her soft voice wrapped in pure malice. "Or you're going to wish like hell you never met me." With that she walked off.

"Where's the rest of the money you promised me?" Naomi called out to her.

"You're wearing it," Vivian said smugly as she slammed the door behind her.

The sound of that door closing was like Naomi's own life ending. She let her tears roll down her face as she stood there. How could he do this to her? How could he go back to her after everything she'd done to him? Didn't he know she was trying to drive him crazy? That she wanted evidence to use against him? That she was an impetuous alcoholic who didn't know a damn thing about loving him.

Naomi needed to talk to him. At least once. She needed to tell him the truth and express her role in all of it. She was willing to take responsibility for her part, but he needed to know that his

28

"Ewww-wee, girl, all these bourgeois bitches up in here," Tiffany piped as they walked through the Bank of America lobby. All eyes were on him and he dared to not notice it.

Ménage walked ahead feeling as if she were the bank's president as all eyes switched to their direction. She was dressed in the finest of fashions, and her hair was combed back in a long straight ponytail that hung to the lower part of her back.

They stood in line and when the two available tellers called them up, they each went to separate windows.

"How may I help you?" the cheerful young, dark-skinned girl asked. She had the biggest ears Ménage had ever seen in her entire life, but she had beautiful dimples.

"Hi. I came to cash my settlement check," she began, handing the woman a personal check written in the amount of $50,000.

The teller looked over the check carefully, maintaining her friendly customer service smile. "Ms. Greer, may I have your right thumbprint here."

Ménage placed her thumb in the inkpad and then stuck her print on the check.

"And may I see two forms of identification."

Ménage handed the teller her driver's license and credit card. She studied them closely. "And here's my social security card, too," she said, laying it on the counter as well.

"Thank you."

The teller began pecking away at her computer, and as she did so, Ménage looked over at Tiffany to see how things were going on his end. She could hear the teller asking him for the same identification Rhonda had just asked her.

"Ms. Greer, how would you like your cash back?" Rhonda asked.

Ménage tried to hold her excitement in. "Whatever's easiest for you, Rhonda," she said politely.

"Okay, Ms. Greer. I'll have to step to the back to get your cash, but I'll be right back."

"Take your time," Ménage said. "I'm in no hurry, honey."

"Please help yourself to some coffee and cookies while you wait. We're also running a great promotion. If you open a checking account with us today, you'll receive a Black & Decker toaster."

"I'll think about it," Ménage said as she made her way to the lobby. Shortly after, Tiffany followed.

"Bitch, we about to be paid!" he said the second he sat down.

"Sshhh! They may hear your loudmouth ass."

Tiffany quickly placed a hand over his mouth. He wrapped his turquoise and fuchsia scarf around his neck and began messing with his eyelashes. "Ewww, chile, I think my lash is trying to fall off. I can't have that. Let me go to the bathroom and fix this hot ass mess."

"Can't it wait?"

Tiffany looked at Ménage as if he had been offended. "Ugh… no!"

"Hurry your ass up," Ménage whispered through clenched teeth.

Tiffany picked up his purse and dashed off to save his artificial eyelash while Ménage sat there patiently waiting for her money. She calculated how much she would have in total. She hated to have to give Tiffany $10,000 of it for coming with her, but she figured there was plenty more where that came from so she didn't sweat it.

Minutes later Tiffany reappeared from around the corner twisting harder than a two-dollar hoe. He reclaimed his spot and picked up a magazine off the table. After fifteen minutes had passed, Ménage finally said something. "What the hell is taking them so long?" she wondered.

"Hell if I know. Go see."

Ménage tossed her napkin and coffee cup in the trash. She strutted back over to the teller window. Rhonda was nowhere in sight. She asked the other teller how much longer the wait would be.

"Let me go check for you, ma'am."

"Thank you," Ménage said, disguising her frustration.

The teller returned rather quickly. "They said they're counting out the money now." She smiled.

Ménage nodded her head. "Oh okay." Satisfied, she walked back over to where Tiffany was. "They're counting the money," she told him.

"Damn, it takes that long. Don't they have one of those machines that count the money for you? Wheww...this is ridiculous!"

Ménage looked at him as if he were crazy. He was acting as if this money was really his and he was a real customer.

Another ten minutes passed. Ménage only knew as she kept sending Slug's calls straight to voicemail. Didn't he get the memo that she wasn't going back to him or Detroit? She was not about to ruin her Hollywood reputation before it even got off the ground. She decided that she was going to go straight to Sprint after all this and have her number changed.

"Ms. Greer," Rhonda called out.

"Mr. Hernandez," the other teller who had helped Tiffany said.

"About damn time," Tiffany huffed under his breath.

They waltzed over to the window and when they got there, there was no money in sight.

"Ms. Greer, I'm sorry to inform you that we are unable to cash your check today."

Ménage drew her neck back. "What! Why?"

"Because these checks were stolen."

"Oh hell no!" Tiffany exclaimed. "I didn't steal a damn thing." Ménage shot him a look and he ignored it.

"So for that reason we're going to have to retain the checks as evidence."

"Evidence!" Ménage and Tiffany said in unison.

When they heard the lobby door chirp, they both turned around to find two Dallas police officers walking inside.

"Fuck," Ménage hissed under her breath.

Tiffany shrieked. "Bitch, I cannot go to jail today! You better tell them something."

Ménage looked back at Rhonda as the officers approached her and Tiffany. "There has to be a mistake. I had no idea," she pleaded.

"Ma'am, place your hands behind your back," the first officer said.

"Officer, there's been some kind of mix-up," Ménage tried explaining. "If you give me a minute to make a phone call, I promise I can straighten all this out."

"Lord, please don't let them take me to jail," Tiffany began praying as he was placed in handcuffs as well. "I'll do anything. I'll stop smoking, I'll stop drinking. I'll even go to church every Sunday," he whined.

The officers walked each of them over to the lobby. "Take a seat," the lead officer instructed. He whipped out his writing pad and then walked over to the tellers to get their statements.

"Tiffany, stop panicking!" Ménage grimaced.

"Bitch, I got anxiety and a bad heart." He winced. "I can't go to jail. Do you know what they do to pretty girls like me?"

Ménage rolled her eyes. If she had never been embarrassed by him before, she sure as hell was now.

"They make us their bitch," Tiffany retorted. "And I be damned if I'm going to be somebody's *bitch* and not get paid. Ooooo, Lord help me father."

Ménage instantly regretted bringing Tiffany's over-the-top ass. She tried to think of a way to get them out of this, but this time when the lobby door chirped, she realized all too soon that they were both going to jail today.

Jeff had the nastiest scowl on his face as he bypassed Ménage and walked straight over to the teller area where the two officers were standing.

"We're so screwed!" Tiffany chimed.

Jeff, the tellers, and the police officers headed in their direction. Ménage tried to show a sense of remorse, although she wasn't feeling it. She did what any other bitch would have done if they had access to that kind of money.

"Sir, do you know these two individuals?" the officer asked.

Ménage could see the fire burning in Jeff's eyes as he darted them from her to Tiffany. His brows furrowed and his nose flared as it always did when he was upset. But Ménage swore she saw fumes coming out his head. He looked at her as if he wanted to choke the life out of her.

"Yes, officer. I know them both."

"It's up to you if you want to press charges, sir. We can take them down and get them processed for check fraud so that you don't have to worry about this happening again."

Jeff continued to look at Ménage with unbelieving eyes. She worked up just enough tears to start a nice drum roll. She heard

Tiffany sniffling; only she knew his tears were real. Jeff didn't look the least bit moved by her performance.

"Those tears don't work today."

She finally averted her eyes, wishing they would get it over with instead of making her and Tiffany the laughingstock of the bank. Everybody that walked in looked right at them. She could hear their snickers a mile away.

"I would have given you my last dime," Jeff said. "I trusted you! My daughter trusted you!"

Ménage couldn't stand to look at him, but she could see Tiffany's face quietly begging him to not press charges.

"I don't want to ever see either of you again," Jeff said. He turned to the officer. "I won't press charges *this* time."

Tiffany exhaled a sigh of relief. "Thank you, Jeff!" he said.

Ménage, on the other hand, didn't utter a peep.

"Thanks for calling me, Rhonda."

"No problem, Mr. Jackson. I'll make notations and freeze all the accounts until we can get them closed out and new ones opened."

"Thank you. Call me if you need anything." He shook both of the officers' hands and walked out of the building.

The officers turned to Ménage and Tiffany. "The two of you better consider yourselves awfully lucky. But before we let you go, we're going to take down some more information in case you get the itch to try this again."

About ten minutes later, Ménage and Tiffany walked out of the bank free as birds.

"Gurl, I thought I was a goner!" Tiffany said as he nervously shuffled through his purse for his keys. As they walked through the parking lot, a BMW rolled up. The driver rolled down the window and Ménage and Tiffany both saw that it was Jeff.

"You wanted my money? Here you go!" he said, throwing out a handful of pennies in their direction.

"Fuck you!" Ménage yelled, grabbing the attention of some of the people in the parking lot.

"We tried that, remember?" Jeff hollered. "Dirty bitch!"

Ménage and Tiffany walked as fast as they could toward the car and got in. She was beyond humiliated, but even more upset that she didn't get the money. They watched Jeff drive off before finally pulling out.

"You think he gon' follow us?" Tiffany asked.

Ménage burst out laughing. "Naw. He just mad 'cause he got his little feelings hurt," she said. "He'll be all right."

"You are one coldhearted bitch," Tiffany said, firing up a cigarette. He offered Ménage one, but she declined.

"I need a blunt after all this," Ménage said before placing her shades over her eyes.

Tiffany looked over at her. "Diva, what you gon' do now?"

"I'ma keep doing what I do best. Get money!"

29

"Daddy, where's Ebony?" Deandra asked the instant she walked through the door. She hadn't seen Ménage's car and Jeff knew she would be looking for her. Especially considering how well Deandra seemed to take to her.

"She's not here," Jeff said as he took his keys and cell phone out of his pockets and laid them on the table. "And she won't be back." Just that quick he'd saved himself from having to answer a million questions.

"But...I thought the two of you were getting married."

Jeff's face seemed to swell. "Married!" He'd banned that word from his vocabulary months ago. So as his cheekbones pushed his eyes into a squint, he looked at her wondering where in the hell that ludicrous idea had come from.

"Deandra, why would you think Ebony and I were getting married?"

"Because she told me you were."

Jeff snatched off his tie. The anger rising inside of him had his blood boiling. He clenched his jaws.

"Ebony told you we were getting married?" He wanted to make sure he'd heard her right the first time.

Deandra nodded profusely. Not an ounce of doubt in her face. "She told me I would be the flower girl and that Nadine..."

"Nadine?" Jeff shot.

"Yes, Daddy. She said that Nadine was going to be her maid and that she would get to hold her dress as she walked down the aisle."

"She lied to you, Deandra, and she used you for information!" He was furious.

Deandra appeared saddened. "Daddy, please don't be mad at me. She told me to pinky swear not to say anything because it was supposed to be a surprise."

Jeff shook his head and walked over to hug his daughter. "Daddy's not mad at you, baby. I'm mad at myself because I should have never brought her here." He kissed his daughter on the forehead. He wished like hell that he had seen this one coming. He was upset with himself more than anything because he'd given her the benefit of the doubt. He thought he was helping her. Now he wondered if she really had been robbed or if it was all part of her scheme to rob him.

"Go on and do your homework," he said. "I need to handle some business."

"Okay, Daddy."

Jeff picked up his phone to call Nadine. He needed to fix this because she was the last person he wanted to believe this nonsense. Not so much that her input would have mattered had he chosen to walk that path again, but she deserved the truth. And the truth was, he wasn't marrying anybody. Not today, not tomorrow, or years to come.

"This is Nadine."

"Are you busy? I had something I needed to straighten out."

"Actually…yes."

"Here, baby, let me get that for you," the male's voice in the background called out.

"Thank you," Nadine said, obviously switching her attention from Jeff to whoever she had been conversing with before his call.

"Ma Ma..."

Jeff froze in his steps. That was his son.

"Nadine, where are you?"

"Jeff, can this wait until later?"

"Where are you with my son?" He didn't mean to sound as angry as it came out.

As if muffling her voice to speak, she asked, "What's so important that you need to talk to me right now?"

"I'm coming over."

"We're not home."

"I want to see my son!" Jeff could hear the rounds of laughter in the background and it made his stomach churn.

"Leonard, I'm going to step out for a minute, baby. I'll be right back."

Jeff could hear her heels patter across the floor. There was an echo as she moved from one area to the other, but even in the distance, Jeff could hear his son laughing, playing, and enjoying, this other man.

"What has gotten into you?" Nadine lit into him. "It's only Monday, and all of a sudden, you want to see your son."

"Don't do that."

"Don't do what? Tell you how I really feel for a change?" She didn't give him time to respond. "I'm sick of you playing part-time daddy to Canvas when it's convenient for you! He needs a father, Jeff. A father! So why don't you, Deandra, and your new fiancée, go on with your happy lives, and let me do what's best for my son. You can clock back in on Friday!"

The only reason Jeff knew Nadine had hung up the phone in his face was he no longer heard his son's laughter. And the only reason he realized how bad he had hurt her was because he could feel his own heart beginning to break as her words echoed in his mind. He could feel that double-edged sword being shoved deeply down his throat. That quickly, she had diabolically cursed him with her anger and pain. Jeff could feel it in his bones. Every fucking ounce of it, he could feel. And the only way he knew the feeling consuming him was the real deal and not a false alarm, was when Deandra walked up to him with her homework in hand. Instead of asking for the help she was seeking, she said, "Daddy, why are you crying?"

30

Five hundred pounds of weight had been lifted off his chest. Greg had been delivered from all the sneaking around and lying he'd found himself doing in order to keep his dirty little secrets safe. It had gotten to the point where he found himself lying to Vivian about almost everything. From his whereabouts, the lipstick print she'd found on his collar last month, right down to his wedding band. It had been one untruth after the other, time and time again. He had lied so much that it was beginning to feel normal. At times he didn't even trust his own tongue out of fear of what lie would roll off of it next. Therefore, when the perfect opportunity came for him to relinquish, he did. Feeling as though he'd perjured himself enough.

After she'd splashed hot coffee in his face, Greg was surprised that when Vivian did finally calm down, she didn't so much as rebut or ask questions. It was as if she had known about his latest affair all along, and his admission had only been to clear his own guilty conscience. They'd talked like civil adults and eventually she agreed that they were no longer good for each other. She'd said they had lost all the fundamental components that were essential in keeping a marriage together. He'd told her flat out—people change. They'd outgrown each other, he had said bluntly. He'd felt the need to remind her how they wanted different things out of life, figuring that would lessen any hurt, but he'd refrained.

Vivian wanted to move back to Connecticut to be near her father while Greg, on the other hand, had other endeavors to pursue. He wanted to settle in California, venture back into the restaurant business, and most importantly, he was ready to start the family Vivian had refused to give him.

The conversation had ended well and they'd promised to remain good friends. After all, he did still care about her. That wouldn't change.

Leonard, on the other hand, had advised Greg wait to tell Vivian that he was seeing someone. He informed him that adultery could have a substantial influence on the outcome of the divorce settlement. But Greg had been bullheaded when he'd admitted to Vivian that he was having an affair. He wasn't thinking about the financial ramifications. He only wanted instant reprieve. Besides, he had taken her through enough already, he could at least be a man and fess up to his wrongdoings for once.

So as Greg killed the engine and jumped out of the car, he couldn't help but imagine the smile he would put on Naomi's face when he'd tell her that he'd told his wife about them. It was official now. He could now make the move to Los Angeles with her so that she didn't have to keep traveling back and forth as she had done for the past few weeks. This would be his first time seeing her this week because she had been so busy, she had told him in a text message. They had agreed on a Friday night date at her place, but he needed to see her now.

He walked anxiously up to her doorstep. Instead of ringing the doorbell as he would have normally, he used his key.

"Baby!" he called out, shutting the door and locking it.

Traces of Chanel perfumed the air. It was the sensuality of the fragrance that always aroused him. Took him places only his mind could go to in 0.2 seconds.

"Naomi, baby!" Greg called out again. He walked farther through the living area, noticing how everything was still neatly arranged and in place. She hadn't packed anything from what he could see. "Baby, you in here!" he called out again. The closer he got to the bedroom door, the closer his hound dog was to being awakened.

He thought she might would have been napping after her usual Friday spa and shopping splurge, but when he walked into that room, all he found was an empty perfectly made-up bed. The bathroom door was slightly cracked and he could feel the steam seeping out as she showered. A John Mayer track played softly. Of all the songs in the world she was playing, "Slow Dancing in a Burning Room." He hated that damn song with a passion. His wife played it all the time, mostly when she was upset or depressed about something. But that's not why he hated it. He hated it because it was sad, tragic, and bleak. Sounded like funeral music for a dead relationship. Then again, maybe that's why Vivian loved it so much.

He walked over to the bed and picked up the folded sheet of paper that had his name written across it in black ink. Was she expecting him to come this early? He read it, then followed the instructions on it, all while wondering what Naomi might have had up her sleeves. The television had already been set. All he had to do was press "play."

He sat on the edge of the bed and waited for the video to come on. Suddenly, a smiling bride and groom appeared on the screen. It had been forwarded to the part where they were reciting their personalized wedding vows.

"I give you my hand, my heart, and all of my love."

"I will always support your endeavors."

"I vow to love you through good and difficult times."

"To be there in your time of need."

"To hold you when you're in pain."

Greg began to tense up. He thought his lungs were going to collapse.

"To protect you."

"Provide for you."

"And I vow…to never…ever leave your side."

Greg's heart began to race. He shot up and stormed to the bathroom to see what kind of sick joke Naomi was playing. How in the hell did she get a copy of his and his wife's wedding video?

When he forcefully pushed the door open, he was greeted by a .45 Automatic Colt pistol. Stainless steel with gold highlights and a wood grain handle. It gave off eight rounds plus a lucky bonus if he'd missed his target the other eight shots. He should know because it was *his* gun. His gun and *his* wife holding it.

Greg's hands shot up. "Whoa, whoa, whoa! Vivian, what are you doing?" Somehow, he still remembered her name. Still remembered how to breathe as his words nearly strangled him.

"Back up!" Vivian ordered. That polished piece of metal in her trembling glove-covered hand was aimed directly at Greg's torso. "Back over by the bed!"

Greg took tiny steps backward. He didn't stop until the back of his legs bumped against the iron rail.

"Sit!"

He sat back down on the bed. The bed that had witnessed his infidelities. If she peeled back those sheets and held up a black light, she would find all of the evidence she needed to write this off. It would have been settled in court. She would end up with everything and it would be the end of their story. But the psychotic look in her eyes, the coldness he felt coming off her body, scared him. It scared him to death.

She looked over at the couple in that wedding video. Neither of them would probably admit now that they knew who they were.

They seemed so in love. So naive and predictable. But here today, Vivian and Greg had made fools out of them.

"To have and to hold, from this day forward."

"For better, for worse."

"For richer, for poorer."

"In sickness and in health."

"Until *death*...do us part," Vivian mimicked.

Greg had thought his confession had been enough. He thought they had agreed on moving on.

She picked up the remote and paused the video. That couple was about to kiss, about to leap into holy matrimony in front of hundreds of people that had been sitting in that cathedral.

"Do you remember that day, Greg?"

Greg only nodded as he sat there riddled with fear.

"You said you loved me and that you would never leave my side."

"I'm...sorry," was all Greg could muster.

Her eyes seemingly turned gray. "You're not sorry. But you will be."

Greg would be a damn fool not to believe her. She had a gun in her hand. That was more than enough to make a believer out of him.

Dressed in black pants, a long-sleeved hooded black shirt, and a short black wig, Vivian looked more like an Asian MMA cage fighter than a wealthy white blonde. Her drunken eyes flared with anger as she wrapped her fingers tightly around the grip of that pistol. Her index finger idled along the curve of its trigger.

The mystery behind her madness revealed itself with every nervous breath she took and the pungent smell of Vodka began to clash with the fragrance he'd smelled earlier as it leaped from her tongue.

"You're drunk, Vivian. Let me get you some help."

"Fuck you! I don't need you to do a damn thing for me."

He needed to calm her. Needed to help her regain her sanity before she did something stupid—like shoot him. But his nerves were getting the best of him. Afraid to move an inch, he coolly paced himself.

"What did you do to Naomi?" he asked, hoping she hadn't been hurt.

"Acgh-kch!" Vivian's laugh sounded more like a single cough. "You're staring down the barrel of a .45 and all you can think about is Naomi? Ha, ha, ha." She shook her head sideways. "Either I did a damn good job picking somebody to screw your double two-timing ass, or you're being awfully thoughtful."

Greg narrowed his eyes. "What did you just say?"

"Ooooh…his head's really spinning now," she taunted. "You heard right. Naomi was a decoy that *I* hired!"

A voice inside persuaded him that he would have a fifty-fifty chance of surviving that bullet that she would unleash right before he wrestled his gun out of her hand and emptied that clip into her. Fifty-fifty were the odds of him escaping that with nothing more than a scrape.

Clenching his jaw, he looked on stone-faced. His breathing grew labored as he sat there feeling so lightheaded, he thought the room was actually spinning. Vivian had set him up—that he might get over someday. But Naomi's deception had his stomach in twisted knots. She was his walking cash vault. He'd transferred stocks, bonds, and several bank accounts, in her name. He put his $5 million house, in her name. A two-karat diamond on her finger. She was, and is, all he had left! And to find out that she was a part of his wife's gambit, infuriated the hell out of him. It was like watching his money burn in his face. At that moment all he could see was red as every drop of blood in his body, rushed to his head. He bet he looked like a vicious pit-bull, ready to attack.

"The look on your face right now is priceless." A conniving grin tugged at Vivian's pout and Greg wanted to smack it clean off. He felt nothing but a rage of fury and every piece of him split in two. He couldn't mask his pain any more than he could his anger. Therefore, she was enjoying the benefit of watching him bear all. Again, he asked himself if he was ready to catch that bullet, or ready to catch that case.

Greg calculated his plan. He had to be precise. Not a second off.

"If you wanted out, I would have given you out," he said calmly. "It doesn't have to end this way."

"You don't tell me how this is going to end, I tell *you!*" She started laughing again.

Greg inhaled. His eyes begged for mercy all on their own while his soul cried for redemption, and all he could do at that moment was hope and pray that God was listening.

Vivian stared at him for a short while. A half-moon smile effortlessly carved in her ruthless face. She looked like one of those women on the FBI's Most Wanted list.

"You know, I thought tipping off those auditors to your old whore's firm felt good. Ha, ha, ha. I was *dead* wrong. This, my dear, will be the best climax I've gotten all year."

"What do you want from me, Vivian?" Greg asked in a low uneven tone.

"Justice," Vivian said as she cocked the gun.

Vivian had an advantage over him. She was standing, he was sitting. She had a weapon and all he had was his strength to rely on. He wasn't afraid to die, but dying at the hands of his wife hadn't been how he wanted to go out. He always thought he'd die of old age or natural causes like his grandparents and great-grandparents had. A life of longevity was in his blood. So he thought.

She took a couple of steps back. "Tear off a piece of that paper," she ordered.

Greg reached behind him and grabbed the note on the bed. He slowly ripped off the lower half. She tossed him a black pen.

"Now I want you to write this exactly how it comes out of my mouth." She paused and dictated what she wanted the letter to read. As Greg wrote the five-line letter, which had been his suicide note, a nauseous feeling swarmed over him.

"Now lay it there on the bed."

They were inches apart so if he was going to take that gun from her, now was the time to do it. It was the only chance he had. She pointed the gun to his head. He held up his hands. "Please don't do this?"

"I was never enough for you," she said. "But it doesn't matter now because I'm going to reunite you with that *home-wrecking* cunt of yours. Although I feel I should get some kind of award for trying to resurrect her black ass for you."

Vivian had lost her mind, Greg concluded. His face tightened as his chest heaved from the pressure pulling at it.

"You have to admit, I did a really good job with your girlfriend." Vivian chuckled. "I knew it couldn't have been anything more than the sweet call of justice because she looked just like that slutty whore of yours," she spat angrily.

"Stop!" Greg said.

Vivian acted as though she hadn't heard a word he'd said. "So I cleaned her up, got her a few nips and tucks, then I put her in this nice lavish condo that *you* leased in *your* name."

"I didn't lease a damn thing, Vivian, and you know that! You did all of this to set me up!"

"All the checks have your signature, honey. Every last one of them." She smiled. "Don't you get it? Neither of those women gave a damn about you. You were nothing more than a paycheck to them, but you were too stupid to realize that. That was *my* money and you had no right!"

"It was ours!"

"No, it was mine!" Vivian lashed out. Greg nearly lost his composure. "But I'll be reimbursed for my troubles once the life insurance pays out, which by the way, I increased after learning of that slut, Denise." She bestowed upon him a twisted condescending smirk.

Greg detested her. The love and compassion he once felt for his wife, seemingly deserted him. He felt nothing. Only saw her for the true evil bitch that she'd always been. The raging veins that protruded from his neck looked more like tiny snakes. His breathing became unsteady as his anger intensified.

"You'll never get away with this!"

"Correction. I already have."

Greg lunged for the gun and when he did...a loud bang echoed off every wall in the house. He collapsed onto the bed as blazing hot lead tore right through his skull. The earsplitting clap of the gun had his ears ringing, but it was a far cry from church bells. It sounded more like a stick of dynamite had exploded right in front of his face. His vision became a clouded blur, somewhat like a thick fog, and everything around him seemed to be happening in slow motion.

John Mayer's lyrics sounded as if they were being played backward as he lay there in excruciating pain. Resistance was futile. His wife wanted him to hurt and he was. She'd sought retribution and with every agonizing breath he took, he knew she'd get that and a lump some of money too. Out of the corner of his right eye, he vaguely saw that their wedding video had been frozen on the part of them sealing their vows. That eternal kiss was the last thing Vivian wanted him to see. The last image she wanted to slow burn in his mind before he succumbed to the fatal gunshot wound.

He couldn't see all the blood spewing from the hole in the left side of his head, but he felt every ounce of it, leaving him weaker by the second. Instead of focusing on the pain, his efforts had been reserved for breathing and trying to remain calm in order to prevent going into hypo-volemic shock.

"Tell Denise I said hello!" she antagonized as she hovered over him. She fumbled around him for a second, then placed his gun in his hand, staging the scene as a self-inflicted gunshot wound to the head. That's what she wanted the police to believe. That's what she would tell family and friends. And that's what she would take to her grave. No one but he and God would really know what had happened here today.

"Please help me," Greg desperately cried out to his wife. He was at her mercy.

He blinked his eyes and Vivian was gone. He couldn't move. He couldn't speak, only writhe in pain. Death had a chokehold on him and he could feel himself slowly losing consciousness. For now, he still had a rhythm to his heart. But that rhythm slowly became more faint with every breath that he took. He was unsure of the minutes or seconds he had left as he began to strangle on his own blood. His body started to grow numb. Then cold.

Just before he closed his eyes, he heard a loud yell. It came from a man.

"Dear God! Umm…hold tight, man. I'm going to get you some help. Hello, operator. My next-door neighbor has been shot." He rattled off the address. "Yes. It looks like he attempted suicide!" Pause. "Yes, he still has a pulse." Pause. "Okay…okay…please hurry! This man is dying!"

31

Naomi shuffled her purse from one arm to the other as she pulled her carry-on luggage from behind. She walked around the airport for four hours waiting on an available flight and as luck would have it, she'd gotten one at the last minute. There was no way in hell she was going to Canada. No way!

She checked the gate information on her boarding pass once again to make sure she was going the right way. She picked up her pace when she saw that they had already begun boarding.

She quickly walked up to one of the attendants and handed him her ticket.

"Thank you, ma'am. Enjoy your flight." He smiled.

Naomi made her way on the plane and located her seat. She then put her suitcase in the overhead bin. She took her window seat. She sighed in relief and laid her head back against the headrest. She had never flown first-class, but she already knew that she was going to enjoy it. Before she could get too comfortable, her neighbor sat next to her.

"Hi," Naomi spoke first.

"Hello," the woman replied, getting adjusted.

Naomi peered out the window, glad to be leaving Dallas, but not the people she loved so much. She had made up her mind that she was going to call her ex-husband, Charles, as soon as she landed. She wanted to check on the kids. See how they were doing in school. She also couldn't wait to tell them that she'd been alcohol free for over a year now. She missed them deeply and she looked forward to being a part of their lives again.

As more people boarded the plane, the woman beside her began putting on makeup. "That's a pretty color on you," Naomi complimented.

"Thanks. I hope the producer I'm meeting with thinks so too." She chuckled.

"Oh, you're a singer," Naomi said.

The woman shook her head. "I wish. I'm actually an actress."

Naomi's eyes bucked. "Wow."

"I'm sorry, let me formally introduce myself because I'm sure you're going to see me in lots of movies soon." She stretched out her hand. "I'm Ebony Greer. But my friends call me Ménage."

Naomi shook her hand. "We haven't even made it to Los Angeles yet and I'm already meeting celebrities."

Ménage beamed. "Lucky you." She smiled.

They both looked up at the flight attendant who had begun her announcement. Naomi peered out the window again. If she and Greg were as in-sync as she felt they were, he'd know exactly where to find her. She closed her eyes, said a simple prayer, and prepared for a safe flight, *home.*

32

She had to be the luckiest woman on the planet. As she sat there allowing him to work his magic down below, Nadine couldn't help but fall into deep thought and mull over everything that had transpired in her life. From leaving Atlanta to come to Texas, to going into business with her best friend Denise, right down to finally agreeing to let him come over to her place. It was true she might have had a few unfortunate mishaps, but in the wake of it all, wasn't that what life was about—living, learning, and growing.

As she stared at his oily chocolate bald head, she knew every moment and every second of her past had been perfectly arranged for this single moment. Many called it destiny, some believed it was luck, and the others felt it was chance. But no matter what it was, Nadine knew without a shadow of a doubt that Leonard Dupree was a damn good man, but an even better feel-good doctor.

"You sure are good with those hands," she teased as Leonard sat on the other end of her chaise, polishing her toenails Soiree Mauve, a fancy way of describing a pearl-like plum. She had just finished beating him in a game of dominos for the third time in a row. So the loser had to give the winner a foot massage. He massaged her feet and polished her toes. He didn't think a sophisticated investment broker like herself would even know how to get down like that. Boy, did she prove him wrong.

Leonard licked the bottom of his lip and let out a chuckle. "Why thank you. And that's not the only thing I'm good with." Sex exuded from his lips and it had been more than enough to entice her. He actually started her bunny to hopping.

"Um, I bet you are."

Leonard kissed the heel of her foot, the center, then worked his tongue along the edge. Nadine laughed softly, then gave into a sensual moan. It was like they were having sex without having sex. He finally kissed the top of her foot.

"All done." He smiled.

Nadine couldn't deny that she wanted more. The passion burning inside had her pussy oozing with sweet joy. She wanted him badly. Canvas was next door with Casey so they had the entire place to themselves. All she had to do was initiate it.

She raised up some, pulled her feet to the floor, and scooted closer to him. She straddled his lap, then began kissing him.

"What are you...doing...baby?" Leonard asked between kisses.

"Make love to me," Nadine begged, her body yearning to be touched.

She could feel him shaking his head, but he didn't stop kissing her.

"Why?" she asked, panting.

Finally, he stopped. He placed both of his hands on the sides of her face. "I told you. I'm going to wait for you. You're not ready to do this."

She started back kissing him. "Yes I am. Trust me. I'm so damn horny I'm going to lose my mind."

Again, Leonard pulled away. Nadine looked at him as though she didn't understand.

"Trust me, baby. It's going to be worth your while. But for now, I'm respecting *your* wish to wait until marriage."

Nadine's face lit up and her heat melted all over again for him.

"You're right," she said, kissing him. "And that's why I love you." Before she realized it, she had admitted her true feelings to him for the first time.

"I love you too. I love you so much, Nadine, that my heart doesn't rest until I see you again. You're like my air, baby."

Nadine's smile radiated all over her body. And as she leaned in to kiss him again, his phone started vibrating. He looked at the screen and looking as if he didn't recognize the number, he answered, "Leonard Dupree speaking."

Nadine quietly slid off his lap to give him some privacy. For all she knew it could have been a client. She made her way to the kitchen.

"Oh my God!"

The panic in Leonard's voice alarmed her. She walked back to the living room.

"Okay. Okay. I'll be right there." He shot up from the chaise.

"Is everything okay?" she asked, although his grief-stricken face told her otherwise.

He shook his head. "No. My best friend has been shot. I'm sorry, baby, but I have to get to the hospital," he said in a panic.

"Okay, but I'm driving you," she said. She rushed over to her purse, slipped into her shoes, and practically beat him out the door.

Twenty minutes later, they arrived at Parkland Hospital. It was the same hospital her own best friend had died in. So as they walked through those double doors, she remembered that final moment with Denise.

She followed closely behind Leonard as he led the way until finally they ended up in the waiting room. A white woman with long blonde hair rushed over to him.

"Thank God, you made it, Leonard!" she said, barely breathing. Her face was covered in tears.

"What happened? How is he doing?" Leonard began to question without giving the woman a chance to get a hold of herself.

"They said...he tried to commit suicide," she said, breaking down again.

Leonard reached in to console her and Nadine stepped aside. It wasn't until she got a second hard look at the woman that she realized she knew her. It was the woman that had flagged her down as she was leaving Kelli's house that day. Her name was Vivian. Vivian was Greg's wife. Now her own mouth was slightly agape as her breathing quickened from the discovery. Greg Adams was Leonard's best friend.

"Can we see him?" Leonard asked.

"He's still in surgery," Vivian cried.

"It's okay," Leonard coaxed.

Vivian began to dry-heave as a mountain of tears poured down her rosy cheeks. He walked her back over to one of the chairs and Nadine followed. As the three of them sat waiting for the doctor to come out, Nadine looked over to check on Leonard.

"Are you okay?" she asked.

The pained look in his face said no, but he told her that he was. "I'm going to step out and make a few phone calls," he said.

"Okay." Nadine nodded. The second he walked out of that room, Vivian turned to her.

"Don't I know you from somewhere?"

"Um...yes. Your husband fixed my tire that day. You flagged me down as you were jogging."

Vivian only nodded. "And you're here with his best friend. Coincidence, I imagine."

Nadine pressed her lips together and forged a smile. "I'm going to go check on Leonard." Leonard was coming from around the corner when she walked out the door.

"No service," he said, making his way closer to her. "Are you sure you want to hang out here? I'll likely be here all night."

Nadine nodded. "Yeah. I'm sure. He was…someone that I knew, too."

Leonard gave her an inquisitive look that suggested he had assumed the worst. "How do you know Greg?"

With sorrow building in her eyes, Nadine believed she had no other choice but to be honest with him. They had said they would leave their past in the past, but she knew that he needed to know. "It's a long, long story," she said.

"And I have all the time in the world to hear it."

With that, Nadine had no choice but to venture right back into the depths of her betrayal.

ABOUT THE AUTHOR

N'TYSE currently juggles her writing career as a full-time mother, wife, and filmmaker. She is the author of *Twisted Seduction*, *My Secrets Your Lies*, and the executive producer of the documentary film, *Beneath My Skin*.